Chosen

Melanie Purser

For my husband, Mark. Thank you for being my best friend, and for being the best father to our daughter.

Contents

Prologue

I could have tried a little harder to enjoy my life, to experience new things, and maybe try to make some friends or fall in love with someone, but what would be the point? Maybe I would have if I'd had the choice.

I'm the Alpha's daughter. I have strong blood. *Royal* blood I guess you could say. Therefore, I am not given a choice. We aren't really kings or queens, princes or princesses but a lot of my people use the terms all the same, especially if they are a high-ranking Alpha.

Either way, my future was chosen for me the moment I was born. I would marry the next Alpha in the pack, or arranged to be married off to another pack in order to establish peace or join forces.

There can only be one Alpha male in the same territory for so long though before one of them attacked the other for dominance over the other. Only pack members can go in and out of each other's land, but they still need to give warning and reason for their passage. The only times Alphas enter each other's lands are for war, or to safely exchange pack members or mates.

None of that matters to me though. I would welcome a war just for the chance to change my future. A war would give me the possibility of escape. I would be able to make my own future, and finally start my life and live it the way I want to.

When I was younger, other pack mates tried to be my friend and invited me to do stuff with them. Things Alphas daughters *should* be doing in case they ever become the mate of a pack leader, but someday I may leave this place, so why bother?

My blood calls to the pack. They can feel what my blood represents. Some want to do whatever they can to please me, while the stronger ones want to challenge me, and the majority that simply want to be near me because I represent safety, loyalty, and leadership. I am not exactly loyal or a leader though.

I'm not and never will be okay with this disgusting arrangement. That's why I have spent all my time training so that if ever given the chance, I could fight my way out.

I train more than our pack warriors and have probably beaten each and every one by now. Dad said I'm not allowed to train with them anymore because of some bullshit reason about it being unladylike. If their prides were hurt, they should work harder if they plan to protect their other pack members.

Dad is the only thing stopping me from running away now.

I'm sure he could probably take me down in a fight, but it would never come to that. Alpha's word is law. As soon as he told me to stand down, my body would betray me and follow his orders.

Sure, I could *try* and break it, but it's very rare that anyone has been able to defy the Alpha unless they were possibly just as strong, or stronger. If someone were able to, it would show the weakness of that Alpha and there *would* be bloodshed.

I don't wish harm to come to any of my pack mates, but I will not hesitate to take my chance at escape if it ever arises. I will be prepared for whenever that moment comes. I just feel bad for any poor bastard who dares to get in my way.

Chapter 1

Ari

My body aches in places I seem to only discover at this time every year. I have been on the edge since the day that I turned 16. When every new birthday comes around, the same feeling hits me like a wrecking ball. Each year I fear that this is the day. This will be the day that my nightmares come to life.

Today I turn 22, and just like all of my birthdays since I was 16, I change into my wolf form and run. Nothing too typical about that exactly, but on days like today I run about three times farther than I normally would.

I don't even bother slowing down to catch my breath, as if something horrible will happen if I stop. Why I think running will change anything, I have no idea. Nothing can change my fate, being the daughter of an Alpha.

This morning I had woken up in a panic. More panicked than I have ever been before, and I pray that isn't a sign.

It was still dark outside, but I could swear I could hear unfamiliar voices and loud footsteps heading in my direction. After running for six hours, I realize it was probably just my heart pounding in my ears, and my own mind conjuring up foreign voices.

I knew no one was coming for me today. Dad would have told me. Or at least I hoped he would. I am running out of time though. Most women in packs are mated by the age of 18, but some are taken as early as 16. It is sickening, but apparently, I seem to be the only person who thinks so. My people tend to be very traditional and it is hard to pull them out of such ancient times.

It's a mystery as to how I haven't been paired yet, though I am unbelievably grateful. It's just that I don't understand the *why*. If I knew that I was going to be unmated at 22 years old, maybe I would have actually tried to make a life for myself here. Instead, I have done nothing but hide from it and learn how to escape from what my future might hold.

Perhaps that is exactly why I haven't been mated. Word must have gotten around to the other Alphas about how *difficult* I am. I feared that some Alphas might see that as an exciting challenge. Thankfully that hasn't been the case.

I should be happy, yet here I am, legs burning and unmoving as my lungs struggle to continue inhaling and exhaling at a normal rate. If a polar bear found me, I would be their lunch.

Hell, if a mouse found me, I would be in trouble, but I would heal before it had enough time to finish me off. Sadly, the polar bear is a higher possibility though being so close to the icy, Beaufort Sea. And if not a polar bear, there are plenty of other species of bears around, including grizzly's, brown bears, black bears, and many other large, frightening animals. Frightening to non-werewolves like myself anyways.

Our land, our territory, consists of mostly all of Alaska and British Columbia, Canada. There are a few free territories around the area for loner wolves, and for packs to use for vacations or hideouts. Every State and Country is required to have safe zones for those reasons.

We are lucky to have this land. It is highly sought after, but we also have a very high number of werewolves compared to other packs. Anyone would be crazy to try and go up against my father's pack, but a lot of Alphas can be a bit insane and greedy for territory, so there is always a small possibility.

Canada has the largest territory, and they may be the only ones that outmatch us in density of wolves.

My family and I are homed in the Arctic Borough of Alaska, on the outskirts of a small city called Noatak. Most of our wolves are in bigger areas, such as Kotzebue, Fairbanks, Anchorage, and Juneau. Many of them are spread out through the British Columbia area as well.

My father keeps his best wolves nearby though. However, he's constantly traveling and visiting with his wolves when they aren't visiting us.

It never made sense to me as to why we were so far away from the edge of our territory. When I got older, dad told me that it is because of all the free territory surrounding us.

Alpha's are very territorial. When others wolves move in too close, things take a bad turn, or so I am told anyways. My father seems to have exceptional control, but if he attacked a member of another pack just for being near our territory, there would be a war.

I understand his reasoning, and there are many of our pack members stationed along our borders to run patrol, and are able to warn us with plenty of time to prepare ourselves if anything were to happen.

However, we are also not far from the coast. They would be insane to, but if another pack wanted to attack from the West side, we would be hit first, and wouldn't even see it coming.

We have plenty of strong wolves on our side for that reason. Dad is a high-ranking Alpha and I can hold my own as well. Or so I think. I have never actually seen real battle since no one will let me. I'm a female *and* a "princess", so apparently, it's frowned upon, but I figure, if I can face the warriors who *have* seen battle, then I know that I can too.

If battle broke out in my town, I would fight and protect who I could, and make my escape when I got the chance.

I have to admit that I do like it here though. I love the wide-open space, and the fact that there's not a very large population of people. Especially where we are. It's like our own private wolf base.

The area is beautiful and I get to explore it every day on four legs. The wildlife has a very high population too. I am really not joking about those polar bears. Many of my kind intermingle with humans, and I don't mind them, but I like the freedom I have here.

Collapsing here by the thawing stream, I attempt to camouflage my brown and gold fur next to a large tree. Of course, it won't matter though if something with an appetite for meat picked up my scent.

I don't have magic abilities that cover my scent or anything of the sort. I am just like any other animal in the woods except bigger, stronger, and faster when I'm not run ragged like this.

After a few more minutes, my breathing starts to settle, but it's counterproductive as my fatigued body loses its adrenaline.

My eyes threaten to close and I am quickly losing the battle.

I shudder awake to snow falling all around me. Slowly rising up on stiff muscles, I shake the blanket of snow off of me. My kind heals quickly with sleep, though better with raw meat.

Us werewolves don't run much faster than an actual wolf, but we can run far longer. However, we aren't really meant to run at a dead sprint for six hours straight. It will be a struggle to get back home, though the nap I took has me feeling much better than before.

The sun is still high in the sky so I must not have slept too long. Maybe an hour or two. I would need to hurry if I wanted to make it home for dinner.

Listening for danger around me, I slowly creep up to the almost frozen stream, lapping up as much water as I can before the journey home. If only I had the time and energy to hunt for a Hare or something. Anything that would help me heal a bit quicker.

I really outdid myself this year and am lucky to be alive, but I still can't help but dread going back. I could keep running the opposite direction, but as soon as my Alpha sensed my intent, he would command me to come home.

It wasn't something he could do all the time, but he could sense us in desperate moments. It's the Alphas way of protecting us. It had the opposite effect on me. I felt like a caged animal waiting to be sold off to the highest bidder.

Even with all the space and freedom, I know that one day soon, I will be forced into something that I don't want.

I've made myself strong. I can protect those that need protecting. Why can't I decide where to live and who to take as a mate? I'm not just a dainty female who needs protecting, and I'm definitely not just going to sit at home all day making meals and babies.

There are other female fighters in the packs; usually just the ones who unfortunately, can't reproduce, or who have already birthed children. Some are allowed to fight anyways, just because of their skills. Sadly, it doesn't matter though because they are still our last resort fighters. None of them seem to mind. So why do I?

Obviously, it's not true that we *can't* carry babies, but with the constant shifting and heightened hormones during the moon phases it seriously disrupts the female's cycles. Basically, most of us can get pregnant, but it may take longer than it would a normal human body.

However, our pregnancies are only half the time of a humans, and that's where another problem lies. Some of the female's bodies don't take well to the rapid change and end up miscarrying or dying in childbirth.

It may take longer for our bodies to conceive, but our aging slows down in our mid-twenties so we get a longer period of time to try and conceive, so trust me, our pack keeps popping out more and more lives to ruin all the time.

Of course, the *non-royal* pack members have more choices than I do, but not always. A few of them still have arranged marriages or get sold to other packs because of a shortage of females, or simply because someone with a higher rank desires them.

We have never had a shortage of females, but some of the smaller packs do. Apparently, males dominate my species. Go figure.

What is the difference between royals and non-royals? According to my dad, we are descendants of the very first werewolves ever created. Because of that, we have more power, allowing us to shift faster, and typically makes us more dominant. Breeding between royals has a much higher chance of producing another dominant wolf. Another Alpha.

Non-royals can produce dominants as well of course, just not as often or just not quite as dominant. That being said, royals can birth a completely average wolf just the same.

To have a royal male and female mated is the key to continuing strong bloodlines. There have even been stories of some members of the royal families possessing certain abilities like super strength and speed. I haven't listened to many of those stories though. All I know is that as a female, it will be expected of me to mate to another royal, and reproduce at least one male heir.

Maybe if I let the line die out with me, there won't be anymore stupid arranged marriages. I won't hold my breath on that.

We, as royal wolves, also have the ability to turn a human into one of us with a simple bite. However, almost being exposed a little over a century ago, biting another human has become taboo.

Due to the shortage of women in packs, one Alpha went crazy, and started turning any woman he came across between the ages of 16 and 25.

The women were taken against their will, away from their lives, and away from their families. To top it all off, they learned that they were no longer human. It's no surprise that some went crazy and couldn't control their wolves.

Other Alpha's had to step in to put them down, including the man that had turned them.

I hadn't even realized I was already running back towards home until I felt my Alpha's anger. We have a stronger connection because we are blood.

He is urging me to hurry home. That must be why I had started running that direction without realizing it. What could he possibly want me home for? He's normally too busy with pack stuff to worry about me.

And that's when I remember that it's my birthday.

He always takes off time to spend with me on this day, and is always mad when I take off, but each year sends me running again. You would think he would have learned after all the years. It's not that marriages are arranged *on* our birthdays. It can happen any time. Each new year just reminds me that I am at the eligible age and that my days are numbered.

There's no way my father is going to let me go much longer without taking a mate. I need a way out, and soon.

I block all thoughts, including his *urging* from my head, and let my protesting legs carry me home, even though all I want to do is run the opposite direction.

I slow my pace when I'm only a mile from home so that I can catch my breath. The snow stopped halfway through my run, but it still left a few inches of fresh powder on the ground. The extra padding on the earth is nice on my tight muscles, but it slowed me down a bit on my journey. Dad is going to be furious.

In the distance I make out our log and stone house, though it looks more like a quaint hotel. It has a huge, wrap-around porch, and it is always lit up like Christmas to look warm and welcoming.

You wouldn't know that you were walking into a house that homed werewolves, that's for sure.

Still in my wolf form, I walk in to find my dad on the phone. I take advantage of him being distracted and stiffly trot up the stairs to go shower and change before he can stop me.

To some, it might be weird living with your parents in their twenties, but it is different in a pack. Even pack members who aren't related feel a pull to be near one another, and mated pairs tend to stick near their parents or close pack mates. It is normal here.

It would be hard on my own away from my family, but I have distanced myself for so long, I've become used to it. I just hope that *they* will be okay without *me*. I also hope that they will let me be and not try to track me down.

I know I shouldn't take too much time cleaning up, but the steaming, hot water is magic on my aching muscles. Letting the water pour over me, I let my body defrost under the blissful heat.

Although I don't remember shampooing and conditioning, the sweet scent of my berry shampoo surrounds me. After double-checking to make sure there is no soap left my hair, I grudgingly step out of the shower.

Quickly, as to not test my father's patience, I throw on some warm sweats, tie my long, wet hair up in a bun, and trudge downstairs. I head toward whatever delicious smell is coming from the kitchen. My senses tell me it is some kind of waterfowl. Duck would be my guess, and I can't help the smile that comes to my lips.

"Have a nice run Ari?" Dad's gruff voice startles me as I enter the kitchen. I wait for the anger to come, but something seems off about him and panic reenters my system as I watch him carefully. He won't even meet my eyes, and I can't remember that happening before. Ever.

My dad looks closer to my age than his actual age. He is half a foot taller than my five feet, eight inches. His hair is still dark brown with no trace of grays. Wrinkles are just barely beginning to form on his forehead, but that is mainly from the stress of the job. He always looked so young but he suddenly looks very old at this moment.

"Yeah. Sorry I was gone so long. Lost track of time."

"Don't you always," he says with a sigh, but he sounds almost amused rather than mad. "Made one of your favorites. Roasted duck. Eat up and get some sleep, sweetie. Goodnight," he kisses the top of my head before turning to go to bed.

"Dad what's going on?"

"You'll find out at the meeting tomorrow."

And just like that, I was dismissed. Not even a "happy birthday" or birthday cake. Not that I need a silly birthday cake, but it had been tradition.

My stomach turns in fear. Something is going on and I hate to think what that might be. I am no longer hungry, but I know I need to eat. I need my strength for whatever is about to unfold.

As I pick at the duck, I can't help but dread the news I was sure to receive in the morning. I knew this was coming. I'd been hoping all the Alphas had heard about the Alaskan Alphas daughter and had just not wanted to deal with someone like me. There were plenty of willing women in our packs, so why would they want me?

Maybe I am overthinking this like I tend to do. Maybe this isn't even about me. Dad would have told me if I had been chosen, wouldn't he? He would tell me if he had picked a mate for me.

A stray tear slides down my face, surprising me. I swipe at it and stare at it in confusion.

Suddenly I am angry. Have I not been waiting for this? Have I not been preparing for this moment?

I would not let my hard work go to waste. I gave up my life up until now so that I could create my own when this day came. Suddenly ravenous, I sink my teeth into the duck and clean it with sharp teeth until there is nothing but bone left.

I could be blowing this way out of proportion. Hell, I can only hope that I am doing just that, but if this is really happening, I will be ready. I have to be.

Chapter 2

By morning, my panic has receded. There is no point fretting over something that has yet to be named. And if it is what I fear, I spent most of the night coming up with multiple plans. Why worry when I am this prepared.

With renewed energy, I slide on a pair of black jeggings, combat boots, and a long-sleeved shirt before bounding downstairs. I make a b-line for the kitchen and snag some hard-boiled eggs and a bottle of water from the fridge where I find a note that attempts to ruin my appetite.

The words 'Meeting at 9am. Don't be late,' crumple up in my hands and soar through the air to the trash bin.

I scarf down my food and am out the door in seconds with water bottle in hand. I set out running towards the woods on two legs. I have maybe an hour to get in a workout before I need to get back.

Snow still blankets the earth, and it is eerily quiet in the woods. I am amped up and on edge.

For once, I almost wish a polar bear or something large would jump out at me so that I would have someone or something to unleash my fury on.

Nothing ever did, so instead, my pent-up energy is taken out on the air and nearby trees and rocks as I release a barrage of punches and kicks all around me. I keep my thoughts clear, and breathing under control as I focus on hidden enemies.

Ugh. This is much harder without dad's men to beat up. It's so unsatisfying when I can't make someone groan in pain. I'm not going to become a better fighter facing off against trees and rocks.

Without a watch, I have no idea how much time has passed, but I know I am running behind. Sprinting as fast as I can back to the cabin, I tense up as the scent of wolves hit me. Pack. A lot of them. I sniff the air again in search of foreign wolves. Thankfully I don't pick up any new scents.

Since we have the largest house, meetings are always hosted here. On top of that, the Alphas home always represents a safe place. We have plenty of rooms so the ones who travel far could stay and rest. Some will come and stay just because they want to be near the Alpha.

I creep in quietly and try to blend in with the crowd just as dad prepares to begin the meeting. His two best wolves, Charles and Niko, flank him. As hard as I tried to avoid my pack mates, there was no hiding from these two.

They were practically my babysitters growing up. Though they preferred the term *bodyguards*, we both knew it was one and the same.

While the rest of the pack saw them as high-ranking dominants, to me, they were just uncle Charlie and uncle Nik. When my dad was gone away for work, they would both come stay with me. We would stay up late and watch movies with giant bowls of banana splits filled with various ice creams and toppings.

They always lasted longer than I would and then carry me to my bed and I'd wake up to blankets holding me captive as my tummy ached with all the sugar from the night before. They always nursed me back to health, but what I appreciate most about them is that they taught me how to fight. On top of that they were always there when I needed someone to talk to or needed a night on the town.

The person who should have been doing all of that was standing directly next to my dad. Long and lean, with honey blonde hair curled to perfection. My mom is beautiful and looks more like she could be my sister with her perfect skin and bright blue eyes.

As the Alpha's wife, you have ultimate protection and get special treatment from all of the pack members. My mother definitely takes advantage of all the disgusting perks. Never had to work a day in her life and spends her days getting primped and pampered, along with throwing parties or other events with other pack women; all on the Alphas dime. She is everything I never want to be.

Her only job was to give my dad a male heir, which kudos to her for doing that on the first try. They had me years later, and according to mom, I was a mistake, but she would never say it in front of dad. In front of him she acted like a perfect angel; the way mates are supposed to act.

My brother is a dominant, and was sent to another pack when I was little. It would be too hard to have another male, even blood-related, dominant in the same pack. It is doable, but challenging. Him and dad were always hotheaded with each other, so it was time for him to go spread his wings. Once he is a little older, he will try to become Alpha of that pack or try to take dad's place here when he is ready.

That fact alone would mean that I would definitely be transferred into a new pack to mate an Alpha. Thankfully our kind isn't sick and twisted enough to make brothers and sisters become mates. I shudder at the horrible thought. If *that* were a possibility, I would have let the bears eat me a long time ago.

My thoughts simmer as I realize the Alpha is speaking. I hold my breath as we all await the news to come.

"As some of you already know, the Canada pack is making moves for more land. We don't know whom they will attack next, but being so close makes us an appealing target. I don't think they are ready for a fight with us, but if they continue gaining, we will eventually be outnumbered."

Selfish bastards. I had heard that the Canadian wolves wanted to expand, but I didn't think they were a serious threat. I mean they are Canadians for Christ's sake. I guess they're not all actually Canadian, but you'd think they'd pick up on their good-natured ways.

Pardon us, but we are deeply sorry to inform you that we would like your land please. Our deepest apologies. Have a great day eh. And then we would slaughter them and take their land.

I laugh aloud and can feel a couple stares from people around me, but I don't care. This is a joke. I don't understand why we are even having a meeting about it, but I can't say I'm not unbelievably happy that it doesn't appear to be what I feared.

Even though we have territory in part of Canada we are still called the Alaska pack. Taking British Columbia many years ago was necessary with the number of wolves we have. I guess now, they want to try and take it back. My dad's deep voice cuts me away from my thoughts.

"Other friendly packs have voiced their opinions and are trying to unite in order to discourage attacks from Canada. I also do not plan to sit and wait for an attack so I have made the decision to unite with another pack in the hopes of helping protect our land and our people."

Oh God. Please don't tell me this is happening. We don't need to unite. We have plenty of land and numbers!

"Alpha King Darien of the Pacific North West United States pack has agreed to join forces," Dad announces and there is a collective silence.

King Darien? As in Darien Shield? The ruthless man that claimed Alpha at the young age of 18? The same man who has increased his packs territory from Washington to Idaho, Montana, Oregon, and Wyoming in just a few years? That Darien? I hear others whispering the same things aloud with worry and fear in their voices.

"And Alpha, what is the price for such a joining? How does this work for us exactly? What will keep him and his pack from turning on us?" a pack member asks.

Oh no. I want to tear the throat out of the idiot who dared ask that question. I'm not ready for the answer.

I want to die when dad's eyes flicker to me, and while I watch mom smile, his eyes fill with guilt. *No.*

"There are things that still need to be worked out, but once we do, you will be able to access their land and they will have access to ours. There will be some established to prevent any confrontations between Alphas," he pauses and my heart stops. Mom chooses this time to take over.

"Alpha Darien is in need of a mate of royal lines and our daughter will make a fine gift for his cooperation. Out of all the offers for mates he has had, our Ari is the one he has chosen. Such a deal will ensure our packs safety."

A gift? Was she joking? I want to vomit and then smash her pretty little face in it.

"Poor Darien, he must not know about her," my heightened senses hear someone whisper in the crowd. How did they go from fear of Darien, to feeling sorry for him? They really think that badly of me? I am too angry about the issue at hand to ponder that any further. Another part of me wants to know why the hell he would pick me out of all the others.

"Where is that beautiful daughter of mine anyways?" mom asks with a laugh, but it doesn't take long for her to find me, as I am already pushing through the mass of people towards her. "Oh! There you are sweetie."

"Oh, cut the *sweetie* crap. Everyone knows you can't stand me and you can forget about "gifting" me to Darien," I stare her down from the front of the pack.

My Alphas guilt-filled eyes turn hard as he steps in front of my mother.

"Young lady, you will not speak to your mother like that, and you will do as you're told."

"This is not fair. I should be able to decide who is to be my mate," I meet his surprised gaze.

"Is there someone you had in mind?" That question threw me for a loop. *Crap.*

"Er, no..." Did I really have a choice before? My mother smirked. They were playing games now.

"Then you will do your part in helping protect this pack, and mate to Alpha Darien," he commands with his Alpha voice. I can feel his words, his will, as it wraps around me and seeps into every fiber of my being.

No! I can do my part to protect this pack! I can fight! I don't need a mate. I won't be controlled for the rest of my life!

Shock fills me as I feel his command start to weaken at my thoughts and emotions. Somehow, I can sense where I need to attack in order to break his command. So that's exactly what I do.

When I look up into his fear filled eyes, I realize what I have just done. He felt what I had done. This is impossible. It would cause chaos. My father could be killed and it would be my fault. With this, I could take my life into my own hands, but are my own needs worth sentencing my own father to death?

"Yes, Alpha," I reply automatically into the deathly quiet room.

Everyone around me is staring in shock at the spectacle I've created. Everyone except for Uncle Charlie and Uncle Nik. Humor was written all over their faces. *They know!* They must have seen it in my eyes that I was able to shake off the command.

Before I can think, I run from the room. I only hope I can trust Charlie and Niko not to pass on the word about me being able to disregard dad's order, or worse, challenge dad themselves.

I run deep into the woods, not caring about the laughter and gossip I have created at my expense. After all, I would be gone soon. With all the plans I made for escape, I never factored in Alpha Darien. How could I possibly escape *him*?

Chapter 3

Dad found me in my room shortly after I came home. It was already dark out so I changed into some warm clothes and sprawled out on my bed to ponder more about what the hell I was going to do. I can't just give up. I won't.

"Can we talk a moment?"

"Do I have a choice?"

"Apparently so, based on what happened this morning," he retorts and my cheeks burn red.

"Charlie and Niko saw. What is going to happen?" I ask, feeling like a little kid even though I am apparently strong enough to break Alpha command.

"First off, thank you for playing it off like it didn't happen. I respect you greatly for that. I've already spoken to Charles and Niko. I offered to let them challenge me, but they were against it. Something about how you would kick their ass if they tried," he says with amusement. I almost laugh, but then I remember what he has done to me.

"How can you do this to me dad?" He sighs loudly and 30 excruciatingly long seconds pass before he speaks.

"I never wanted this to happen, Ari. I know the rules suck and if you found someone you truly cared for, I would do whatever I could with my power to make it possible, but you are 22 now and haven't even tried to find interest in the pack."

"Don't blame this on me!"

"I'm not! It's not your fault. I would have done the same thing if I was in your shoes, and for a while I was, but as an Alpha, I had to follow the rules. Even Alphas don't get to choose their mates sometimes," he says with a wink and I realize he is talking about mom.

"You mean you didn't choose mom?" He looked like he wasn't going to answer but he finally caves.

"No, I did not choose her. My father gave her to me when we were both only 16. I didn't become Alpha until I was 25, but my father knew I would be Alpha one day so he wanted to give me a gift. I was dumb, and well, you know what it's like to be 16. Carrie, your mother, was only 17 when we had your brother, Daniel.

We had nothing in common, but our wolves were mated and I would do it all over again if I knew I would get you and Daniel out of the deal."

"Oh please, we both know I'm a pain to deal with." I hang my head.

"You are *different* than most of our kind, but I see much of myself in you. You are strong, smart, and I know you will become something greater than anyone would believe. There is a reason I have not had you mated yet." I look at him in surprise.

He has *kept* me from being mated?

"There has been many Alpha's pining for you because of your bloodline, but I told them that none of them were good enough. There was nothing they could offer me worth your value."

Time seems to stand still as the last 22 years play through my head. I can't believe my ears. I wish I had known sooner so that maybe I wouldn't have been so bitter to him and everyone else. I wanted to hug him for what he'd done for me, but there were still things I needed answered.

"So, what makes Darien good enough?" I try to hide the emotion in my voice, but fail. His eyes soften.

"I don't think anyone will ever be good enough, but this threat is real and I want you and our pack protected. With Darien's help, I believe we can do that."

"I can't mate to him dad."

"Sure you can. I know he is ruthless in his quest for more territory, but he can protect you. Besides, if anyone can handle him, it's you. I have heard many say that he is quite the looker."

"I don't care if he's the hottest man on earth, he is still *Darien Shield*! He killed his own father and like three other Alphas shortly after. He could kill *me*."

"How do you know so much about him?" he eyes me warily.

"Because I'm not going to let anyone make my decisions for me. I knew this would happen someday and I wanted to know what I would be up against, but I never expected Darien Shield."

"Calm down, Ari. Just give the guy a chance. Maybe there is more to him than you think. Who knows, maybe you could actually fall in love with someone as strong as him."

I want to hurl at his words. As far as I know, Darien is nothing but a killer. If he could turn on his father, he could turn on me, and not in the good way.

There were rumors of his father being a cruel and ruthless man too. Apparently, his son grew up just as dark as he was.

How on earth could my father think that I would fall in love with a murderer?

"When is he coming?" I ask with renewed anger.

His face pales at my question.

Shit.

"Tomorrow? Seriously dad?" he nods his head in confirmation and I want to cry and vomit at the same time. I am so not ready for this, but I have to be strong for my dad and for what was to come.

"Well, just so you know, if he turns out to be the guy that I think he is, I will kill him," and I am dead serious.

"That's my girl," he says proudly before kissing my head and walking out the door, leaving me standing stunned in my quiet room.

H e is coming *today*. Since I couldn't sleep last night, I packed all my stuff that I would need to take with me and tried to mentally prepare myself for this. Who am I kidding? Nothing could possibly prepare me for Alpha Shield.

It is true that I have heard stories of his seriously good looks but as far as I knew, he didn't give any woman the time of day. Why is he looking for a mate now? Why do I care? If he truly is a monster, I will take him down, or die trying.

I give up trying to sleep and start the shower before standing under the spray where no one can hear my muffled cries.

At least I wasn't leaving behind any friends or a mother who would be heartbroken at my departure. No, the only one who will miss me is my dad, and maybe my "uncles," but I'm sure they will be happy enough not to have their asses handed to them by me again.

Maybe my mom would have loved me if I liked to do all the things she did. Or even if I enjoyed *one* of the things she liked to do, but we did nothing together. Part of that was my fault though. When I was younger, she always asked me to come shopping with her or the spa to get our nails done, but I never wanted to.

The only time we ever did anything was when I would need to go shopping for new clothes, but those trips always ended up in a fight about one thing or another. She finally stopped asking and would just bring me whatever she picked out for me.

I got a lot of my features from her. We are the same height and are both lean, but still blessed with the right curves. We have the same hair texture but mine is a soft brown, and I have hazel eyes next to her blue ones.

Over the years, I have gotten many compliments on my looks, but it wasn't a blessing to me. It was a curse. If I were ugly, maybe I wouldn't be forced into this. It's not that my picture has been passed around, but the rumors spread. News definitely would have gotten out about the grotesque Alaskan Alpha's daughter. Then maybe I could have had my own life.

Apparently, the sweats and combat boots that consist of my main attire didn't get spread around to help me out. I downplayed my looks as much as I could, but with the benefits of being a werewolf I never had to worry about acne or scars or getting fat. All werewolves are beautiful in their own unique ways, but there are some, like my mother, who stand out above the rest.

I wish my mom and I could have been closer, but I will never be like her. I won't ever agree with arranged marriages. I'm sure some work out, but what about for the rest of us? My simple-minded mother would never understand.

As for my dad, he taught me all about pack politics. Everything I know about our kind, I learned from him or my uncles. We had a lot in common. We like the same food and both prefer our wolf form to our human form, and love to fight.

Sure, he was gone a lot for work, but he always made time for me when he was home.

Now I would have nobody. I almost hoped that Darien would be someone I could fall in love with and that my life really would start with him and wherever he is taking me.

That hope is what inspires me to wear something other than sweats. Today, I chose to wear my nice jeans with a teal hooded jacket but I keep the boots. And if it turns out Darian really is the monster that I believe him to be, I can at least trick him into thinking I'm just a pretty bimbo before making my move. I guess it can't hurt to hope for the best though. Unfortunately, I don't think I inherited my dad's optimism.

I walk downstairs to find Charlie and Niko in the entryway. Any silly thoughts I had about this being a start to my happily ever after, are shattered at the words "He's here".

The minute he stepped out of his hummer, I hated him. Maybe it was even before he stepped out. He's wearing jeans, a thick leather jacket, and a smug smile that reads *asshole* all over it. I want to punch that grin right off his face.

In due time, I try to wipe the glare from my face and force a fake smile.

"Alpha Shield," my dad greets him with a handshake.

"Pleasure to finally meet you, Alpha Wilder" he shakes my father's hand.

"Thank you for making the long trip. I hope it wasn't too unpleasant. Please, come meet my daughter, Ari." The man takes my hand and kisses it before I can stop him.

My inner wolf growls. What happens if our wolves don't want to make nice? My parents may not love each other, but it is obvious that their wolves accepted each other.

Our wolves are an extension of our human-selves but their thoughts and needs aren't quite so complex. Rather than love, they seek strength, power, submissiveness, or loyalty, depending on the personality of the wolf. I could definitely sense power from him, but something about him was putting my wolf on edge. Or maybe it is just my strong feelings that are feeding her attitude towards him.

"It is lovely meeting you, my beauty," he purrs, causing my stomach to roll in disgust. Sure, he is handsome with a strong build, though he looks older than I thought he would. There's something about him that is sending creepy crawlies down my spine.

I glance at my father who simply shrugs at me. He's clueless. Whoever said this guy was hot, definitely does not share my taste in men.

He's definitely not ugly. His features are dark with eyebrows that make his light blue eyes pop. Plus, he's a decent height, with broad shoulders. He could be handsome, but he looks a little rough around the edges for someone I believed to be only in his late twenties. Maybe the stress of all his conquests at such a young age have aged him, or he's just one of those unlucky men who don't age well.

Two expressionless men flank Darien just as Charlie and Niko accompanied us for safety. I try not to be surprised that mom isn't here. I guess she couldn't even spare a few moments to say goodbye to her only daughter.

"I would invite you to stay for lunch, but I don't know how much longer I can keep the wolf under control. You are taking my only daughter after all," my dad laughs at his own ridiculous offer.

"Understood. She will be well taken care of. We have a long trip ahead of us anyways. I look forward to doing business with you," Darien says before they shake hands again, and my uncles start loading my stuff up. I only packed two bags since we are taking a plane back to somewhere in the United States. We know his territory, but not exactly where he resides.

It finally dawns on me that this is actually happening. I don't know what I was thinking would happen. Was I expecting dad to not like him and tell him no and that the deal was off? Did I expect a hole to open up in the ground and swallow Darien and his cronies?

Fuck! This is really happening!

My body shakes involuntarily and I'm suddenly in Niko's arms. I didn't see him come in for a hug, but I could tell it was him just by his familiar scent of spicy cologne and coffee.

"Shh. It will be okay. Just be yourself, sweetie," he tries to calm me but how could I possibly be calm? I have no idea where I am going, nor do I know anything about the people around me aside from the fact that Darien is a cold-blooded murderer who is greedy for territory.

Charlie hugs me next, telling me to make sure to keep in touch and visit soon.

Dad is up next but just gives a quick hug and swift kiss on the cheek. He says nothing, but I know it is only because he would break down if he did. I know because I am on the verge of doing the same thing. *I'm* allowed to cry, but if *he* falls apart, it would show a great weakness to Darien and his companions. I won't show him my tears either. No one gets to see this girl cry.

It took me until now to realize that if I run away and break this deal, the pact between the two territories would probably be null and void, leaving my pack vulnerable to Canada. When I imagined how I would be sent away to another pack, there was never any imminent danger in the scenario. I might actually have to try to make this work for my family's sake.

Dazed and defeated by my new revelation, I subconsciously let the Alpha take my hand in his elbow and lead me to the car.

I look back once more at the only three people I considered my family, wishing I had tried harder to be a part of their pack, but it was too late now. I give a weak smile as I try to memorize every detail about them before stepping into Darien's Hummer, and into my new life.

Chapter 4

Darien

It was weeks ago when we started hearing from the other packs. Due to too many dominance games, Alphas never talked to other Alphas over the phone. Therefore, their advisers and mine, the eldest, or most educated in the pack, are the ones who do all of the talking.

The Canada pack appears to be making a move, which we have suspected for some time, but we were hoping that those suspicions were just nonsense.

Whether it is true or not, our territory borders to theirs, along with a couple other packs, but I don't want to risk *us* being the territory they try to take.

Rumor is that they are going after the Alaska pack, which makes sense since they had taken part of Canada. However, if they take over Alaska, they will triple my packs size.

We have grown significantly from where we started, but we are still new, and therefore seen as weak to some. Regardless of how much we have grown, I don't think we are ready for a war with a pack as large as Canada's. We are too spread out and vulnerable to counter an attack.

Over the past couple years, I have had countless packs offer me their top eligible female, in order to unite my pack with theirs, but have turned them down. There was no immediate threat at the time, and I don't want a mate. Not then, and not now.

However, when the Alpha King of Alaska said he was looking for a pack to unite with, there was no way that I was going to let that chance pass. Their territory borders ours, and between our numbers and theirs, only a fool would mess with our packs and territory.

For some reason though, the Alpha of Alaska seemed to believe *we* were doing *them* a favor. To me, I saw it as equal, if not *them* doing *us* a favor. We have a lot of territory now, but the number of wolves in that territory is not as dense as the amount in Alaska. Not all wolves remained after we took out their leaders. Some fled to other packs, while others tried to retaliate, and lost their lives along with their Alpha. We just recently took a new territory so we are still figuring out our numbers.

My advisors took advantage of the situation and asked if they had an eligible royal to be married while I was away dealing with new pack members. When they told me that they asked for such a request, I blew a fuse.

We argued back and forth, but in the end, I knew they were right. Mating to the Alpha's daughter from the Alaska pack would make a stronger pact between us. Everyone would be much less nervous all around with a woman to seal the deal.

It doesn't change the fact that I don't want a wife. Taking a mate is the furthest thing from my mind right now. I don't need that distraction, but I can't deny that it's a good move for this deal to work.

Refusing them at this point would be a sign of disrespect, and then we would never join forces. There was nothing I could do about it except suck it up and deal with it. As long as she stays out of my way, how bad could having a woman by my side possibly be?

Then I remember the stories I have heard about Alpha Wilder's wife. Sure, she plays the part, but when he is gone, she does nothing but throw parties and spend his money. She actually believes herself to be Queen of the pack. I'm sure the apple doesn't fall far from the *queen* tree herself.

I had immediately started asking around about what others might know about Alpha Wilder's daughter. I had to know what my advisors have gotten me into.

The Alpha offered to have her sent on a flight next week, but something about that didn't seem right to me. Typically, dealings like this are done in person. I would go get her like a man should do. Besides, this way I can meet the man that I will be joining forces with in person, if only for a couple of minutes.

Now that we are almost there, I am ready to turn the plane around and call the whole deal off. If Canada decides to attack, so be it. I don't need some royal, high and mighty, spoiled brat, coming into our territory, especially as *my* mate. I am doing things just fine on my own. Sure, it would be nice to have some release every now and then, but not with the price tag attached to it.

Being an Alpha for over six years now, I should have already taken a mate, but I have been busy straightening out things in my pack, and increasing our territory so that what happened before would never happen again.

I feel wrong leaving my territory and pack for so long, but I told them to be on alert while I'm away. Together, they will be fine for a couple of days. Traveling to Alaska is no quick journey, which is why Alpha Wilder had offered to fly his daughter to me versus typical protocol. Staying and resting won't be possible, so we will be traveling back as soon as we pick the girl up.

My two right-hand men and I had landed in Anchorage not too long ago where we boarded for our next flight to a city called Kotzebue. From there, we will be renting a Hummer as they recommended due to the snow and icy roads.

Being in northern territory, we are used to the ice and snow, but I'm sure that here in Alaska, it is a whole other world. Us wolves don't mind the cold, but I don't think I could live in it every day for the rest of my life. So far, the scenery has been something else though.

Minutes later, the plane lands a bit harsher than I am used to, and I realize it is due to the snow-powdered runway. Back home they would have just cancelled the flight, but it's a whole new playing field up here. These pilots do this almost every day.

I am less than an hour from meeting the girl I will have to spend the rest of my life with, and I am suddenly feeling queasy. Maybe she won't be that bad. Maybe I wouldn't even notice her presence. And then I remember that royal women always make their presence known in a pack. *Shit.*

Our pack doesn't need that right now. We are still building up from nothing, so we don't need someone coming in and causing drama and wasting all of my and the pack's funds on whatever they want.

There are definitely going to have to be some rules. If I have to put her in her place, I will. After everything I have done, I will not tolerate a self-righteous brat just because she thinks she is royalty. I'm "royal" born as well, but I don't think of myself as a King.

I don't remember exiting the plane or getting in the large SUV, but here I am in the backseat, dreading what will happen about 30 minutes from now.

Shoving down my poor attitude, I prepare to be on my best behavior and put on a good face for the Alpha. I need to show them that I am confident and capable of keeping her safe. However, nothing could have prepared us for the surprise that awaits us.

We pull up to the spot the Alpha directed me to meet him and his daughter. We had agreed on only two wolves each, aside from his daughter. So why on earth are there a dozen men waiting for us here? *Fuck.* I don't even see the female. Did we walk into a trap? Was this all some set up to take me out?

My men become uneasy beside me. If this is a trap, their deaths will be on my hands. We slowly step out of the truck, prepared to shift if anyone makes a move towards us.

"Why is there another Alpha on my territory?" Alpha Wilder practically growls at us, or at least I assume that is who spoke.

Is he mad? He must have lost his damn mind. The other Alpha's hostility triggers my dominant side. My wolf tries to take over but I force him back.

"What are you talking about? I am Alpha Darien. We were supposed to meet today to receive your daughter. And the deal was that you were only supposed to have two extra wolves," I growl right back. I may be in his territory, but I will not show weakness.

"Alpha Darien was already here over half an hour ago and left with my daughter," anger fuels his words and I can see his canines sharpen. What does he mean she already left? Does that mean someone posed as me and took her? How could someone have even known that we were meeting today?

"I'm sorry Alpha Wilder, but *I* am Alpha Darien Shield. Someone else took your daughter, sir," I stare him straight in the eye.

The anger remains on his face but slowly changes into confusion and disbelief as he hears the conviction in my words. Werewolves can sense when someone is lying and he now knows that I am not. And then his anger returns tenfold. *Shit.*

Ari

Almost an hour or so has passed since we left my home. Well, the only place I really knew as home anyways. I don't think it ever really felt like home until the moment I was removed from it. I tried to never let myself hold that attachment, and for this reason exactly. I didn't want to be sad about leaving. I need to be strong and prepared for whatever comes next.

We should have reached the airport a long time ago, especially with how insanely fast the driver has been zooming through the mild snowstorm.

"I thought we were going to the airport in Kotzebue," I question suspiciously. Had dad given me the wrong details?

No one answers, putting me even more on edge. What the fuck is going on? The whole car ride has been quiet, and the tension in the air is suffocating me. Darien punches buttons on his phone, and continues to ignore me.

"Someone please tell me what the hell is going on!" I demand.

"We are taking a different route back, *princess*," the Alpha finally answers me through gritted teeth. My fists clench in my lap.

"Don't call me *princess*."

Darien laughs at my threatening tone.

"Oh, I am going to enjoy you, *princess*," he says the word slowly for effect. I am about to sock him square in the jaw, when suddenly the car stops. "It won't be long now. Our ride will be here soon."

We all exit the vehicle and I have to fight the urge to shift and take off. I need to accept this as my life now in order to unite our packs and provide safety for everyone. Mostly I am just doing this for my dad. However, if he continues to call me that stupid term of endearment, deal's off.

Not five minutes later, a small plane or a large jet lands in the distance. Dad never said anything about giving them clearance to bring a private jet.

If they had a jet all this time, why wouldn't that have been their transportation the whole way to and from the chosen location?

Something is definitely wrong here. I don't need my wolf senses to tell me that.

Darien's two men, whose names I discovered to be Garrett and Ryan, grab my two bags out of the trunk. If I had known we would have a private jet, I may have packed a few more things.

Darien takes my arm a little too roughly and hurries me toward the jet. I pull my arm free, but keep his hurried pace just so he won't try to touch me again. Though he gives me a hard glare, he lets it go.

He rushes up the ramp before me, and with his back turned, I play with the idea of running again. Suddenly Garrett is behind me, reminding me that I am definitely not alone. Not that I couldn't outrun them all, but I have a job to do.

Are they really just going to leave the hummer stranded out here? Oh well, I guess it doesn't concern me. Apparently, I wasn't privy to all of the details of this arrangement.

With a defeated sigh, I continue up the ramp.

"Are we ready for takeoff?" I hear Darien ask the pilot as I step into the cabin.

"Almost sir, I just need to double check a few things and top off on fuel, and then we will be off."

"Fine, just hurry up," the Alpha dismisses him. *Asshole.* "Come sit, my pretty," he calls to me from the luxury bench seat.

Instead of obeying, I just stare at him like he is out of his mind, which he is if he thinks calling me stupid pet names is going to work for him.

Strong hands push me from behind and deposit me on the seat beside Darien. *Damn.* This man handling shit needs to be dealt with and soon. Clearly these men think they can push me around, and I was going to play cute and innocent, but I won't stand for this treatment.

"You are a feisty one aren't you," he smiles wickedly. *Yes, I am, and I want to scratch your eyes out right now.* I settle for just glaring in response.

Apparently, he took that as a sign for him to straddle me. His movement catches me off guard. I try to push him off but his weight pins me down.

Gathering my strength, I prepare to knock him off using one of the moves that my uncles taught me, but Ryan and Garrett grab my arms from each side as Darien holds my face still. His disgusting breath hits me at full blast.

"You were going to be a gift to my son, but sadly I will have to give you to him *used.* I've never had a woman quite as spunky as you, and I just have to try you out. It's been a long time since I've had a virgin. Don't worry though, he's not a virgin either."

What? Since when does Darien have a son? He definitely isn't old enough to have a son near my age, that's for damn sure.

Then everything begins to make sense; the Hummer they abandoned, the tense atmosphere since we left my home, the fact that he definitely doesn't look like he's in his twenties, and now the unplanned jet. I don't know how it is possible, but this is *not* Darien Shield. *Shit.*

Darien

"Which trail is theirs?" I sniff around in anger. I should have been happy about this turn of events. I should be thrilled that she is gone, and let things be as they were. After all, she isn't my problem, but for some reason, I feel like it is. Spoiled brat or not, no one deserves whatever she might be going through right now.

"What are you doing?" Alpha Wilder questions me.

"What does it look like? I'm going after them. Now, which trail is theirs?" I ask impatiently.

"This is it," one of his wolves' call, and I hurry over to check it out. I pick it up easily as it is the strongest scent from being the most recent.

It's obvious that the woodsy, berry scent must belong to the female. My wolf rumbles in approval. He is angry that they took what is his. I shake his thoughts from my head.

My eyes search the darkening sky. Hopefully the snow stays at bay to keep from covering up their fresh tire tracks.

"You would do that? You will go after my daughter?"

"I'm sure going to try," I start undressing and find the Alpha's confused gaze. "I will be faster on four legs in this weather and terrain," I explain to him.

"Take my two best men, Charles and Niko," he calls them to attention, and I don't argue his request. "I would go too, but if we both go as the wolf, one of us may not make it back. I will follow behind you shortly."

It is true that we are both close to reaching our limit. I can't help but wonder why he would go after her. Though it's not strange for a father to want to protect his own daughter, it is not protocol. She was no longer his responsibility once he handed her over. It must be because of the fact that he had been deceived. I couldn't see my parents doing the same for anything other than that reason alone.

I can't help but wonder what is so special about this girl that he has kept her untouchable until now?

Before anything else can be said, I change into my wolf form and sprint at full speed down the trail with four wolves on my tail as we set out to rescue the Alpha's daughter; my future mate if I can get to her in time.

There were many possible situations I could have come upon, but I would have never guessed in a million years that this is what I would find. I am amazed that we even got here in time, but I am even more amazed by the scene that's taking place in front of me.

Chapter 5

Ari

"Who are you?" I question the asshole gripping my face between rough hands. Panic sears every cell in my body. I am alone, up against at least four wolves, though I have no idea if there is another pilot that I didn't see.

"Alpha John Flint of the Canadian pack, Miss," he laughs as he moves in to sniff my neck and I try not to faint with repulsion.

"What do you want with me?" I try to distract him.

"I want your land little pup. I want *my* land back. Plus, I heard that you, the Alaskan Alpha's infamous daughter that is too good for everyone, was going to be part of the deal. It was so perfect that I just had to interfere. You are my bargaining chip, my dear. Without you, the PNW US pack can't join forces, and I can get Alaska to surrender to my will," he laughs like a maniac, but he is surprised when my own laugh joins his. He stares at me as if I have gone mad.

"You think they will surrender just because of me? You are even stupider than I thought!" I continue to laugh but am cut off by a sharp pain against my cheek. I move to retaliate, but the two goons keep me pinned in place.

"I think you have done enough talking for now. Obviously, your dad has some soft spot for you, or else he would have given you to me a long time ago. I will get what I want, and right now that's your body, sweet Ari," he growls before tearing through my favorite top, leaving me in just my bra. Big mistake.

From the moment this prick showed up today, my anger had been ignited. The flames burn hotter and hotter with every passing second. First the *princess* comments, the manhandling, the slap, and now *this*. The only thing keeping me cooperative was the fact that he is supposed to be Darien Shield, which he apparently is not. Even if he was the real deal, I have officially been pushed over the edge. Enough was enough. It's time to show them the *real* Ari.

This time, I catch *him* off guard as I slam my head into his nose, causing blood to gush down his face and onto my bared skin. I then remember that two dominant wolves are still here, and hold my arms hard enough to leave bruises.

Fuck it. I don't care if I die fighting. I will not let them have their way with me. These meatheads messed with the wrong girl.

Alpha Flint howls in pain and I watch as he struggles to keep his wolf under control. Ryan and Garrett pull me to my feet. *Just what I needed,* I smile to myself. I use the momentum to do a split jump, kicking both legs straight out. I make contact to each of their stomachs, causing meathead one and two to release me, though they about pull my arms out of socket as they fall.

Catching myself on one knee, I am back up in an instant. Garrett reaches me first and I land a hard punch to his face, followed by a swift kick to the groin.

Thankfully a lot of males underestimate me for being a female, or else I might not get such easy shots. I use my training and search for a weapon, but the space is clear of objects aside from a couple of pillows. Unless they are going to lie down and let me smother them to death, I am stuck with my fists alone.

I leap for the door in order to create more distance, but the pilot's return catches me by surprise. My fist thrusts out reflexively, effectively knocking him back down the ramp. He is definitely a submissive wolf. He stood no chance, even when catching me off guard. If I had told him to fling himself down the ramp he probably would have. I almost felt bad for him. Almost.

Yanked back by my hair, I again use the momentum to slam my back into my attacker, throwing elbows and aiming for the soft spots.

He grunts, releasing me, and it turns out to be Ryan that I have knocked down, but he will be up again soon.

It takes a lot to keep a dominant wolf down, which is why I would not live to see another day again. Fighting my pack mates, I learned their fighting styles, but these are new opponents, and these intend me serious harm. It's because of that, that I would not deceive myself into thinking I could make it out alive tonight. I will definitely be giving them hell though. I wanted to see real battle, and I am getting my last dying wish, and enjoying the shit out of it.

I turn my attention to my other attackers just feet away from me and move back into fighting position. Instead of charging me, I find them glaring at the open door to my back left. They almost look nervous now. I let my gaze follow theirs.

In the doorway stands a large man, easily a head taller than me, with dark brown hair, and bright, emerald green eyes that seem to glow with intense anger.

He is beautiful and terrifying at the same time. He looks dangerous. Those emerald eyes seem to burn brighter when they meet mine. My wolf eyes surface to meet his. I realize then that he is buck ass naked, and I make an effort to keep my eyes on his face and no lower, even if my traitorous eyes do want to wander.

Deep down in my soul, I know that this man is the real Darien Shield. That fact scares me more than the three dominant wolves I'm fighting off. This is the actual man who is to become my mate. How the hell did he find me here?

Hearing movement behind me, I quickly drop down and kick out a hard sweep, knocking Garrett on his face. Before I can move to strike again, the real Darien is on him, quickly knocking him unconscious before leaping over me toward the now wolf form of Alpha Flint.

I barely get the chance to take in his dark gray wolf with those piercing, ice blue eyes before Ryan is back up and moving to help his Alpha. However, four more men suddenly appear and it takes two of them to get him outside of the small cabin. *Was that Charlie and Niko?*

Now that I have been kicked out of the fight, I am very aware of my state of dress. *Dammit all to hell.*

That was my nice outfit too. And the real Darien didn't even get to see it. Why do I care? The excitement of the fight must be getting to me, or maybe I'm annoyed that his first image of me is in shredded clothing and covered in blood. I'm not used to showing so much skin.

I try to shrink into myself and cover up, though I don't know what the big deal is, when my soon to be mate is as free as a jay bird.

Us wolves get over the nakedness pretty quickly, but since I avoided everyone, no one has ever seen me naked. Not passed the age of like two anyways. Now I kind of wished someone had just so that this wouldn't feel so damn awkward. My shyness is a hindrance on my current situation. Who would have thought?

In the blink of an eye, Darien shifts into his wolf form. He is even more massive now, with fur so dark, it is almost black, and his eyes really are glowing now.

His wolf form is beautiful, and the sheer size of him is intimidating. Not only that, but I can see the absolute fury in his eyes as he faces off with the other Alpha. Even after appearing to have run all the way here, he still has enough energy to take on another high-ranking Alpha.

They both move with great force and incredible speed. Darien is obviously the stronger of the two as he backs the gray wolf into a corner, but he is blindsided by a swift bite on the arm before being tackled across the jets cabin. *Cheap shot, Alpha Flint.*

I am too busy watching Darien get back up to realize that Alpha Flint is now charging to attack me. To kill me.

Before I can retaliate or move out of the way, Darien's body takes a protective stance in front of me, and he braces for impact. My eyes widen with fear. Fear for Darien. And that terrifies me even more. Why on earth do I care?

Darien

We had crept quietly up to the unmarked jet in the middle of the field. If we lose the element of surprise, this rescue will not be much of a rescue at all.

The other men and I change back into our human forms so that we can climb the narrow ramp without our claws scraping at each step. Hell, they probably smell us by now, but they haven't peeked out the open door yet. It's as if something is distracting them. I'm afraid to find out what that distraction might be.

As I am about to start our climb, a man, a werewolf, is flying down the stairs. Backwards. I prepare to attack the enemy, but he isn't moving. Unconscious. What in the hell is going on up there? I hurry up the stairs and take in the scene before me.

Blood is everywhere. The one I assume to be Alpha, due to his substantial size, is soaked in the blood, while the others each look a little worse for wear as well.

I search for the culprit who caused the gore and my eyes land on a lean, muscled masterpiece of perfect curves, rocking jeans and sexy combat boots.

When she turns, and those hard, hazel eyes find mine, I feel like I am having an out of body experience.

The fight around me is nonexistent and for a split second, it is just me and *her*. The woman before me is absolutely breathtaking. I can't help but memorize every detail of her luscious dark lips, bright eyes, and brown hair that I want to run my hands through.

As I look her over, I notice that she has no shirt or jacket, but is wearing blood, and matching bruises on each arm.

My anger comes swift and wild and I am moving the moment I see one of the males make a move toward her. Before I can reach her though, she is down low sweeping the males feet out from under him.

I am on him the instant he hits the ground and land a blow that I know he won't be recovering from anytime soon.

Wasting no time, I am up leaping over the fierce woman before the Alpha can reach her. No one is going to touch her like that ever again.

Tackling the gray wolf away from my mate, I simultaneously shift into my wolf form. *My mate?* Strange how easy the word comes to me in this moment, but somehow it feels right.

Mine, my wolf growls. Shit. The Alpha catches me during my revelation and tackles me away, leaving her wide open, and she isn't watching him, but *me*. Is that worry in her eyes?

The gray wolf makes a b-line for her and I am up in a flash, moving faster than I ever have before. Blocking his path, I shield her from him, and brace for impact. After this hit, I'm going to need my men to help me finish him off.

No one is more surprised than me when her hands grip my fur. She uses my body to leap over me and lands a clean kick straight into the wolf's face.

It's enough force to keep him from slamming into me, but not enough to take him out, and he is already going after her again.

He has her pinned in an instant, a claw digging into her bare stomach. Fury erupts in me like white-hot lightning.

I don't know how or when it happened, but the Alpha's throat is suddenly in between my teeth and I am seconds away from ending his pathetic life, like so many Alpha's before him. He snarls at me, but I can feel his fear as he desperately tries to free himself.

"Wait! Darien!" I am caught off guard by hearing my name from her lips. She knows that I am the real Darien? "If you kill him, you will start a war."

I growl in response. Like I care after what he almost did. Her eyes bore into mine and I can feel the strength she holds.

"Trust me, *I* more than anyone agrees that he needs to die, and would love to kill him myself, but think about your pack. I won't stop you from killing the bastard. He is more than deserving of death. I just want to remind you why you and I are here. To prevent a war; not start one," she soothes with her hypnotizing voice.

Before I can consider her words, she lands a swift roundhouse kick to the Alphas head, narrowly missing my face, but something tells me she would have hit me too if she wanted to. My wolf's excitement is unlike anything I have felt through him before. He wants her now.

The Alpha now lies unconscious in my grasp and I harshly toss his body aside. My, um—ah hell, who cares—my *mate* is rubbing at the bruises on her arms and I involuntarily move towards her. She stops when she sees me take notice.

I sniff her sweet scent, in search of hidden injuries. She has a large wound on her stomach from the claw mark, but it's already healing. The majority of blood I noticed when I first found her, I can smell is thankfully not hers, but the Alphas. When I find nothing life threatening, my nose presses against her belly in relief. I immediately regret it when I startle her and she flinches away from me. *What am I thinking?*

I turn and growl as two men that aren't mine run in, but they stupidly ignore me and head straight towards the girl.

My snarl cuts off when I realize it is the men who were sent with me by Alpha Wilder. Their scent was not recognizable at first because they appear to be wearing the Canadian wolves clothing since they had shredded theirs in their shift.

"There's our girl," they snatch her up, and I have to fight to keep myself in check. Maybe it is time for me to find some clothes and shift back to something a little less hostile than my amped up wolf right now. Normally I have perfect control on my furry half, but I don't feel so in control at the moment.

Hopefully when I return to her, I will be a little less frightening. Why do I care if she is afraid of me or not? Didn't I want to keep her at a distance? A few hours ago, I did, but after laying eyes on her, I am not sure that I will be able to keep myself away from her side.

Chapter 6

Ari

I embrace my uncles, unbelievably happy to see familiar faces here. Moments ago, I thought I was doomed, and in the next I'm the one saving the stupid asshole that started this whole mess. I couldn't just stand by and let Darien start what we are trying to prevent.

Or maybe I just didn't want to see him as the man I know him to be. A murderer.

Maybe I should have just let him kill him. Then maybe my wolf would see the man for what he is and calm the fuck down. She is fighting to come out and meet the new wolf, but I push her down.

It is hard to imagine that someone so willing to run all the way here to protect me can be a murderer. Of course, that is probably just my stupid raging hormones wanting to overlook that fact. There is no denying that Alpha Darien is ultimately the most attractive man I have ever laid eyes on, and there are a lot of attractive men in my father's pack.

This man killed his own father. He has killed other Alphas to take their land and wolves. He almost killed the Canadian Alpha, and he could easily kill me. I can't afford to look past that.

He may have protected me tonight, but Alphas can be unpredictable, especially if the wolf side doesn't accept the female as his mate. He could have come after me simply because he didn't want someone stealing his *things*. Dominant wolves tend to be a little possessive.

"Are you okay?" a deep, concerned voice asks from the jet's doorway. The voice caresses my soul. It's Darien. Clothed now, and still sexy as sin. Remembering his wrongs might be harder than I thought when he has a body like that. Before I can respond, uncle Niko steps up and answers for me.

"Course she is. She's our best female fighter," he slaps me on the back proudly and I feel my cheeks start to burn so I look away.

"Best *female* fighter? She has handed our asses to all of us several times," Charlie corrects him. I look up and I am surprised to find a look of awe in Darien's eyes, but there is something else there mingled with a hint of edginess. This is going to be a long trip back to his home, wherever that may be.

"So, what now?" Darien asks impatiently, directing his question at my uncles. I'm sure he is in a hurry back to his own territory.

"Our Alpha is on his way. You are free to leave once he arrives. They are bringing the SUV you came in, along with all of your belongings," Charlie reports.

Dad is coming here? Who would have thought I'd be seeing him again so soon?

"Can we get out of here?" I ask, suddenly needing some fresh air. They each nod. I look down at myself as we all start to move toward the exit. I then realize that I am still covered in blood and have only a bra covering my top half. "Actually, I'll meet you all outside in a minute 'kay?" They all stare at me in confusion for a second before obliging.

Grabbing one of my suitcases, I open it up, and grab the first shirt and jacket I can find. What am I going to do about the blood though? I walk over to my torn clothes and pick them up. Asshole ruined my favorite jacket. I move to go kick him again—

"Here," Darien's voice surprises me and I jump, but quickly find my composure. Once calm, I notice he is holding out a bottle of water and I stare at him questioningly. "For the blood," he explains, staring at me as if I am some sort of puzzle.

I take the bottle slowly as if it would bite me if I moved too fast. The bottle might not, but the man holding it just might. I just don't know if I liked that idea or not. I do know that I *shouldn't* like the idea.

Turning away from him, I twist the cap off before pouring some water onto my ripped shirt. Using it as a towel, I wipe up as much as I can and use the torn jacket to dry off.

Once clean and dressed, I make my way back to my luggage and find Darien with one bag in his hand and he is about to pick up the other with his free hand.

"I got it!" I say a little too abruptly, and am surprised when he doesn't argue. He motions for me to head out first, but before I go, I take one last look at the unconscious Alpha. *I did that*, I smile. Even if I did have some help in the end. Satisfied, I turn and head down the stairs with my head held high.

"Ari!" my dad's voice shouts, and half a second later I am in his strong arms. "Are you okay?"

"I'm fine da—

"Oh Ari! You're a mess! How do you always find yourself in trouble, sweetie?" mom cuts in with the *sweetie* crap again. The rest of her words have me just as puzzled. The only trouble I ever get in is being out in the woods too late, which I'm sure she hoped every time that something had eaten me.

Why is she even here?

"Oh, you must be Darien," mom giggles and offers her hand. Question answered. Wonderful. I give my dad an "are you kidding me" look and he just shrugs in response.

"Alpha Shield," my dad cuts in before Darien can take her hand, and I want to kiss him for it, "I can't thank you enough for saving my daughter. I hope this wasn't too much for you, and I hope we can still keep our deal."

"No trouble at all, Alpha Wilder. Your daughter had it all under control, and our deal is still intact if it's all the same to you," Darien replies without hesitation.

"She does have a way about handling things," dad says proudly. "I hope you'll do well to remember that, Alpha Shield. And yes, I do wish to keep our arrangement. I hope the rest of your trip is a smooth one. We will take care of everything here."

"Thank you, Alpha Wilder. I would suggest you find a new location for you and your wife now though."

"I agree. Now that the Canadian Alpha knows my location, it is probably best to move elsewhere," dad says before he hugs me and kisses the top of my head like he has done so many times before, and I didn't realize how much I was going to miss that. I may never see any of them again. If I escape Darien, I won't be able to go back to them. I would have to remain in hiding, because I would be wanted for my head, and even my father wouldn't be able to protect me then.

"I love you, Ari. Be happy," he whispers.

"I love you too, dad," I whisper back and choke back tears.

"Bye, sweetie," mom calls, but when I turn to look back, her eyes are all for Darien even though his back is turned and depositing my luggage in the trunk.

I wave to a smiling Charlie and Niko before sliding through the door Darien is holding open for me. He climbs in on the other side while his two wolves hop in the front to drive us away from the chaos.

Darien

I could have gone the rest of my life without meeting Carrie Wilder. She looked as if she wanted to eat me, even with her husband standing right there. Was she trying to cause a fight? She was everything I worried her daughter would be, but even *she* seemed embarrassed by her mother.

Maybe Arianna isn't like her at all. Do I really need more proof? Ari took on an Alpha and two dominants. Not to mention the fact that she knocked a submissive wolf unconscious with one blow.

On top of that, when I stayed in the jets cabin, and she assumed I had left with the others, I saw another side of her. There was no way I was going to leave her there where the unconscious Alpha remained there.

Her kick knocked him out good, but Alphas recover quickly and if he came to with her there, he would kill her. Or rather he would *try* anyways, and I wouldn't leave her to face him alone no matter how strong she is.

Anger sparked in me tenfold when I had spotted her ripped clothes. *She is fine*, I remind my wolf and myself before taking a deep breath.

She had walked over to her torn clothing and I quietly grabbed a water bottle from the snack cart to offer to her. I regretted it when I made her flinch yet again.

After she cleaned up, I watched as she pulled on a fresh shirt and jacket. She had intrigued me again. Most female wolves, especially female wolves looking for a mate would flaunt their blessings. Ari has definitely been blessed, but there was no flaunting. I curse myself for actually wanting to see more.

Did that mean that she doesn't want this? What female wolf didn't want a mate? Especially a mate with land and power like myself. Maybe she is upset about what just happened? I laugh at myself. You *didn't want this a couple hours ago*, I point out to myself. How had things changed so drastically?

How could a woman affect me so quickly? The women I have known have been nothing like the one who stands before me.

I suddenly felt like an asshole for taking her away from her father who obviously adores her. Then I remember the two men who came with me that were all over her, and I don't feel bad anymore. *Mine*. It had taken all of my strength to keep my wolf under control when they touched her.

Hopefully my wolf will calm down once we mate. *Oh shit. Deep breaths.* I attempt to keep my hormones under control, but I know she must have sensed it from her close proximity in the cab. I need to stop thinking.

"So, princess—," my second in command, and our driver, begins.

"The last person who called me princess is unconscious and bleeding in his private jet," she growls.

"I'm sorry, er, I just meant—never mind," I have never seen him so flustered before and I can't help but laugh, but he continues on, "my name is Trace, and I just wanted to say that I am glad to have you on our side, Miss Wilder." There is a pause and he turns his attention back to the road.

"You can call me Ari," she says softly before blushing.

"Welcome Ari, I am Asher, but you can call me Ash, and if you don't want grumpy ol' Darien here, I'll be happy to—

My growl surprises even me, but it shuts Asher up. And then I want to smack myself. What if I scared her?

Slowly, I turn my head in her direction and stare in surprise. Her face is turned away, but I can see her reflection in the window. Is that a smile?

My heart soars at the sight of that small smile, and I want to touch those lips with mine. Once again, I am fighting an erection. I try to look away but her glowing hazel eyes hold my gaze.

After some time, her eyelids begin to flutter before finally closing. Now that she can't see me, I take in her long, thick hair that rests on strong arms and shoulders. She is lean and curvy, but up close it is obvious that she is made of muscle.

I had expected either a bitchy or bubbly, designer clothes wearing girl who wanted nothing but money and power.

Not a quick-witted, combat-boot-wearing beauty that could be *my* security detail. It is still early though and I don't want to get my hopes up. We will see what happens once she settles in to her new home.

Her head rests against the window, but the bumpy terrain keeps jostling her. I move closer and shift her sleeping form so that her head can rest against my chest. I slide my arm over her shoulders to keep her still. She doesn't wake, but cuddles her body closer to mine. That, mixed with her scent filling my nostrils awakes another hard on. Shit.

I look up to see Asher open his mouth.

"Shut it," I say before he can utter a word.

Chapter 7

Ari

I wake up to a comfy bed and a foreign, yet familiar, scent. Not ready to move quite yet, I let myself explore each new smell. There is a combination of thousands of people that I don't recognize, cheap laundry soap, various cleaning supplies, and still a hint of Alpha Flint's blood, but most of all, I smell *him*. Darien Shield. *Oh God.*

Though I'm afraid of what I'll find, I open my eyes to check my surroundings and confirm my suspicion. I find bare walls, a dresser with a TV on it, a small table and chair, along with ugly, fuchsia drapes over the window. I was right; I'm in a hotel room, with Darien Shield himself plastered to my side.

I should be appalled and disgusted, which part of me is, but another part of me doesn't want to move a muscle. Dammit, he even looks sexy when he sleeps. This needs to stop.

Very slowly, I try to slip out from his grasp, but his heavy arm wrapped around me holds me tighter. I freeze. *Please don't wake up, please don't wake up,* I chant. I try not to think about how I seem to fit perfectly in in his arms. Maybe I am still sleeping and just having a silly dream. That makes more sense.

If I am dreaming, I will myself to be bold and touch him. His body is all muscle but has just enough give in the right spots. Touching him feels right and wonderful, and—*oh shit.* I quickly stop touching him and try thinking about something else as my body begins to tingle all over. And then I realize his breathing has changed. He is no longer asleep. *Crap.*

Suddenly his face is close to mine, staring hard at me and I can't do anything to stop my cheeks from heating under his gaze. And then I feel his arousal join mine and my panic begins to set in.

Of course, I knew when this moment came, I would have to make a decision to either let it happen or kill him and run. I didn't expect the moment to come so soon though. I'm not ready. I haven't decided, though I don't know why. He is a murderer; a man capable of killing me with his bare hands. How could I give my body to someone like that? I shouldn't even hesitate to try and kill him. So why do I?

As I wage an internal battle, he slowly slides his body off of mine, and retreats to the edge of the bed. He must have sensed my fear. Why would that stop him from taking what he obviously wanted though? Alphas tend to always take what they want.

"Where are we?" I ask to just stop the voices in my head, and try to keep my emotions in check.

"At a hotel in Seattle," he says softly in his husky morning voice.

"Is this where you live?"

"In a hotel? No," he laughs.

"No, smart ass. Do you live in *Seattle*?" So, he likes to play, does he?

"No, *we* don't live in Seattle." He is testing what little patience I have.

"Okay, well, from what I'm aware of, your territory consists of Washington, Idaho, Montana, and Oregon. We are in Washington now, so do you live somewhere here?"

"No, we don't live anywhere in Washington either," he corrects me again, "and we also have territory in Wyoming, along with territory in northern California, Nevada, and Utah now."

"Well, haven't you done well for yourself," I drawl before rolling my eyes, but feel immature when he raises an eyebrow at my tone. "So, where do you actually reside in?"

"*Our* home is Priest River, Idaho." He says fondly, and my stupid heart flutters at the words "our home." I'm sure he just means the pack.

"So close to the border?" I ask in surprise and his brows narrow in confusion, but he answers anyways.

"Yes. As you've witnessed, our biggest threat is to the North so I want to be nearby just in case of an attack. Plus, I don't think I could leave Priest River. It's beautiful. You will see once we get there," and a part of me is excited to go, just from the way his voice changes when talking about it. I have never been outside of Alaska, and while it's beautiful there, I am up for a change.

It's strange how different he is from my dad. My dad is no coward, but he chose to place his location far from the border, whereas Darien is on the front line.

And that makes more sense to me. If I were Alpha, that's where I would be.

"So how are we getting there?" I ask a little too anxiously, and he smiles, causing me to blush. *Murderer!* I remind myself. I'm already letting him get to me.

I can't forget what he has done. I look down away from him, but he instantly lifts my chin, forcing me to look into his intense eyes. If I had more sense, I might be scared of that look, but instead, I am swept away by the power in them. There is a story behind those eyes, and if I stick around long enough, I'm going to get that story.

"Are you okay?" he asks. *Damn he's perceptive.*

"Just fine," I lift my chin and square my shoulders, surprising him, "just ready to hurry up and get things situated." He gives me a knowing look.

"I have a friend with a helicopter. He will be picking us up shortly and taking us directly to our ranch in Priest. We will be home soon," he says with relief before rising up and moving towards his small suitcase and pulling out clean clothes.

Home. It would be nice to have a place to call home. Why did it have to be here with someone I was terrified would kill me though, or that I *should be* terrified of at least, but I'm not. If this worked out however, I wouldn't have to hide anymore. I could finally start the life I have always wanted.

Now that the time is here though, I don't know how to go about it. As the Alpha's mate, *this* Alpha's mate, what did that mean for me? I won't ever be like my mother, but what would I be allowed to do without getting killed?

Darien's sudden close proximity pulls me away from my thoughts. Intense eyes glow with heat as he leans over me. He reaches towards me and I know that I should stop him, but I'm too stunned to do anything. His scent is intoxicating, and deep down I almost want him to touch me.

His hand reaches for my shirt, slowly lifting it up, forcing me to choke back a moan. This isn't happening now. I'm getting ready to pull back to throw a punch, but his hand gently sliding over my belly gives me pause.

He softly runs his hand over where my skin was torn open yesterday, but it has already healed over. Only faint traces of blood remind me that there was ever anything there.

"Ari, do you want first shower?" my eyes snap to his as his sexy voice says my name.

"Um, I'll let you have it," I stutter, afraid to move with his gaze on me, but I regret my decision and I spend the longest ten minutes of my life thinking about his hot muscled body in the shower. *Just perfect.*

Darien

I had to get out of the bedroom. Her sweet scent and the memory of her touch on my skin is driving me mad. I thought the shower would help, but so far has been a failure as I can't stop thinking about her just outside the door, and how badly I wanted her in here with me.

I hadn't meant to fall asleep in the bed with her, nor did I plan to practically smother her to death, but I can't say I didn't get a great night's sleep.

We were actually supposed to meet up with my friend Gray last night with his helicopter, but Ari was mentally and physically exhausted. The helicopter would have woken her up, or maybe not. I've never known a wolf who slept so hard.

To be safe, we decided to stay the night here in Seattle. We could have stayed with a pack member, but I didn't want to freak Ari out by making her stay in a new place with more foreign wolf smells. Foreign to *her* anyways.

Of course, there were only two single bedrooms left. I was going to sleep on the floor, but now I just look like an asshole. Although it was nice waking up to her touching places that I never thought were sensitive. I almost lost it the moment I scented her arousal.

How have I gone from not wanting a mate in my life to completely *needing* this woman? I didn't want to force her to stay if it isn't what she wants, though why anyone would want to run from a life of luxury and safety is beyond me. Maybe I just hoped the girl I imagined wouldn't want to stay. Now that I have caught a glimpse of the real woman, I'm not sure that I could let her go now, even if she wanted to leave.

I walk back out into the room after drying off and changing into a fresh pair of clothes. Her scent, her arousal hits me full force and I can't help but smile. It's good to know that I am not the only one struggling with the heat between us.

My wolf and I want to just take her now, and claim our mate, though another part of me wants to run before I scare her off. This isn't the place I want it to happen. I need to wait until she is comfortable, and based on her fear I that sensed earlier; I know she isn't ready yet. Hopefully she will be soon because I don't know how much longer I can wait for her. Ari's wolf, her strong blood, calls to us.

She walks on shaky legs passed me to the bathroom and I fight the urge to grab her and kiss her until I can't feel my lips anymore.

I need to taste her, but I know that once I start, I won't be able to stop.

That helicopter better be here soon before I lose my mind to my wolf.

If I sit here and wait, thinking about her naked body in the shower, and then have her come out with sexy wet hair I really am going to snap. I decide to leave her a note telling her to meet me at room 141 when she is done.

Grabbing my bag, I quietly slip out the door. At least around my other wolves I should be able to clear my head a little better. Or so I thought.

Thirty minutes later I am seated at the hotel room's desk talking to the guys about plans for when we arrive back home, when Ari walks in. She awkwardly pushes her way through the door handling her bag and two suitcases. *Shit.* I am such an asshole. Apparently, I have a talent for mucking this up. Goes to show how much experience I've had with women in my past. Pretty much, zero.

"Nice job boss, making the poor girl carry all of this by herself," Asher laughs before groaning from a quick strike to the gut.

We all stare at Ari in attack position, prepared for a counter-attack from Asher. Silly girl. No one would dare mess with the Alpha's mate. Not without a death wish.

"I'm not a *poor girl*," she growls, "I can take care of myself."

Asher looks at me with amusement in his eyes, and I see red as he steps towards her.

The bastard reaches a hand out to grab her. He's my best friend, but can't they see that I'm prepared to kill for this woman?

After what happened to her last night, no one is laying a hand on her if I have anything to say about it.

I move to intercept him, but before I can get there, she grabs his outstretched hand, pulls him towards her, and uses his momentum to flip him on his back.

"Clearly," he laughs appreciatively from the floor. "Lucky bastard," he mutters after glancing at me standing above him. He is lucky she got to him before I could.

Turning my attention to her, and stepping back to calm my nerves, I shift my attention to her. Not like I had a choice. The woman is testing my control with her sexy wet hair pulled up into a messy bun. Her white blouse flows over tight, blue, jean shorts, and she traded out her boots for white flats.

I can't decide which outfit I prefer more. She looks absolutely breathtaking right now, but the combat boots were pretty hot, and a pleasant surprise for a royal to be wearing. I'm curious as to what she will surprise me with next.

Glancing around the now quiet room, I notice Ari tensely standing in the middle, with Trace and

Asher both staring openly at her. They both look dazed, and seem to be struggling with their control.

And then I remember that they are both unmated, dominant males. Dammit, why am I so stupid lately?

"Ari, would you like to come get some breakfast with me?" I practically yell the question at her in my panic.

"Yes!" she snaps a little too quickly. She knew just how dire the situation was about to get. I grab her hand, and we practically run out the door before Trace or Asher can even react.

Ari

Darien and I run down the hotel's hallway. He looks back to make sure that his men didn't follow us. Last thing we need is a brawl between a bunch of dominant werewolves in a hotel full of people. We can't ever let the humans know we exist. They are better off being blissfully unaware of the creatures that lurk in the night.

As we sprint away, I'm definitely regretting wearing these stupid flats. I can run just fine in them, but they are not meant for their durability. I only put them on because I stupidly thought that I could get Darien's attention. I don't want his attention. I *shouldn't* want his attention, but a subconscious part of me apparently does.

My wolf and I need to have a talk. She may want the powerful, sexy Alpha, but this girl knows that this man is dangerous.

Not only do I have to deal with him, but now I have two dominants *and* the Alpha lusting over the untouched, unmated female. Can you say déjà vu?

"Sorry. I didn't think about Trace and Asher being unmated," Darien apologizes awkwardly.

Because Darien and I are technically not mated yet, I am still considered fair game.

Back at home I stayed away from everyone so I had forgotten what it was like for a single male. Well, so much for dragging out the mating process as long as possible. If we don't mate, or if I don't leave soon, Darien will be at risk for a challenge from his men.

While a part of me thinks that wouldn't be so bad since that would mean I wouldn't have to mate to a monster, another part of me knows his men may not be any better. In fact, whoever bests him could be a monster far worse than Darien himself. Not to mention the fact that someone innocent could get killed, and it would be my fault. Hell, he had murder in his eyes with his own men just moments ago. If I hadn't put a stop to it myself, who knows what would have happened?

Maybe a fight between him and his wolves would be a good distraction for me to get away though. Either that or I would have every single male in the pack on my tail, and I'd never get a moment of peace to escape.

I *can* say that I am honestly surprised that Asher is even interested in me, especially after I flipped him on his ass. Apart from my uncles, most men have either tried to fight back dirty, or their pride would be too hurt to feel any attraction afterwards.

"It's strange. I have never seen them so interested in a mate that they almost lost control," he says suspiciously, "maybe it has something to do with your bloodline."

"Couldn't tell ya. I didn't spend much time around the males in my pack. Or the females for that matter."

"Really?" he asks in disbelief, and I don't answer. I don't have to prove anything to him. "Why not?"

"I just didn't," I reply sharply so he will let it drop, and I keep on walking.

As we make it to the lobby, all of the breakfast setup is being put away. I know Darien was just trying to save me from all of the building testosterone, but I am actually starving. I haven't eaten since yesterday morning.

To prove it, my stomach growls, and I blush.

Darien grabs my hand and leads me outside. I resist the urge to rip my hand out of his. It's not hard, because I actually like the feel of my hand in his.

Am I a monster for being attracted to one? How could this happen to me; the girl who doesn't give anyone the time of day unless it's for a sparring match? The girl who doesn't bow to anyone, not even my own Alpha. I wonder if I could break Darien's control. Now that would be a sight to see.

"Come on. Let's get you some food. Although I am afraid of what you can do to my two best men on a *full* stomach."

"It's not my fault! He was asking for it," I feel like a child defending myself to my dad, like so many times before.

"Hey," he cups my chin, effectively stunning me. My eyes are lost in his as they hold me captive. "I'm not mad," he soothes.

He isn't mad? I mean, he *shouldn't* be, but Alphas aren't usually too pleased when their men get beat up by a single woman. I always thought it would be better to put that anger towards the one who lost. That just makes too much sense though.

My heart rate picks up when his hand doesn't leave my jawline, and his deep sea-green eyes still hold mine. Those intense eyes shift to my lips, and right before I think he is going to kiss me, he pulls away.

"Hell, I'm thrilled. I'd make you my second if that were allowed, and if it wouldn't terrify me to put you in harm's way."

"I'm not afraid to fight," I stand straighter. My tone brings his eyes back to mine.

"I didn't figure you were. I would never forgive myself if something happened to you, though."

His words throw me off and he tugs me along before I can respond. It doesn't matter right now anyways. I most likely won't be sticking around to be a fighter for him anyways.

I try to focus on my surroundings to try and calm my racing heart.

Large buildings and shops surround us, along with thousands of cars and people just on this one stretch of road. I feel like I am in what I picture New York to be like. The sky is overcast and the saltiness from the ocean gives the air is muggy and stinky scent. The ocean smells a lot cleaner and fresher back home.

I'm glad Darien's base isn't in Seattle. This small-town girl wouldn't survive here.

Darien brings us to a halt in front of a small bakery, and holds the door open for me. The smell of warm dough and sugar makes me smile. I must admit that it is convenient having everything you need right at your fingertips. We have to travel to Kotzebue or Anchorage for most of our things such as clothes and more variety of foods to stock up on. You can forget finding anything as fancy as a bakery in Noatak.

I check out the bakery's display of goodies and order two bacon, egg, and cheese croissants with a hot chocolate.

"Make that two," Darien adds in before handing the cashier his card. Shoot.

I forgot all about having to pay. I've never worried about money before. Of course, I never really asked for anything growing up. I just wanted to be in my wolf form away from everyone, but every now and then mom would bring me clothes and other things she thought would make me happy. I never really thought about it much, but now it suddenly bothers me that I don't have any money of my own.

"Are you okay with hanging out here for a few minutes?" Darien asks me as the lady starts putting our food in paper sleeves. I nod my head.

The cashier hands us our croissants while another lady retrieves our drinks.

Darien takes the hot drinks and kicks out a chair for me at a quiet table in the corner. I take the seat he offers and he takes the one opposite of me before setting my hot cocoa down in front of me.

I agreed to stay here so that I could ask him something, but I'm regretting that now. Even with all the people around, it feels way too intimate sitting across from each other in this dimly lit area, with all the sweet smells surrounding us. Is this what a date feels like? *Pull yourself together, it's just breakfast*, I scold myself.

I'm not even sure why I am entertaining the idea of staying, but I guess I'm curious about his answers to my question all the same. The question will also keep him from suspecting my contemplation for leaving. At least that's what I tell myself.

I take a sip out of my steaming cup and my empty stomach swoons with delight. I grab my sandwich next and nibble on it a bit as I try to gather up the nerve for what I am about to say.

"So, Alpha Shield—

"Darien is fine," he cuts me off, and I take a deep breath to calm myself before I blush bright red. It shouldn't be that big of a deal. I mean we are supposed to become mates. That is, if I decide to stick around.

Hopefully no one is holding their breath on that, but if I do, there are some things I want to discuss.

"Right. Darien. I have a question," I begin awkwardly. What is it about him that continues to set me on the edge? I'm never this jumpy. Maybe it's just because I'm not used to being around others or because I'm afraid of the person he is hiding under this cool, friendly mask that he is wearing for me. Or maybe it's his insanely good looks.

"Shoot," he says before bringing his cup of hot cocoa to his lips.

"I was wondering, for when we get back, if there is a job that I could do to earn some money," he spits his drink straight back into his cup, causing some of it to splash onto the table, "Oh my goodness, are you okay? Is it too hot or something?"

I grab some napkins and hand them to him. He quickly starts cleaning it up instead of answering me, looking too bewildered to reply. Did it taste bad? Mine had tasted fine and the temperature was perfect.

"You want a *job*?" he asks in disbelief after settling himself.

"Well yeah, I feel like I should earn my share. I *want* to earn my share," he narrows his eyes at me, but is that relief I see in them too? No, that wouldn't make sense. Plus, if I had my own money and ever needed to run, I would have the means to do so.

He doesn't say anything for a while, and I wait for him to refuse and tell me that my job is to be home taking care of things there and having children, and pampering myself so that I keep up my youthful features. I almost want him to say exactly that because it would easily make my decision for me.

"Sure. When we get home, if you still want a job, we can figure something out," he replies hesitantly. Well that wasn't so hard, but I don't know what is up with the strange way he is reacting. Is he really going to be okay with this or is he just saying it to appease me?

If he is serious though, what does that mean for me? Will I stay? I guess it's a reason to try and make it work if he isn't lying to me.

"What are you so happy about?" he asks making me realize that I am smiling. I quickly smother it and look away as I finish my food. Darien pulls his flashing phone out of his pocket and checks the screen. "Our ride is here. Are you ready to go?

Chapter 8

Darien

SHE WANTS A JOB? Since when does an Alpha's mate, a royal, want a job? She must be pulling my leg. There must be some ulterior motive, but I can't think of what that could possibly be. This woman is a puzzle and I don't know if I will ever be able to solve it.

First, she can fight just as well, if not better than probably most of my men, and then there was her comment about never hanging out with anyone in her pack. Most royal females take advantage of their strong blood to show off in front of their pack. Royal females are hard to come by, so they know they are guaranteed a life of high status.

As a male, we work hard and fight to become the strongest in order to become Alpha one day, but the females don't have to worry about such things.

This girl is already an enigma, but now she tells me she wants to work. Not to mention the fact that she seems to be nothing like her mother, which I am very okay with that aspect.

If it weren't for how easily her blood is threatening to rip apart my control, I'd almost think she wasn't the Alpha's real daughter.

Is this some trick to infiltrate my pack? You'd think she would want to at least *try* to hide her abilities if she was undercover.

Until my wolves mentioned it, I had almost forgotten he had a daughter because he kept it on a low profile. There were a few Alphas that had asked for her hand in the past, but they were all turned down. Could this be why? Everyone thought it was because of all the rumors about how stubborn and crazy she is.

Meeting and observing her now, I can see where the rumors came from, but I can tell that they were exaggerated and that they left out all of the good qualities she has that I've witnessed thus far.

Can I really be lucky enough to get a mate like her? If I had known there were women like Ari out there, I would have searched for a mate a long time ago. It's as if I have been waiting for *her* this whole time. I don't think anyone else could hold this power over me. She is *it* for me.

Now I just need to figure out why she is keeping her distance from me. I've somehow won a couple smiles, and I can tell that she is attracted to me, but she is definitely holding herself back.

Almost four hours later, we are landing in Priest River, Idaho. Trace and Asher both took sleeping pills for the ride so that they would be unconscious while in a secluded area with Ari and I. Our metabolism is faster than normal human's though, so the pills would burn off just in time for landing. I only wish that I had taken one too.

Ari and I spoke briefly in the beginning of the trip, but for two hours, I watched as multiple emotions played across her face while she stared out the window, thinking, or daydreaming about who knows what. I wanted to know each thought she was having, but couldn't find the nerve to ask her. Just thinking about the possibilities of what could be going through her mind was driving me crazy.

To top it all off, halfway through the trip when she got bored of the lack of conversation, she took down her partially dry hair and fiddled with it. She must know exactly what that scent is doing to me. I'm sure she got an idea a few different times when I couldn't control myself in time, and now she's torturing me.

Thankfully we are back on the ground and finally home. Now that we are here, I realize the impact this might have on our lives. Things are about to change.

We have joined ranks with a strong pack with a lot of territory, but more than that, I will never crawl into an empty bed again. Ari will be my mate and my pack will look to someone other than me.

Just yesterday morning I had expected to be annoyed or angry returning with the bratty mate I assumed I'd be inheriting, and who would automatically have almost as much power and control as me.

We're not mated yet, but I am happy to have been proven wrong, and strangely excited to share my life with her. She may be just what we need around here. Or so I hope. She could be playing me for a fool for all I know. Women are definitely not my forte.

While everyone unbuckles and stands to stretch, I make my way to Gray to thank him for the ride. Everyone including Ari follows suit. Gray bows, earning a laugh from us all.

"Take my truck and go grab some lunch before you head back," I half command, half suggest as I hand him my keys.

"Yes sir," he agrees without hesitation and shuts down the chopper.

Asher and Trace hop out of the helicopter first, followed by myself. I turn to help Ari out, but she just glares at my outstretched hands before gracefully sliding out on her own. Her hostility surprises me, but I figure she's probably nervous about stepping foot in a completely new place with no one she knows anywhere nearby.

Before she can stop me, I grab her two suitcases, and just leave her shoulder bag for her to carry. I meet her fierce eyes and know that I am testing her patience, but I won't give in. Bracing myself for attack, she takes a deep breath, and pushes passed me in a huff. *Smart girl.*

She may have held back this time, but I foresee a challenge coming soon. Obviously, she needs to get something out of her system.

If it were anyone else in the pack, they would have already been taken care of, but this is something completely different. This is my soon to be mate. A challenge between mates is unheard of. Why does that excite me? This woman is definitely going to be interesting to say the least.

Ari

"Where are we?" I ask as I take in the sight of beautiful, endless green fields and trees. There's a partially frozen river running up to a large house in the distance.

With my wolf eyesight, I can see that the house is actually a huge log cabin that reminds me of my parents' house back in Alaska, but without the stonework. There is lots of river rock surrounding the home though. The property is set far back from the roadway, which has a wall of small hills and trees bordering it, leaving plenty of privacy still.

"This is my ranch," Darien says warmly, "Welcome home, Ari." My body tingles all over at his words. I take a closer look. It's beautiful, and apparently, it's mine now. It doesn't look like a monster's home.

Lanterns run all the way up the walkway and around the house. I bet it's quite a sight when it's all lit up at night. And lucky me, I'm sure I'll get a chance to see it if the Alpha doesn't kill me before nightfall.

We make our way through the field towards the house after Darien thanks the pilot. The house grows more beautiful the closer we get.

The sound of horses in the barn reach my ears, and I instantly smile. Dad always offered to get me one, but we both knew it was pointless. It was unknown how long I'd be around to take care of it. Plus, anywhere I wanted to go, I preferred to run on my own four legs. I have a feeling that I won't have that luxury here though, so at least I'll have another option that I can accept.

From the corner of my eye, I notice Darien watching me, and I quickly hide my smile. After a few seconds go by, I dare a glance at him to find him smiling, though I have no idea why.

He carries my heavy bags effortlessly, and I think back to how I acted moments ago, ready for a challenge before I remembered his men nearby. My nerves of setting foot in an unknown area amplified the moment we landed.

I've already fought and broken my father's control. I don't want to give away my secret quite yet. Not over something so silly as a man doing what men are "supposed" to do anyways. Even if that is so, I don't like feeling useless.

Darien and I step onto the generous sized porch where I find a bench and porch swing. It's strange how similar this place is to my parent's place, but for some reason this house feels more like home and I haven't even seen the inside yet.

Trace and Asher both remain at the bottom of the steps with their small suitcases. They don't look like they will be joining us. *Shit.* Soon I would be truly alone with Darien, and while my wolf seems to be excited by that, the human me is on edge.

"Remember what we discussed earlier," Darien regards his men, "We'll talk soon." Wait, what did they discuss? Why don't I know what's going on? This isn't helping keep me from the edge. It's like being back at home, kept out of the loop.

Maybe now that I am technically higher up in rank, I can demand the information. *No. I won't do that.* That has my mother's name written all over it. If

Darien has anything that he wants to share with me, then he can. If not, then so be it. I just hope it's not something that comes back to bite me in the ass.

"Yes sir," Trace says, followed by a "Have fun you two," and a wink by Asher.

I look longingly after them. I'm not ready for this. I would rather go shopping with my mother than face whatever may be coming. Maybe Darien's so far sweet and calming demeanor was just an act in front of his men.

I hear the door open behind me, and Darien goes inside where I hear him set the bags down. My body doesn't move.

"Ari. You're going to have to come in sooner or later," he calls softly from inside. *Damn.* I was hoping that maybe he would just leave me out here to sulk like a child. *No such luck.* I suck in one last breath of freedom before stepping over the threshold.

Inside Darien's beautiful home, I feel trapped, or at least that's how I imagined I'd feel. In truth, it feels like a home. Plus, it's not exactly the cold, bare-walled dungeon I had pictured in my head. I guess murderers can have nice homes too.

He asks me if I need anything, but I am distracted by all the fine detail. Its familiarity settles me a little. I comment on the beauty of the home and he replies with information that surprises me before he offers to show me the rest of the house. Apparently, he did a lot of the updates himself. Once again, I am impressed.

Nodding absentmindedly, he grabs the suitcases and leads me around. The rooms he shows me are all tastefully done although a little bare and cold perhaps. I'm no interior designer, but it just feels like they are missing something. I guess it's not a big deal since they seem to only be used by pack members passing through or needing a place to stay for one thing or another.

"So where am I staying?" I ask wanting to settle in, and ok, maybe I need a reprieve from his intoxicating scent and heated gaze.

Any other male Were, I would have picked a fight with by now for looking at me like that, but Darien's heated stare ignites other things in me. Things I don't want to feel for a guy like him.

"This way," he grabs my hand with his free one, and tugs me along up the stairway. I should flinch away from his casual touch, but his hand is large and rough. I can feel the strength and safety in his grip. It irks me to my core that I can't sense the evil that I know he is capable of.

It's a mystery as to how he hides his true self so well, but my irritation is redirected when he leads me into a room that smells very strongly of him.

The room is spacious and beautiful with its own fireplace, a large log wood bed, and a bay window looking over the river. I don't have to see it to know the on-suite bathroom is probably amazing.

I try to hide the horror on my face when I look at him, but I have no idea if I pull it off or not.

Most arranged marriages, I had heard that the female is offered a separate room in the beginning so that the woman can ease her way into the dramatic life change.

Eventually they typically end up in the same bed, but right off the bat is virtually unheard of. I know we somehow ended up in bed together already due to interesting circumstances, but he can't seriously expect me to share a room with him, can he?

Darien

We are finally alone, yet Ari doesn't seem too thrilled about it. Maybe I'm not as lucky as I thought I was. Yes, she is indeed the perfect woman for me, or so it seems, except for the fact that she looks like she is ready to bolt at the first chance. *Would I try to stop her?*

"Can I get you anything?" I ask gently as she takes in the entryway.

She ignores me so I follow her gaze around the large room. As soon as you walk in, you are met with a large rock fireplace that dominates the living room. Everything else is made of wood. Wood floors, log walls, and a wooden staircase leading to the second floor. There is a basement as well, which is accessible from the trapdoor hidden by the fireplace.

This room is decorated with leather couches, a few framed pictures on the wall, and lantern style lighting. I'm sure she will want to make some changes though. I'll do whatever keeps her from wanting to run away. I may not deserve her, but I *want* her.

"Beautiful," she says shyly.

"Uh, thanks. I updated most of it myself," I reply stupidly. Smooth.

"Really? That's pretty amazing," she says, and our eyes meet before she turns in on herself again. She is going to have to talk soon. I can't take her tip toeing around me much longer.

"Want to see the rest?" I offer and she nods without looking at me, so I grab our suitcases and head up the stairs without looking to see if she follows. I stop at each room and bathroom.

Aside from my master suite, there are another six rooms, along with two more bathrooms. There's also a king size suite in the barn with a pull-out couch for just-in-case situations.

Saving my room, *our* room, for last, I set our stuff against the wall for now. Before I met her, I had fully intended to give Ari her own room far away from me. I like my space, but I'd rather chain this timid vixen to me than let her sneak away or get snatched away by my already interested pack.

However, the shock on her face makes me think that I made a big mistake. Pushing her might not be the best idea. My wolf can feel her wolf's attraction, but her human side is resisting. Hell, if you had told me two days ago that I would be rock hard, and practically salivating over my arranged, soon-to-be wife, I would have laughed hysterically.

Only my true mate could elicit such emotions from me. If that's the case, why is she about to leap out the window?

True mates are rare, but a few of us have been lucky to experience what most would call 'love at first sight'. Two wolves see each other and it's like they instantly know that they belong to each other. I knew as soon as our eyes made contact that she was mine. There's no other explanation, but wouldn't her human side realize it just as mine has?

"We don't have to do anything until you're ready," I try to reassure her. After saying that aloud, I wonder how many lovers she has had. I know that like most packs, the males outweigh the females, and she is a grown woman with needs so I can't hold it against her. I won't lie that I am still curious though.

Of course, she said she didn't spend much time around the males in her pack, but that doesn't mean she didn't take a lover. I also saw how she was with the two men that helped find her last night. She is too beautiful to not have had every male in her pack after her.

She doesn't speak for a long time, but when she does it's not what I expect to hear.

"I can see why you wanted a woman here," she laughs, but quickly cuts it off with an apology, and her cheeks redden.

"What's that supposed to mean?" Here we go. She is ready to start spending my money. Maybe she is not much different from mommy dearest.

"Er, just thinking the rooms could use—well I'm no expert, but it needs *something*. Unfortunately, you chose the wrong girl for the job."

"I know the others need some work, but what's wrong with this room?" I ignore her other comment.

"Nothing's wrong with it per se, it's just missing something. Like some curtains, a mirror, or some pictures on the walls," she shrugs. I guess she has a point.

"What kind of pictures?" I ask intrigued.

"Of your family—uh well I guess that probably wouldn't be the best idea," I flinch at the word *family*, but what is she talking about?

"Ari?" she looks at me, and though she says nothing, I can see her form tense. "What is going on?"

"Why don't *you* tell *me*?" I watch as the little bit of control she has snaps. "I didn't choose to come here. I was sent here and I have no idea what happens next."

"Your dad offered you to me. I didn't force him into anything. If you don't want to be here that badly we can try to figure something else out, but will you not even try?"

I feel pathetic using that line, but I don't know what else I can do. She wanted out just like I did only yesterday, so why am I trying to guilt her into staying? Just because she appears to check everything and more on my interest list, doesn't mean that is who she is. For all I know, she could be a spy sent to win me over and then stab me in the back. Maybe we aren't true mates, and this feeling is just some kind of trick.

I step towards her and she retreats with a wary look in her eyes.

"Dammit, Ari, why are you so afraid of me?" she glares at me, but I glare right back. I am the Alpha here and I can't let her make me weak.

"I'm not afraid of you," she grinds out, but I can smell her fear, even as she is preparing for a fight. Fine, if that's what she wants, that's what she will get. We need to be done with this.

This time when I step towards her, I do it with purpose. She holds her ground. The look in her eyes hardens.

I reach out with both hands to grab her, but she knocks both arms aside with surprising strength before delivering a swift kick to my chest. If this were my first time seeing what she could do, the surprise would slow me down, but I have an idea of what she is capable of, and I don't give her time to plan her next move.

I move in close, startling her but she throws out a quick fist that I barely dodge. I catch the next hand coming at my face and use it to spin her away from me so that I can grab her from behind, but now I'm the one caught off guard.

She holds me tightly and uses the force of the spin to pull me down. Damn, I forgot that she knows how to use my size against me. Taking us down to the bed was a mistake on her part though.

I fall to the bed, but I am able to retain my hold on her and pull her down with me. She collides against my chest, and I quickly roll us to position myself above her struggling form. I hold her legs down with mine, and pin her hands above her head.

"Ari," I try to calm her, but she continues to struggle. "Please, tell me what I have done to upset you so badly. If it's something I can't fix, then you can leave."

"Oh please. Just try to kill me already. Let's get this over with. Stop feeding me lies." She snarls at me with watery eyes, but no tears fall.

"What the hell are you talking about?"

"You are a murderer!"

Her words catch me off guard.

"I'm an Alpha, Ari. At some point we all end up killing." She knows this. I don't know every detail of her father, but I do know that he has killed his fair share.

"And what got you that role of Alpha? Oh yeah, killing your own father! Then you killed other Alpha's for more land."

My body stiffens above her. "That's what this is about?" I ask incredulously.

"Um yeah Darien, it's kind of a big deal," she replies, too tired to struggle anymore, unless she is feigning exhaustion. I hold on tighter just in case she gets any ideas.

"Well you are right. I killed the fucking bastards. I would do it over and over again if I could. I didn't do it for the Alpha position though. Any person, human or werewolf, that abuses and rapes women and children should be tortured slowly and painfully. I did him a justice he didn't deserve," I shout at her, barely hanging onto my control.

So, this is what she has thought of me all this time? She is going to side with my father? My wolf threatens to surface when she doesn't say anything for a while.

"If that is a problem for you, then by all means, please leave," I release her, stepping out of her reach.

Ari

He told me to leave so I do what I do best. What I had planned to do all along. I run. Out of the room, down the stairs, and out the front door. I want out of my skin, but it's too light outside to shift in a place I am unfamiliar with.

I'm not at all surprised that he doesn't try to follow me, considering I basically just shamed him for doing the right thing. Word about his father had never reached my ears.

This is why I should know better than to listen to gossip. There's always another side to the story.

Frustration and anger pushes me to run faster. How could Darien's father do that? Alphas are supposed to protect their pack. I should have known there was a reason Darien did what he did or else someone would have stopped him.

My head is clearer now with some space. The electricity between us has been way too intense. Now that I can breathe, I feel stupid for running like an immature coward.

All I've ever wanted is freedom, and the moment he provided that opportunity, I jumped at it. The only problem is that now I'm not so sure that I want to disappear anymore. Not from him.

From the moment our eyes met, I felt like when he looked at me, he saw the real me. Not only saw, but accepted me for who I am. For the "me" he knows so far anyways.

My guarded heart wanted to believe he was wearing some mask to fool me, but I knew deep down that he couldn't possibly be the monster everyone portrayed him to be. I was afraid of being tricked. Even now, I don't want to let my guard down with him, but my wolf trusts him. One thing I know for sure, is that I trust my wolf. Plus, I can't deny that he intrigues me. He's not like most male wolves, let alone any male Alpha I have ever met or heard of.

Sounds of a road nearby makes me slow my pace. After a few miles of running I've come to the edge of the property. If I cross over, I may never come back. Is this what I want?

A single day isn't enough time to get to know someone, but in that short time, he has given me a glimpse of the man he is.

First, he flew all the way to Alaska for me and went above and beyond to find me when I was taken.

Second, he has been nothing but kind and respectful to me, even with both of us having our emotions amped up by the attraction to each other.

Third, watching him with his men and seeing the affection they hold for him says just how good of an Alpha he is. Just like how my uncles interact with my father.

Last but not least, he took it upon himself to destroy evil men in order to help his and other packs suffering from the same problems. And what does he get in return? A stubborn, selfish brat that runs away at the first sign of trouble. Darien deserves better than me.

If I leave, perhaps I may find the freedom I have always dreamed of. If I stay, I could have a home I never knew was within my grasp.

I hadn't even realized that I had started running back until I could see the house in the distance. Slowing down again, I contemplate what I need to do. If I run away, I may always wonder what could have been. I could actually fall in love with Darien. Something I thought would never be a possibility for me.

My insecurities flood my thoughts.

What if he doesn't want me anymore? After all, he didn't come after me when I ran. What if my accusation sealed my fate? He may never forgive me for what I said. I'm not sure I can leave with that guilt. Whether he wants me anymore or not, I have to at least apologize. He deserves that, and more.

I've made up my mind, but I'm too afraid to go back inside. I'm not ready to face him and have him tell me to leave and never return. I know remaining here is hopeless. If he wanted me to stay, he would have run after me.

I hate that he is making me feel this way. I hate that I'm letting myself be so stupid and weak.

Instead of going in, I sit on the porch swing and rock slowly back and forth in order to help calm my nerves. The last thing we need is another heated fight before inevitably parting ways for good.

Darien

She actually ran. All this time she has seen me as nothing more than a murderer. Part of me wanted to stop her, but if she wanted out, who was I to stand in her way?

I thought she was different. How could I have read her so wrong? I promised myself I would keep the past in the past and keep moving forward, but now it has all come crashing back. All thanks to *her*. I should have known she was too good to be true.

Lying back on my bed, I try to clear my mind of the painful memories.

What do I do now? Call her father and tell him it didn't work out? Would he hunt her down and kill her for betraying him? What will I do about the pack?

I could accept another pack's offer, but I think it's safe to say that I'm just not cut out for the relationship life. Though things didn't work out, I don't think anyone could measure up to Ari.

With her sweet, intoxicating scent heavily lingering, my thoughts can't help but drift back to her.

My mind replays the instant we met. Seeing her first smile that I glimpsed in the reflection on the car window. Waking to her soft touch. And, *wait*.

I abruptly sit back up before concentrating on my thoughts, trying to remember everything she said and did.

She was obviously very wary of me, and for what I now know why.

However, she also touched me gently, and I know for a fact that she was attracted to me, just as I am to her. Would she really be attracted to me if she truly believed I was the monster she accused me of being?

I then consider everything I know about her.

One, she is a formidable fighter. She even got a couple shots on me minutes ago, which is not an easy feat.

Two, she wears a tough front, in part, because she actually *is* tough, but also to hide her vulnerable side. I mean, she chooses hot cocoa over a cup of coffee. Plus, it's obvious that she is uncomfortable showing her skin.

Remembering her shyness last night and this morning brings a smile to face, extinguishing some of my anger.

Three, it's obvious her father and those other two male wolves I met adore her. Behind her ferocity I can see that there is a sweet, caring woman in there. Even if she doesn't know it yet.

Though it's a small list, I keep coming back to how advanced a fighter she is, and not only that, but how quick she is to take matters into her own hands. Maybe my assumption was wrong. She doesn't seem the type to just stand by idly by if someone needed help. No one trains themselves to be as strong as she is for no reason.

Why else would she run though? Did my reaction scare her?

Putting myself in her shoes, I try to imagine if I had to be sent to a foreign place with strangers, and expected to mate with someone I just met. On top of that, ending up kidnapped and fighting for my life. Against an Alpha, no less. I would probably bolt at the first chance I was given too.

Granted, I too am expected to mate with a stranger, but I don't have to leave everything I know behind. Plus, the moment I saw her, she was no stranger to me. She was everything I never knew I wanted or needed.

What if that's not the reason she took off though? Of course, there's only one possible way to find out, and I let her get away. I basically kicked her out into a whole new world with nowhere and no one to turn to. I'm the biggest idiot in the world, either for making her run, or for wanting to drag her back here. I may have lost her forever, but I need to try to fix this.

Before I can talk myself around in more circles, I sprint out of the house, nearly taking the door off its hinges with me.

Ari

After a couple minutes of gathering the strength to confront Darien and apologize, I'm finally ready. Before I can even stand up, a large blur of motion smashes passed the front door, straight passed me, and hurdles towards the woods.

Feet away from the tree line, he suddenly stops in his tracks before turning back towards the house. My eyesight is pretty good but I can't read the expression on his face from the distance between us.

He starts to walk back towards me. Taking his time now. I decide to just stay put, letting him ponder what made me return. Just the same, I ponder the fact that he was actually about to come after me. I just am not sure if it's a good sign or a bad one.

His eyes are averted as he steps up on the porch, but doesn't come any closer. I try to read his features now that he's closer, but he gives nothing away.

"Just tell me one thing," he finally meets my eyes. "Did you know about what my father had been doing? Did you know why I killed him before today?"

If I hadn't paid close attention, I might not have heard it, but there is a faint hint of raw, vulnerable, emotion behind his hard gaze. He is honestly concerned about my answer.

"I had no idea," I tell him truthfully, and I can tell that he's paying close attention to my tone, and listening to my heartbeat to make sure that I'm not lying.

He sighs, the weight on his shoulders seeming to lighten slightly.

"I'm sorry for judging you without knowing the whole truth. That information never made it to me. To my knowledge, no one else in my pack knew that either."

Relaxing more and more by the second, he comes to sit beside me on the swing.

"I'm sorry for my intensity earlier. A lot has happened in a short amount of time, and have us both pretty riled up, but that's no excuse for me to snap at you."

His apology floors me. We're both silent for a while as the electricity between us becomes apparent again. Maybe he hasn't noticed, or just doesn't care anymore.

Standing up, I move to lean against the pillar to put some space between us. His scent is too intoxicating and I can't let myself feel anything for him again.

I'd already known that I had messed things up when I insulted him then ran, but I hate that the next words out of his mouth actually sting.

"I can try to arrange another place for you, whether somewhere else in the territory I control or in one of the free zones if you wish."

It takes everything I have not to react to his words. When I don't respond right away, I hear him stand and move behind me.

He catches me off guard when he gently turns me to face him, forcing me to meet his gaze.

"I don't want you to go, though," the huskiness in his voice is my undoing, and it's my turn to catch him off guard when I rise onto the tip of my toes to press my lips against his.

I can feel his initial shock before I'm lifted into the air with my back pressed against the pillar that I was leaned against moments ago. His mouth roughly melds to mine, feeding hungrily from me. It is the most intense feeling I've ever experienced in my 22 years on this Earth.

My wolf writhes against the surface, and I can feel her excitement at finding her mate. Our mate.

Darien's muscled form pressed against me has me completely at his mercy. Our mouths move together in perfect unison as if we were made for this moment. The heat between us rages like a wildfire and I can feel my body telling me to kick things up a notch.

This girl has zero experience with boys though, and I hardly know this man kissing my lips as if he needs them to breathe.

Reluctantly, I put my hand on his chest to push him away and he backs off immediately. How could I have been so wrong about him? I wave him off when he tries to apologize. I probably want it just as much as he does.

"I'm sorry," I begin breathlessly, "I just don't know you that well, Darien."

He smiles kindly before taking my hand and leads me back inside the house and into the living room. He deposits us on the couch. I'm not one to be led around like a dog on a leash but I hold back my annoyance. I can't help but want to follow after him anyways. No longer seeing him as a monster, I can fully appreciate his perfect body without feeling guilty.

After sitting me down on one end of the couch, he sits himself as far as he can from me before asking, "What would you like to know?"

With the heat dying down, my shyness rears its ugly head. Aside from my parents and uncles, I didn't spend much time talking, playing, or doing anything close to flirting with anyone. Fighting and running is all I know. His close proximity, and his arousing scent is not helping my nerves.

"I guess start with your family, but you don't have to talk about that if you don't want to." He sighs in exasperation, but I need to know who my soon-to-be mate is.

"There's not much to tell, Ari. I'll leave out the gory details, but just like I said, my father and some other Alpha's had been taking advantage of women. Since there's a shortage of female wolves, they were secretly meeting in undisclosed locations, bringing a new woman from their pack each time, and taking turns," his voice falters on those last words.

"It took me a long time to find proof, but when I did, I killed him. I hadn't planned on taking the position as Alpha, but if I hadn't, they were going to kill my mom too," his voice chokes up on the last bit, but his features harden a moment later.

"That's awful. Why would they do that?"

"I don't want to talk about her," he says sharply, and his expression tells me not to push the matter.

"Fine, then tell me about yourself. Any siblings or weird hobbies I should know about?" I try to lighten the mood back up. He gives a small smile and I wait patiently, praying he doesn't actually have any weird hobbies.

"Since I became the Alpha at such a young age, I unfortunately don't have many hobbies or fun, happy stories to tell," I continue to wait, and he rolls his eyes before he finally gives in. "I like movies, especially old westerns, but the horses in the barn probably gave that away already. Let's see, my favorite food is a toss-up between steak and chicken wings."

"Well yeah, depends on the quality of steak, and what type of sauce is used on the wings," I chime in, happy to hear that we already have a couple things in common; movies and food.

"Exactly. See, you get it," he laughs. "That's enough about me. Tell me about yourself."

At that moment, my stomach growls after talking about food, and my cheeks burn in embarrassment.

Chapter 9

Darien

Shit. I'm not doing a very good job at taking care of my woman.

I leap up from the couch, and without thinking, start removing my clothes.

"Hey, whoa! What the hell are you doing?" Ari yells and covers her face with her hands. I laugh at her modesty and quickly shift into my wolf form, letting out a yip to get her to do the same.

She stares at me with arms crossed before twirling her finger at me, telling me to turn around. I do as I'm told, and I can hear as she rapidly undresses before shifting.

When I turn back to her, I am completely mesmerized by her wolf form.

She has a beautiful brown coat, with cute black tipped ears and a black tipped tail. There are also highlights of gold throughout her fur that lightens her stunning color.

Most female wolves are half the male's size, and while Ari's wolf is still considerably smaller than mine, she is taller and stronger looking than most I have seen. She is also more beautiful than any other wolf I have seen, and there are no ugly wolves. She stands above the rest in more ways than I thought possible. And she is *mine.*

Maybe she is right about adding some art and pictures to my bedroom. Little does she know is that she will end up being the object of my inspiration. Side by side pictures of both of her beautiful forms. Now that would be a great addition to my walls.

After I realize that I am probably staring at her like an idiot, I quickly snap myself out of it and turn to head towards the kitchen. I hear her follow behind me. In the wall next to the door that leads out to the back porch lies a secret wolf-sized doggie door. I push through it and wait for Ari on the other side where we will hunt.

Ari steps out cautiously and takes a whiff of all the scents that are new, but will soon come to be normal to her. Already, the sun has begun to set, but we still have a little bit of daylight. Not that we will need it. In fact, complete darkness would be better in order to avoid being spotted by a human. The property has lots of tree coverage, but we still don't want to risk anyone calling animal control. Hopefully it's dark enough that anyone around would just think they saw a large dog.

Early spring here is really just an extension of winter. It's April, and the snow is mostly gone, but the air is still frigid, especially at night. Hell, it's probably nothing to Ari after living in Alaska. She doesn't even flinch at the bitter chill.

I check our surroundings, suddenly feeling very cautious in my own town, and I realize that it is because of Ari.

My wolf's protectiveness is kicking into overdrive now that we have a mate to watch out for. Even if we haven't mated quite yet, my wolf recognizes her as so. I know that she is tough enough to take care of herself, but she is mine now, and it is my job to protect her.

She brushes up next to me, reassuring my wolf and I. Her confidence in her wolf form surprises me. At her request, I try to relax. I take the lead and quietly creep towards the woods surrounding the Ranch. I don't usually hunt so close to home, but I didn't exactly have any time to grocery shop before leaving for Alaska, and my mate is hungry *now*. We could have ordered a pizza, but then I wouldn't have gotten to see her stunning other half.

Before Ari came around, all we cared about was taking out the bastards bringing shame to our race. Like me, he didn't really care to find a mate, but now that she is here, he wants to claim her just as much as I do. He knows we must wait though. For now, he is satisfied with the chance to interact with Ari's wolf. He licks her nose to prove it.

Technically the wolf and I are the same. Our thoughts and actions are the same, but sometimes my wolf feels and reacts more strongly than a human. My wolf senses things that I might not, and he can try to take over and control me like the hulk, but as an Alpha, I can hold on to my control better than most.

There are people out there who have completely abandoned their wolf side because they didn't want a life controlled by the wolf. They had other dreams and goals. Strangely enough, they are technically considered *strong* to have the ability to control their wolf, but I can't understand wanting to abandon your own kind. I could never do that to my wolf. He is as much a part of me as I am a part of him.

Of course, there are those who either can't control the wolf or choose to let it take over. Those wolves are dangerous and have to be hunted and killed or placed in the wild, away from civilization to remain as wolves.

As for the last group, there are the lone wolves. They use their wolf and human form just like me, but have chosen not to live in a pack, or they found a human mate. Humans aren't allowed to know about us, but we don't tear apart mates. Instead, they are banished to only live in the free territories, with only their mate being allowed to know what they are.

Before, I didn't, but I can understand that one a little better now. If Ari were human, I may have given up Alpha for her, or tried to change the rules to be with her. She is definitely a wolf though. A strong, beautiful wolf who has the potential to be a great asset to our pack.

Ari bites my ear, capturing my attention and I realize again how much more comfortable she is in her wolf form. Most females don't like being in wolf form, but this girl is extraordinary. I nip her nose playfully before running full tilt through the woods. She keeps up easily, but lets me stay ahead. She's smart and is aware that I know the area better than she does.

I slow when I pick up the scent of a deer. I warn her with a low growl and leave her here near the water as I hunt for my prey. It doesn't take long to find her. She is small and young, which I try to avoid, but she is for my hungry mate. I can't be picky right now. At least she doesn't have any babies I would be taking her from.

She is on the run a mere second after I charge, but I am fast for a male wolf. The doe never had a chance. I dive for her, taking her down with my claws before I sink my teeth into her. My jaws grip her by the throat and I break her neck with a hard shake to end her suffering.

It takes a few minutes for me to drag the doe back to where I left Ari. When I get close, I smell blood, and it's not coming from the deer. I sprint after her trail the moment the scent hits me, completely abandoning and forgetting my kill.

In a full-blown panic, I follow Ari's scent. It leads me closer to the river. Awful visions fill my mind of someone or something hurting her and throwing her body in the river. *Shit.* If anything happens to her it will be my fault.

One of my wolves could have scented her, realizing she's unmated, and forced her into mating. They would pay with their life. I run faster and almost stumble over Ari's body on the ground.

Blood and feathers surround her. Wait, feathers?

I find her staring up at me. With a feather sticking out the side of her mouth she tilts her head sideways at me like a German shepherd would, and it's ridiculously adorable. I stare back at her, asking how she could just take off like that.

Uh, sorry, I was really hungry and well, there were these ducks sleeping here, and I couldn't resist, her panicked rambling makes me want to roll with laughter, but I am too stunned at the fact that I actually heard words in my head. Her words.

Ari? I say wondering if I just imagined the whole thing.

What? Oh my God, I can hear you! Why can I hear you? Can you hear me too?

I nod, still in shock.

I have heard of this before. It is rare, but every now and then, an Alpha can reach their pack through their mind. It's easier when blood related, but even that can be hard. There have been stories about mates who can talk to each other in wolf form as easily as being in human form. Of course, the stories don't say why this occurs, or at least not that I have found. It must be a 'true mate' thing.

I focus back on Ari who has blood and feathers in her sharp teeth, and this time I do laugh. She growls at me, making me laugh more. Even looking like that, I am still mesmerized by her. She is so different from what I imagined and from what my mother was.

What's wrong? Ari asks, picking up on my sudden mood change as she polishes off her kill. Damn, I was really hoping to avoid this subject for the rest of my life.

I was just thinking about my mom. Ari gets up and walks over to sit beside me. *She was nothing like you.*

I know, she hangs her head, *I'm weird.*

I growl before nipping her ear.

You are mine, *and you are nothing short of amazing, Ari. You are strong, where my mother was weak. She let so many be tortured before I found out what was happening.* Ari whines in sympathy. *I'm glad you are different, Arianna. You are better.* I lick her nose affectionately, tasting blood from her kill.

So, where's that deer I smell on you? She asks, making me rumble with laughter again, and completely lifting my mood.

Ari

I don't know what has come over me. A couple hours ago, I despised Alpha Shield, though he turns out to not be what I thought, and now I am flirting with him like a wolf in heat, which I guess I technically am. The really strange part is that I feel like I have known him all my life. Hell, I wish I had known him all my life.

I'm amazed at how comfortable I feel with him, while at the same time, excited about the newness of it all. Darien is so much more than I expected. Sure, he can be a little intense at times, but also charming and strong. He also seems very protective, which I never thought I would like before today. On top of all that, he is the hottest man I have ever laid eyes on.

We are now both still in wolf form, cleaning our muzzles in the slow flowing river after feasting on the deer Darien provided. Darien's wolf form practically blends in with the night. He is a large male, even larger than my dad's wolf. I am tall and more built than most female wolves that I know, but my head barely reaches his shoulders. I feel tiny next to him.

Even being in an unfamiliar territory, I definitely feel safe with him around. However, I also feel weak in comparison. Not just physically, but when he spoke about his mother betraying her pack, I felt as low as her.

I'd like to think that if I had known something was going on like that in my father's pack, I would've done everything in my power to put a stop to something as horrendous as that.

It doesn't make me any better though when I never even tried to be a part of the pack. Not since I was old enough to learn my fate anyways.

Whether out of selfishness or hate, or anger, I was weak for casting myself out. Aside from whispering about me being a loner, my pack had done nothing to me to deserve what I had done. I don't know if anything would have changed if I had tried, but now I regret the fact that I basically ran away.

Absentmindedly, I follow Darien back to the house and I watch him jump through another hidden doggie door. I quickly follow suit and he catches me on the other side with his body before I can slide into a wall. When I look up at him, he licks the side of my face.

Your stuff is still upstairs if you want to get ready for bed. I'll be up there soon, Darien says. I take him up on his offer and am in heaven when I step into the large spa bathroom. There is a his and her sink with plenty of counter space, a walk-in glass and stone shower with water that spays out of the sides and from above with a rainfall setting. In the corner is a wood paneled Jacuzzi tub.

On a night when I am not so tired, I will be taking full advantage of that tub. I opt for the rainfall setting for a quick shower instead. Suddenly the past 24 hours has caught up with me, making my eyelids heavy. I grab my soaps out of my bag and hop into perfection.

After showering and throwing on shorts and a tank top, I head back out into the bedroom. I feel nervous walking back into the foreign room that I said I would not be staying in just hours ago. To be honest though, I thought I would be more on edge than I am in a new place. The comfort I feel is astounding. I want to look at my surroundings more, but my tired eyes don't want to focus.

Thankfully Darien isn't in here yet as I crawl under the covers that smell like his sweet and spicy, woodsy scent. I know he will come to sleep with me again tonight, and all the other nights that I will be here from now on.

Am I really going to stick this out? So far everything has been more than anything I could have imagined. Though I want to trust in him, it's still very new. I have to stay prepared. Things could still change.

I wake up to a hard body pressed to mine for the second morning in a row. Sunlight creeps through the large window. I shift to look around the room, but Darien pulls me in tighter, and his hard length presses against my hip. I blush crimson. It doesn't help when I realize that he is stark naked. I try to relax, but my body aches for him to be inside me. What am I saying? I'm not ready for that!

He stirs awake, probably because my hormones are spiking the air around us, and tempting him without my approval. I want to know why the hell he is naked, but I already know the answer. Wolves are used to being naked around each other and he most likely shifted out of wolf form and came straight to bed. I on the other hand, did not grow up walking around in my birthday suit so no one has seen me naked before.

We are still strangers to each other. You'd think he would at least keep boxers on. Is he just trying to tempt me?

"I'm all yours today, and the pack is coming over today," Darien's sexy voice in my ear makes me shiver, "so what would you like to do until then?" Of course, my stomach is the one to answer with an obnoxious growl. My cheeks heat up in embarrassment.

"Food it is," he laughs as he gets up to head to the kitchen. Thankfully he throws on boxers and a shirt. I get dressed quickly before I meet him downstairs and find him searching through the contents in the fridge. "Sorry about the lack of groceries. I haven't had much time to shop, but I should have made time when I knew you would be here once we returned from Alaska. I guess I wasn't thinking."

"Don't worry about it," I wave off his apology.

The fridge is practically empty aside from half a gallon of milk, a stick of butter, a carton of eggs, and a few other random items. He grabs for the milk and eggs before reaching for something in the cabinet.

"Why don't you go find something on TV or make a grocery list or something? I'll take care of the cooking," he smiles before handing me a pen and paper that had been magnetized to the fridge.

"Can you cook?" I challenge.

"I have been cooking for myself almost all my life. I can handle it," he winks.

Not 20 minutes later, Darien brings us each a cup of hot cocoa, a bowl of scrambled eggs, and one big plate of blueberry muffins. The smell from the kitchen has been making my stomach roar in anticipation.

After devouring my food like a pig, I am stuffed, but everything was so good that I can't help but want more. I don't feel as bad when I see that he has scarfed down his food too when he had an even larger serving. He really does know how to cook. This man is just full of surprises.

I hand him the grocery list when we are both finished eating. He takes his time to look it over and I realize that I must have gone overboard.

"Sorry, I have never really made a grocery list before," I panic.

"Actually, I was going to say that we are going to get along great. There's not one thing on here I don't like, and I can be picky," he says in amazement.

"So, what you are saying is that we are going to fight to the death over the last bowl of Lucky Charms," I laugh.

"I wouldn't dare touch the last bowl," his laughter joins mine, and my jitters start to appear. *I've never done this before! I don't know how to flirt!* Jumping up, I take the dishes to the kitchen. "Hey, I can do that," he follows after me.

"You cooked. I can handle the cleanup." He doesn't stop me, but instead leans against the counter to watch me. I focus on keeping my nerves in check so that I don't drop the dishes or crush a plate in my hands.

"Why are you so tense?" he asks with amusement.

"Because you are watching me."

"Well you are going to have to get used to that. You are hard not to look at," I blush at his words. "Come on, we will do this later," he grabs my wet hands and steers me back into the living room. I'm too caught off guard to stop him.

"I want to get to know you, Ari." He sits us down on the couch and looks at me expectantly.

"Well there's not much to know. I'm really boring," I reply sadly, crushing any hopes he had before things get serious.

"Now I already know that that's not even remotely true," he laughs.

"It is true though. I'm nothing, but I want to be something," he moves towards me, and I flinch when he takes my face in his hands. He scowls at me in confusion.

"I have only known you two days, Ari, but you are most definitely not *nothing*. You have intrigued me from the moment I laid eyes on you. You are strong, funny, and refreshingly different from anyone I have met. I wonder why that is," he muses. Well, I guess I better tell him now so he can stop thinking I am someone I'm not. I can't handle him saying all those sweet things anymore when they aren't true.

"It's because I am weak, Darien," I say, catching him off guard. "I'm no better than your mother. From the day I was told that I would have to mate to whoever was chosen for me, I chose to run away and learn how to take care of myself. I trained every single day in the hopes that if ever given the chance, I could try to escape," I say, watching his expression carefully.

He doesn't respond for a while, and his expression is unreadable.

Oh my God! What am I thinking? I am an idiot! He is going to kill me or tie me up and lock me away so that I can never escape or have the life I have always dreamed of.

"I don't think you are like my mother, Ari. I don't think anyone should be forced to mate with someone they don't want. I told you last night that I would help you. You are no prisoner here. You are free to go back home or be a lone wolf if that is what you choose," he says emotionlessly before he rises and turns to leave me here to sulk and hate myself for my big stupid mouth. I'm not having any of that though.

"Darien!" I say suddenly angry now. I grab his arm to stop him and he looks at me with surprise. I continue to glare at him, but I am just as confused as he is.

"Why are *you* mad?" he asks and I feel stupid for my craziness, but my mouth doesn't know how to stop. "You are the one who wants to get away right? Is it to be with someone else? Are you already involved with someone and you just used me as your escape?" The questions keep coming and hit me like daggers. He is really mad at the thought of me having another man in my life apparently. He really has no idea how I have lived the majority of my life.

"What? No! I've never been with anyone! I'm telling you this because I want to stay. Would you really just let me leave when we have this connection?" And the hidden truth comes out. Yesterday he said he didn't want me to go.

All along I have been unconsciously waiting for someone to want me, to fight for me, and to love me for who I am. I want Darien Shield. A man I thought would be the death of me, but his very being calls to me and comforts me, making me feel like everything is finally right in the world.

I watch as clarity lightens his features, and with complete seriousness he growls, "No. I wouldn't."

The next thing I know, I'm in his arms and his lips crush mine.

"You. Are. Mine" he growls between kisses and carries me up to his bedroom. I should be putting on the brakes, but I don't care anymore. I've only known him for basically minutes, but it feels like so much longer. I need him now before I shatter into a million tiny pieces.

He lays me on the bed and I pull him down to me. With a deep, sexy groan, he kisses me with a passion that melts my bones. All of the tension of the last 48 hours has built for this moment. Before the day is over, I will be the true mate of Alpha Darien Shield.

I feel small, but powerful in his arms as his hands and mouth explore my body. He kisses my lips until they are numb and swollen before making his way down to press hot kisses into my neck. His arousal fuels mine, making every inch of me hot with need.

Darien's heated eyes meet mine. They are literally glowing with hunger. I know that mine must be glowing right back. Since I had never expected this day to come, I forgot that our wolves would be present for our first bonding in becoming mates.

He practically tears my clothes off. His need sends a blazing fire straight to my core.

"You are so beautiful, Ari," he moans as his eyes rake over my nearly naked body. I'm glad that I decided on my favorite undies, but they don't stay on long as Darien sets to covering every inch of me with his lips and greedy tongue. All the while, his hands work to remove the remainder of my clothing away.

I take a sharp breath as his teeth graze my hardened nipple, then moan when he takes the whole thing into his mouth.

"I need to taste you," he groans before moving down my body to the heated area between my legs. He looks up at me and smiles wickedly. It's sexy as sin, but...*Oh God. Is he going to do what I think he is? I have never had sex before. I can't start by doing something as intimate as that!*

"Shh," he soothes, and I realize that I am making a soft whining sound, "I'll take care of you." And then his hot mouth covers my opening. He has to restrain my hips, to keep me from rising off the bed. My entire body tingles with bliss. I can feel myself burning with embarrassment, but it feels too good to stop.

He moans as he licks and sucks all of the right places until I scream and shudder from the most intense orgasm I have ever had. He continues to swirl his tongue around my clit as shock waves course through my body.

Darien finally releases me from my torment when I can't take it anymore. He stands and begins removing his few articles of clothing. I watch him carefully, hungry for more of him, but I begin to panic when his hard cock is free. *That's not going to fit*, I back away, but he is on top of me the instant I try to move.

"Ari. You are a virgin, right?" he asks, and even though I already said earlier that I have never been with anyone, I nod to confirm. I want to die of embarrassment, but then he whispers in my ear, "You are my first too, Ari." Those words send a wave of tremors through me and I stare at him in disbelief. I see in his eyes though that he's telling the truth. "I have an idea about what I am doing. It may still hurt, but you can handle me, baby. Just trust me," he reassures me.

I don't have much time to dwell on the fact that this is his first time, as his tip pushes against my wet opening.

"Holy fuck, baby," Darien practically growls as he slowly, yet firmly, pushes his hard length into me. Tears sting my eyes, but don't spill over as he breaks through the barrier. He stops when he buries himself to the hilt, and lets me adjust as we both breathe heavily. My body throbbing around his, I pant, taking in as much air as I can so that I don't pass out from pleasure.

He presses his lips to my forehead, then to my own swollen lips, and down to my neck where he breathes in my scent. I jolt slightly as his teeth sink into my skin, and it sends a tingle all through my body. I tighten around him as he drinks me in.

The fullness of him being inside me, combined with his teeth claiming me is almost enough to make me come again. Who would have thought the mating bite would be so erotic?

Sharpening my canines, I take my turn biting into his neck, taking a pull from his blood; his essence, and he groans before starting to move above me. Pure ecstasy replaces the pain.

I writhe and moan beneath him as I meet him thrust for thrust. He starts slow and soft, but as my body expands for him, he pumps harder and faster into me. His movements become wild and the moans of pleasure he makes push me to the edge.

All too quickly, I am exploding around him and screaming his name. He growls before biting into my neck again just before spilling himself into me.

He collapses on the bed next to me as my body continues to spasm.

We don't move for a while as we try to catch our breath, and calm our racing hearts.

Our bite marks have already healed. When I learned about the mating ritual, I had thought it to be so weird and gross, but not only was it intimate between the two of us, I felt more one with my wolf than I ever have before. It was another thing that I never thought I would have the chance to experience before. Not like this anyways.

I feel complete as I lay here next to the sexiest man alive, and think about how much has changed since I left the place where I had spent my entire life. First, I am kidnapped by the Canadian Alpha, and then rescued by Darien, who turns out to not be the crazy-ass murderer I thought him to be. Instead, he is truly my mate. And now I am his.

Chapter 10

"Want to go for a run?" His question elates me.

"Is that a serious question?" I practically leap to my feet. He laughs at my sudden burst of energy and joins me. "Can we actually do this here?"

"Certain places, yes. It's probably a bit trickier than where you're from, but for now, just stick with me or someone in the pack until you learn the ropes."

We shift then, and Darien leads us to the same exit as before.

The sun is almost at its highest point in the sky. We bolt across the field in broad daylight. Darien is fast. Faster than my old pack mates, but I'm still faster. I trained myself to run faster and longer than any wolf in my pack. I wonder how *he* got so quick. I know he wasn't training to run away like I was. And then I remember our ability to speak to each other, so I ask him with my mind.

He takes a little time before responding and I wonder if last night was just a fluke. We reach the forest and dart through the trees before finally slowing our pace.

My father was training me to be strong enough to help him take out the surrounding Alphas so that we could have more land. I didn't know any better.
Then as I got older, I started to suspect what he and the other Alpha's were doing. That's when I started doing extra training on my own, and with Trace and Asher, so that I would become stronger than he was. I took him out, along with all the other Alpha's involved. I just wish I had accomplished it sooner.

You were just a kid, Darien, I say, but he remains quiet for a few moments.

Since then, I have continued training for the sake of my pack and any others that might need help in case there are any other Alphas or wolves like them.

And now you have me here to help, I say after listening to his story. How could I have seen this man as a killer? He is a much better person than me.

I appreciate it Ari, and you will be a great asset to the pack, but we both know that women, especially you as my mate, are not allowed on the front lines. I have sworn to protect you, he says and what happened next was out of my control.

I attack. Being behind him, I have the element of surprise when I leap onto him, knocking him over.

*Ari, what the—*we tumble together, but I am on my feet first, and already charging again. I aim to sink my teeth into his throat, but he turns just in time, and I end up with a mouthful of his shoulder fur instead. He growls and turns on me.

I wait for him to attack, but he just stares me down, using his Alpha abilities to make me calm down. Surprising him again, I charge once more.

He braces for me, prepared to counter, but I spin away at the last second before maneuvering myself behind him.

When he turns to find me, I clamp my jaws onto his exposed throat.

He freezes. I could easily rip out his throat, but that is not my goal and hopefully he knows it as well. Getting my point across that I can be on the front lines is the true reason for my attack.

I can be of more use than you think. I don't need protection, I release him.

What just happened?

Don't sweat too hard about it. Most people underestimate me, and you weren't trying to fight back anyways.

No, not that! How did you ignore my control? Oh that. I hoped that this would never come up, but once I figured out how to break my father's control it was a piece of cake to do it again. I can't tell him about my father though. That could cause a whole new war.

I don't know. Maybe because we are mates now, I wave off his question.

No, that's not it. You don't seem surprised by it either. Have you done this before, Ari? I don't answer, but he guesses on his own. *You broke your own father's control?*

Once. Just recently, actually. He would sense it if I lied. Hopefully he realizes he can't take on my dad since I broke *his* control just the same. So much for trying to prove a point. I don't currently yearn for war, but I hate that I can't even be considered because of my position and gender.

What does this mean? He asks, and I shrug in response. I honestly have no clue either. It's unheard of. Never before has a female broken an Alpha's control. Hell, few males have even been able to accomplish that. My father's control is one thing, but Darien's too?

Darien

We continue to run, both lost in our thoughts. Earlier, I thought she was trying to kill me. Hell, she *would have* killed me if that were what she was really trying to do. Though I didn't want to have to use my control on her, I was left open due to the fact that I hadn't expected her to break through my control. Once I think I have her figured out, she throws me for another loop. Damn woman has my head spinning in circles.

Ari's words from before keep playing in my head. *From the day I was told that I would have to mate to whoever was chosen for me, I chose to run away and learn how to take care of myself. I trained every single day in the hopes that if ever given the chance I could try to escape.*

I can't blame her. After all, I felt the exact same way not long ago because I didn't have much of a choice either. If I did have a choice, I would pick the woman I was somehow lucky enough to get anyways. She really is different, and not because she thinks she is weak. The more I think about it, the more I admire her for what she did. It takes a strong resolve to continue down the path she started. If she had ended up with someone like the Canadian packs Alpha, I would be glad she had the skill to free herself. If she had been caught, she would have been killed though.

Arranged marriages have been around for a long time, and wolves don't change as quickly with the times as humans do. I believe most werewolves want to pick their mates, but not many royals have complained about the benefits of their positions. Ari wants something different from power and money though. She wants something real, and that's definitely not weak in my eyes.

If she wants something real, I will do whatever it takes to give it to her, but I don't think I could ever let her leave. I *know* I can't let her go, but I also don't know if I can allow her to fight alongside me and the rest of the pack if there was ever a war. She is strong and crafty, but she is also too important to risk. I'd worry too much about her, and that would hinder my own fighting ability.

Though we have only been together a matter of days, and I hadn't even wanted a mate in the first place, my wolf and I would be seriously wrecked if anything happened to her.

Somehow, I am going to have to tell her that it's just not possible. The only problem with *that* is I've learned she can break my control. Granted, I didn't put too much force into the command, it still should not have been possible. She is not the first skilled female I have met, but there is something different about her.

Most female wolves are very obedient, and even the strong ones have a need to please or keep the calm. I can't say that I don't like her rebellious side though. It is sexy as hell, but her safety must come first.

However, her ability to break my control, along with her own father's control has me stumped. Not to mention the fact that we can communicate in wolf form as well, which is a rarity in itself. Who is this woman of mine?

I have no idea what any of this means. Even she doesn't appear to know. And the only other time she has broken an Alpha's command was apparently recent, but is that because she couldn't before or just hadn't tried? Maybe if I knew more about her, I could at least guess at a possibility as to how she can do that, but I know next to nothing of her past.

All I know is that I am mesmerized by her strength and endless abilities. There is something about the way she always looks ready for anything while also so unsure of herself at times, just like a new pup. In a way, that is kind of what she is since she has hidden most of her life. She is more wolf than woman, and I think I love that about her.

I also can't seem to stop thinking about this morning when I finally made her mine. I knew sex would be better with a woman versus the palm of my hand, but holy shit, that was like nothing I have ever experienced before. That moment, and the sexy look of pure ecstasy on her face, when she came undone beneath me, will be forever ingrained in my memory.

After hours of running and chasing down small critters for lunch, I lead my mate back home. I need to take the time to get her to talk about her past so that I can try to figure all this out. I don't like the feeling of being in the dark. I also want to get her back in my bed, but the pack will be coming over to meet her soon.

Once in the house, she follows me back to the room so that we can change back into our human form and get dressed. Ari, still in wolf form, drags her bag into the bathroom and closes the door. Still a shy thing, is she?

I am the only one who has seen her naked body since she chose to grow up away from her pack mates.

Is it wrong that I am happy about that fact? I go downstairs and outside to give her some space in order to try to clear the increasing dirty thoughts from my head. I breathe in the fresh air and sit down on the porch swing. The sun is bright and warm as it cuts through the cool air.

Minutes later, Ari meets me on the porch, wearing jean shorts and a long t-shirt with her long hair flowing down to her waist. She looks beautiful, and I am too stunned to look away from her. There is nothing flashy about her outfit, nor is she wearing makeup to enhance her beauty, but that is the part that captivates me most.

"Are you okay?" she asks with a raised brow, completely oblivious to her effect on me. *Thank heavens*. I pat the empty spot on the swing beside me and she takes the hint. At least she won't ignore everything I ask of her. She keeps a little distance from me, and I don't move to close the gap. If a few inches of space will make her more comfortable, I could afford her that.

"So, what did you do all day in your old pack?" I ask a little rougher than I intended. She tenses and eyes me warily.

"Where did that question come from?"

Damn I should have eased my way into this. I'm not just the Alpha. I am her mate.

"I'm sorry, I was just thinking about what you said earlier and I want to get to know you." She curls back into herself, but answers anyways.

"When I was younger, I stayed close to home by order of my dad. I hunted and ran as far as I was allowed when I wasn't picking fights with my pack mates," she pauses and I wait. "When I got older and stronger from all the training with the other fighters, dad let me run some of the territory lines, not that anyone has ever been dumb enough to attack us until now."

I was shocked to find that her dad allowed her to do such a dangerous task, but I was more curious about something else.

"You never did *anything* with your pack?"

"Aside from a few pack hunts and training, no. Some tried inviting me along for stuff, and I wanted to, but what would be the point? I wouldn't be staying. I'm surprised I stayed as long as I did."

"Well, I'm glad you did or I might have missed my chance," she turns bright red, and I realize what I said aloud, but I am not ashamed of it. I truly am glad she has been saved for so long. And then something dawns on me. Something I should have realized sooner. "Wait. Does this mean you have never been on a date?" my heart stops as I wait for her response. She shakes her head from side to side and I leap off of the swing. "Oh my God. I am such an asshole!"

"Excuse me?"

"Go get ready to go! Wear something warmer," I pull her frazzled form up off the swing, and start pushing her towards the stairs, and practically shout at her in my panic. Of course, she stops and turns around with hands on her hips.

"What is going on, Darien?" she snaps at me.

"I'm taking you on a date, woman, which is the first thing I should have done if I had known, so I am sorry for that. I will make it up to you now, Ari," I kiss her hand, but she pulls away.

"It is not necessary, Darien. I don't need all that fancy stuff. I just want to start my life."

"Well, that's exactly what we are doing. We are going to start your new life as my mate. And as my mate, you deserve to be taken out on a proper date. Now get your butt upstairs and get ready or I'll never let you out of my bed."

"Is that supposed to bend me to your will?" she laughs, a seductive laugh that goes straight to my groin. Maybe that's not such a bad idea. No. I need to do the right thing. Ari needs to go on her first date, and I want to be the man to take her on her first, her last, and all of the ones in between. She is mine now, and I have to take care of her, starting with all the things she missed out on.

"Just move it, woman," I swat her on the butt playfully and she rolls her eyes before finally complying. "Oh, and wear your hair down," I command, and wait for her to challenge me. She turns and stares in confusion, unsure of what to do, and I think we are both surprised when she blushes and quickly runs up the stairs.

While Ari gets ready in the bathroom, I call Trace and Asher and tell them I'm postponing the pack meeting until tomorrow night and that they need to contact everyone for me. I change in the bedroom before going downstairs to wait for my hot date.

About 25 minutes later, she comes down looking absolutely perfect. She doesn't wear any make-up aside from maybe mascara, but, just like I asked, she let her long brown hair fall free over a long, loose t-shirt that bares one of her shoulders.

I'm not surprised that she wears jeans, tight jeans that fit her amazon legs perfectly, and her combat boots to complete the outfit. God help me, we may never make it out the damn door.

Chapter 11

Ari

Walking down the stairs in a huff, I find Darien staring at me like an idiot. I can't believe he is making me do this. I like the idea of staying in his bed better. Would you look at me, one time, and I'm already sex crazed. It doesn't help that Darien's muscled body makes me drool and his scent drives me crazy. Even his voice sets me on fire, especially when he says my own name.

He is dressed much nicer than me, with dark blue jeans, a light brown button-up that makes his eyes pop, and cowboy boots. His dark hair looks messy but styled at the same time if that's possible. All I know is that it is sexy as hell and he looks like one of those men featured on the covers of romance novels.

If I had to describe him, I'd say that he mostly resembles Theo James, but taller and buffer, and has green eyes rather than brown of course. I feel like a little girl standing next to a gorgeous, full-grown man.

"Sorry, my best outfit was destroyed by Alpha Flint," and I immediately regret my words when his teeth suddenly elongate and he growls in disgust. Damn, I can't do this. He knows I have never been on a date. I'm going to ruin this night and shatter whatever image he had of me. He puts himself back together before taking my hand in his and leads me out the door.

I let it go once again, avoiding angering him further.

Darien drives us to a restaurant that looks more like a shack. I step out into the cool night and his warm hand takes mine before leading me to the building. He releases my hand so that he can open the door for me, and I step inside with arms crossed over my chest awkwardly.

Every eye in the place lifts to me, to us. I take a deep breath before letting my arms fall to my sides. I glare at them all before lifting my head as I walk past them to a quiet table in the corner. I ignore the looks that follow me and focus on my surroundings. Among the humans, I can smell werewolf in here but there are too many smells to determine how many and what is old and what is fresh.

I take my seat and trust that Darien can pinpoint who is who better than I can. After all, they are his wolves.

The table in front of me is made of wood with carvings of mountains, trees, and a moose on the surface. It is very well done, which makes me feel nervous about eating on it. A candle is lit at the far end of the table, creating a romantic mood, and I'm reminded why I am here.

Darien sits in the booth across from me with a wry smile on his face.

"Sorry, it's nothing fancy, but it's the best we have," he apologizes.

"Darien, I'm from Alaska, not France," he smiles at my response, "This is perfect, so stop worrying."

"Well, they don't serve duck either," he says and in the next instant he is grabbing my hand to pull me back down into my seat. "Very funny Ari," he chuckles, and I shrug in response.

"I guess I can live with my second favorite," I see the spark of interest in his features.

"And that is?" he asks impatiently when I don't expand further.

"Elk of course," I grin at him.

"Good choice," he smiles back.

A young woman with big hazel eyes like mine and curly brown hair walks up to our table with a determined look on her face. I sit up and prepare for whatever she wants. Darien catches the change in my posture and turns to face our company.

"Alex," Darien greets her.

"Darien. Glad you're back home safe," his presence seems to stun her momentarily before her features soften.

"Thanks. It's good to be home," he waits a moment to see what she came over here for, but he gets impatient. "Is something going on?" and her determined look returns.

"I was just wondering if it was a good idea to be on a date when you just brought a royal home to be your mate," she says curiously, slurring her words slightly. We both stare at her dumbfounded.

I can smell the alcohol on her, and though I haven't done much drinking, I have heard that it dulls our senses a bit. She must not be able to smell that we have mated.

"Alex. This *is* my mate," he motions towards me and the woman's eyes widen.

"Oh, thank God! I figured so, but I thought it was too good to be true. We were expecting a snobby, Prada-wearing, ice queen from the north, and while that may work for other Alphas, that would never work for you, Darien," she says with laughter and relief before sliding into the booth next to me. "Hi, I'm Alexia, or just Alex for short," she smiles at me and holds out her hand to me.

"Ari," I take her hand in return. Her sass and boldness make me like her instantly. She is beautiful, though I sense she is older than me, and Darien even, but not by much. It's hard to tell since the aging process slows down in our 20's.

Alex tells me about how she's new to the pack. She lived in Northern California where Darien has just recently claimed territory in the past year. She didn't run into trouble with her old Alpha, but she knew the rumors.

She came here to meet her new pack mates, fell in love with the town, and never left. No one in my pack had ever tried so hard to talk to me before, and I didn't have to run away anymore. As of today, I was starting my life and I may already be making my first friend.

She tries to ask about me, but Darien clears his throat loudly and raises a thick eyebrow at her.

"What? Cool your jets. Am I not allowed to talk to your mate?" she asks in a snarky voice.

"Um, we are kind of on a date," he says trying to keep hold on his temper. Alexia's face turns bright red as she looks back and forth between us.

"Whoops, my bad," she says, and now I wonder if she's closer to my age than I thought, or perhaps younger even. "I guess that's why you cancelled the meeting tonight. Sorry, it was nice to meet you though, Ari," she surprises me with a hug and whispers in my ear before disappearing from our booth.

Darien gives me a curious look. I smile shyly back at him.

"What did—," he tries to speak, but the waiter arrives at that moment, causing him to swear under his breath in frustration. Our waiter is definitely human, but he smiles at Adam as if he knows him. With this small of a town, he most-likely does.

I order lemon water when he asks what I'd like to drink. Darien does the same and puts in our food order as well so that we don't get interrupted again I assume.

"What did she say to you?"

"Nothing much," I play coy and try to change the subject. "So, the pack meeting is tomorrow then?" He frowns at my withheld information but lets it slide for now.

"Yes. This was far more important. Besides, we have already mated so the worry of someone else trying to claim you has dissipated," I blush at his words and look around to make sure no one heard him. "Don't worry," he grabs my hand "no one here heard anything. Any wolf that sees you will know you're mine because of my scent now mingled with yours."

Even those words have me blushing, and I turn away when the waiter deposits our drinks on the table. Darien thanks him before he turns to leave again.

His hands reach for mine across the table and mine automatically comply. His touch makes my skin tingle, and when he looks into my eyes I want to melt in my seat.

"You are absolutely breathtaking. How did I get so lucky? Please, tell me more about you. I want to know everything," he says seductively. He keeps forgetting that I'm boring and a pain in the ass. Does he not remember I've attacked him in as many days as I've known him?

"Like I said, there's not much to tell," but I give him what info I can. I tell him about my Dad and my brother, along with my coldhearted mother, and my uncles that he got to meet. He listens intently as I talk about how they took me under their wing, and that I loved watching movies of all kinds, eating banana splits, playing cards, and beat boxing.

He raises his brows in either surprise or horror, or probably a combination of the two. I enjoy watching him squirm as he tries to recover his panicked features.

"Okay, maybe I'm pulling your leg on that last one," I laugh and he breathes a sigh of relief. "Everything else you pretty much already know. Fighting, running, getting abducted, and now here with you." I pause and try to think of anything I might have missed and realize I have. "Oh, and fishing, though I've mostly only done ice fishing."

"Nothing boring about you, Ari Wilder. However, very soon I'm going to change your name, and now that you're where you belong, you might find even more hobbies and learn even more about yourself. Someday you will see yourself how I already see you."

My heart threatens to beat out of my chest at his sweet words, and I'm so awkward that I don't know how to reply. I'm saved by our food arriving just in time.

For a little hole in the wall place, it is well decorated and the food is top notch. I went from one small town to the next but I have no issue with that whatsoever. If I ever was a runaway, I planned to go somewhere warmer. As a wolf I don't mind the cold but the feel of the sun, and the magic of the ocean calls to me.

The beauty of coastlines and beaches in Alaska can't be beaten, but even us wolves can't tolerate the cold waters without a wetsuit on. I want to be able to go to the ocean and feel the cool, salty water on my bare skin.

"What are you thinking about?" Darien asks, taking notice that I have drifted off to dreamland. Again, I shy away at revealing each and every detail about me, but one look in his beautiful, intrigued eyes beg for my secrets, and I want nothing more than to give him everything.

"I was just thinking about how I have always wanted to go to the California and Oregon coast."

He smiles brightly at my admission.

"I can grant that wish," he says happily, and my insides dance with excitement. "Unfortunately, not right away, but I promise that we will go someday soon." I want to kiss him right then and there but the table between us allows me to only reach my hand out to his.

"I'd like that. Thank you," he takes my hand and squeezes.

"However, I have a favor I'd like in return," and the dangerous look in his eyes has me wary. I tilt my head as I await his request. "Before we go to the ocean, would you teach me how to fish," he asks a little embarrassed. I grin from ear to ear, pleased that he is interested in something I like, and not afraid to ask for my help versus having a male teach him.

"I would be happy to," I continue to grin and squeeze his hand back. Neither of us lets go as we one-handedly finish eating the elk, cheesy garlic mashed potatoes, and chopped asparagus.

When we finish, and he pays the bill, I'm reminded again that I want a job. I decide it's not best to bring it up while we are on a date. I will have to find a newspaper or get online to hunt for jobs.

Still holding my hand, we head back to the Toyota Tundra he drove us here in and is about to open my door, but instead pushes me up against the truck and captures my mouth with his.

My body, apparently having a mind of its own, grinds against him as I kiss him back with equal need and passion.

"Damn," he reluctantly pulls away, and I want to pull him right back to me. I ask him what's wrong with a subtle tilt of my head. "I want to take you home, or just take you right here and now in my truck, but this is your first date, and I want to do it right," he admits.

While I am having a good time, I want to beg him to do one of the first two options, but I hold my tongue. He kisses me once more, softly this time, and then opens my door for me to climb in.

He hops in the driver's seat and drives away from the direction of home, and I try not to be bummed out by that.

We arrive at a large beach area next to a wide part of the river. I assume it's probably a popular spot in the summertime. I follow his lead and exit the truck. A muscular arm wraps around me, and together we stroll down towards a grassy area where Darien pulls us down into a sit. I take in the sights, smells, and sounds all around me, enjoying the beauty of nature in my human form. In this moment, I feel at peace next to my mate.

"You have done this before, haven't you?" I accuse playfully.

"Only a couple times, but I've never taken them to that restaurant or this spot. Nor did I get any farther or want to go any farther than a kiss. I saved a lot of firsts for you."

"Apparently I saved *all* my firsts for you," I retort.

"Thank heavens for me," he pulls me in for a sweet kiss, and for some reason the combination of our surroundings plus his touch has my head spinning, and hormones raging. He looks at me with pure sexiness and I know he smells my arousal, just as I can feel his.

"So, what did you do on your other dates," I try to distract him and myself. As much as I would like to give myself to him right here, we are too close to the main road for my comfort.

"Usually just a movie at the theater and maybe dinner or dessert at a fast food place or diner; nothing too intimate. I wasn't interested in any of the women I dated, but being an Alpha, even a young Alpha, I have been pressured into dating to find a mate and create an heir." His mention of a baby stuns me for a moment. I never considered finding a real mate, therefore never considered children. I will be expected to birth that heir.

Werewolves almost never use protection. Pregnancy is few and far between for us but also a blessing, so why would we, unless you're like me and don't want to be used for your womb?

I want to be more than just a tool to create a male heir. Staying home popping out kids and playing my mother's role is exactly what I don't want to end up doing.

"I know it sounds crazy, but I can't help but picture a little girl with your beautiful blue-green eyes and wavy brown hair," his words shake me out of my inner tirade.

"You mean *after* I give you a male heir?" I taunt, and watch his reaction closely. He shrugs his shoulders as he stares out into the night, and I'm left speechless at his indifference over the situation.

"To be honest, I never really thought or cared about bringing children into this world. Not until I met you, that is. I want to see you pregnant with our child, but if you couldn't or didn't want to, I would be content just spending the rest of my life with just you." He looks at me when I don't respond for a while.

Everything I had ever known or thought was being blown to pieces. A few words from my mate and all my fears seem to wash away. This man wants me whether I can give him an heir or not, where other women who couldn't produce have been shoved aside and replaced by another who could. He is turning my world upside down. Once again, it's making me question everything I have done in my life up to this point. Could I really have choices?

I let myself picture it for a moment. I see the look in his eyes when he sees me round with his child, *our* child. Then flashes of him holding our child, loving them, and helping guide them through this life. It's a beautiful dream that I had never let myself witness before.

"Are you okay?" he asks with genuine concern, shaking me out of the chaos in my mind. I don't know how to answer yet so I just smile reassuringly at him. He knows there is a storm going on in my head, but he doesn't pry. Instead he wraps me in his arms, my back to his chest, and our hearts beat in the same rhythm as we watch the constant changing river run free.

Darien

Ari is still lost in thought as we pull up to our home. I knew change wouldn't come easy. Growing up I had no idea what love was. My parents had never really gotten along but they stayed out of each other's way. Of course, my mother always stood by his side as a show of support whenever needed, but it was all a front, and I hated it.

I imagined Ari, a girl even younger than me, having nothing in common, and her pretending by my side just to reap the benefits of being an Alpha's mate. How could I have been so wrong?

I assumed it would be a long time before we even felt comfortable to mate. We don't even need to hold a pack meeting. Any wolf that crosses paths with her will know that she is mine, and I am damn pleased by that.

She makes me feel things I never thought I could feel. Every breath she takes, every word she speaks gives my life meaning. Dating I assumed would be a nuisance and unnecessary, but it felt so easy with her silly humor, warm smiles, and her appreciation for the simple things. I only wish I knew what she was thinking at times like this.

I shut off the truck, and together we exit. Quickly meeting her on her side, I take her hand to walk her up to the porch.

"Thank you," her words stop me, and I turn towards her, looking into her beautiful sea glass eyes.

"For what?" I stare at her in question.

"For my first date," she blushes and looks away. She is so confident and fierce all the time, but I am the lucky bastard who gets to see her insecure, awkward moments, and it's simply adorable. "I had a better time than I dreamed possible." Her sweetness floors me, and I'm pleased to know she had a good time, regardless of our lack of fancy amenities in the area.

Pulling her in close, I gently kiss her lips before I say, "Silly mate, the night's not over yet."

She has no time to respond before I lift her in my arms, open the front door, then carry her over the threshold. Not even bothering with the lights, I close the door and move into the living room. I set her on her feet near the fireplace and cover her lips with mine before she can speak.

I reach my hand along the wall for the switch to the gas fireplace. After finding it and turning it on, I back her up towards the couch without breaking the kiss. Ari meets my passion when my hands grasp her perfectly shaped ass. Without missing a beat, she wraps her legs around me without a fight, and I guide her down onto the cushions.

She writhes against me in need, and I plan to fulfill that need soon, but I want to show her what she means to me.

My hands are in the hair that I have longed to run my fingers through from the moment I laid my eyes on this wild woman. I caress her face and body, as our lips and tongues move in sync together. Mine. My Goddess. I claim this woman with every part of my being. She could be the Goddess of Destruction and I wouldn't care in the slightest.

I lift her shirt over her head, breaking our kiss, and then my lips find her neck. Her hands hold on to me as I kiss and suckle her exposed skin while I work her bra off. Her upper half is exposed and I take a second to look at her. Beautiful skin, sexy messy brown hair, and hungry eyes stare back at me. I lean back down to kiss her again. The vibration of her moan against my lips melts away the last bit of my control. I can't wait any longer. I need her now.

Still holding her sweet lips captive, I start unbuttoning my shirt. Impatiently, she steps in to help before quickly unbuttoning my jeans as well. When her hand glides down my length over my boxers, I am almost done for. I stand to remove my boots and the last of my clothes and then throw a blanket and some pillows on the area rug.

I take off her boots as well, and then rip off her jeans that she has already undone for me. It is then that I find my little vixen went commando this evening. She smiles wickedly up at me.

"You are going to be the death of me, Ari," I breathe before lifting her off the couch and moving her down onto the blanket and pillows. I cover her body with mine and her fingers reach for me, tickling my skin, making my whole body tighten with pleasure.

I watch the light of the fire dance on her skin as I firmly enter her, forcing a sexy moan from her lips. She is soaking wet for me, and it takes everything I have to resist letting go right then and there. Her insides squeeze me tight, and I start to move as she pulls me in deep.

She moves with me, her hands searching my body for God knows what, but it feels heavenly.

Her wild need for me makes me even harder, and I know I don't have long now. I find her dark swollen lips and capture them, biting and sucking as I push deeper and harder into her.

She takes everything I give her and every movement and sound she makes brings me closer to release. I want this moment to last forever, but the feel of her is making that impossible.

I pull her tight against me, burying myself in her as deep as I can, and she moans my name along with curses of pleasure.

"Ari," I call her name. Her heated gaze meets mine as I stare into her soul. "I love you, Ari," I pronounce and her eyes glisten with tears that she forces back. She grips me harder and I say it again as I pump furiously into her.

Ari screams my name as she comes undone, her orgasm squeezing me for all I'm worth as I release into her.

I collapse next her when I have nothing left to give, and pull her into my arms. She doesn't resist, and with my free hand, I tickle her sensitized skin before pressing my lips to the top of her head.

Only a few minutes pass before she is softly breathing as she sleeps in my arms. What I said is true. I love her. I probably loved her the moment I saw her on that jet. I didn't expect to hear it back, and I won't hold my breath waiting for her to return the sentiment. She will say it when she's ready. Until then, I will show her my love and make sure she is safe and happy.

I gently lift her in my arms, carry her upstairs to my bed, and I resume my position next to her, all without waking her in the slightest. It helps that she is a deep sleeper for a werewolf.

Ari

The next morning, I had barely come out of my sleep when I find Darien exploring my body for another round of naked fun. He's extra greedy today, tasting and caressing every inch of me. He grows harder inside me every time he makes me moan, but he refuses to move.

Images of last night flutter through my head, and I can't wait any longer. Gathering up the strength in my newly found muscles, I grip him with all I have, causing his form to shudder above me. If he was standing, I don't doubt that I would have brought this beautiful man to his knees. It makes me feel powerful.

So, of course, I do it again. And again, until, with a heated growl, he finally gives me what I want.

I hold on tight, feeling nothing but solid muscle, and it makes me tighten even harder around him. We become frantic with need, and I'm full of pure bliss when we both come undone together.

Apparently, he's not done with me quite yet. I'm panting, trying to catch my breath, when suddenly he lifts me in his arms and carries me into the shower for a slower, gentler round two. Is it wrong to wish for every morning to be just like this?

I thought it was a dream, but the way he looked into my eyes this morning reminds me that his words from last night were indeed real. He said it with such ease, and I couldn't find the words to say it back. Did I *want* to say it back to him? Do I love Darien Shield?

If I do, I don't think I am ready to admit it. It's too early to be sure of anything, but I can't deny that my feelings are rapidly heading that way.

There's still a lot that I don't know about him, and I haven't even met his pack or seen how he runs things. Yes, he is definitely strong, and insanely attractive. So far, he has taken good care of me, and we are already mated, but there could still be sides of him that I haven't seen.

Wolves, especially Alpha's, have tempers and are capable of losing control. Very bad things happen when an Alpha loses control. Only a strong wolf can take out as many leaders as he has, but the more wolves under him, the harder it is to keep control.

For now, I just have to keep being who I am, watching and listening to detail to protect myself. He may already be my mate, and I may be ready to start the life I never dreamed of, but I won't be blindsided either.

If Darien can prove to me that he is the man and Alpha I hope he is, then I will gladly take his last name and give him the "L" word.

"Come on," Darien says, snapping me out of my thoughts. I look at him questioningly, but he just gets up and starts getting dressed.

When I don't move, he goes through my clothes, and throws me underwear, jeans, and a long sleeve shirt. I flush bright red and I'm not sure if I'm embarrassed or angry that he just went through my undies as if it were no big deal.

"What the hell do you think—"

"I thought we'd go take the horses for a ride. Unless you're not up for it," he backtracks, but I'm already up dressing. I throw on my combat boots, and he smiles before we hastily make our way to the barn.

The scent of hay and earth fills me. Even the horses have a unique scent that is wild yet calming.

Two giant, beautiful horses stand before me that look like Appaloosas, but I'm not positive. I've looked at many pictures of horses, but have done only minimal research on them, so I can't be sure.

Both of them are brown, but one is much darker than the other and they both have the white, leopard-spotted rear. The lighter brown also has more white showing in its coat than the other, but they are both stunning.

"AraAppaloosa's," Darien says, answering my unspoken question. At least I was partly right. I remembered reading that there was an Arabian and Appaloosa cross breed. Araloosa was the term I had heard before, though. There must be multiple names.

I can't resist touching their soft muzzles and talking sweetly to them as Darien saddles them up.

They are sweet, and there is obvious intelligence in their eyes. They know what we are, but they are not afraid like most animals tend to be of our kind.

As Darien preps them, he tells me how they belong to the whole pack. Everyone pitches in to take care of them and gets to enjoy the benefits of riding them. It's obvious that they get plenty of exercise based on their lean, muscled form.

The lighter colored one is a female whose name I learn is Princess Lightning. I wrinkle my nose at the princess part, and opt to just call her Lightning. She is the one I want to ride.

Darien shows me how to climb on, and excitement courses through my body as I diligently follow my mate's directions. I succeed on my first try, and I am now at the mercy of this beautiful beast.

Darien confidently, and probably more graceful than me, leaps up onto the male whose name is Royal Thunder. I laugh at the creative names. He explains that it's partly because Princess is faster than Royal. Lightning always comes before the thunder. My insides are practically dancing in anticipation for our ride.

We start off slow, but with Darien and Lightning's help, I pick it up quickly, and soon we are galloping through the fields. The power of this magnificent creature is nothing short of amazing, and the feeling is almost as freeing as running on my own four legs. I make the mistake of looking over at Darien. My energized mood turns into something else as I take him in.

Darien looks sexier than sin itself in his tight jeans, cowboy boots, black t-shirt, and messy wind-blown hair. He notices me staring with a heated gaze that I try to put out before he sees but he does, and winks before sprinting back to the barn. I watch the way he moves, fully in control as Royal moves fiercely over the terrain.

I squeeze Lightning's sides briefly but sharply to kick up the speed. I imitate Darien's movements as we race after them.

Thrilling sensations course through me as we move faster and faster back towards the barn. We are right on Royals heels as I gently pull back on the reigns.

I am breathless right along with Lightning when we come to a stop even though I wasn't the one running full tilt. Riding is even more exhilarating than I thought it would be.

Darien awaits me with a sexy grin. Though I don't need it, I let him help me dismount before we walk the horses back to their stalls. Together we remove the saddles, and Darien shows me how to clean their hooves along with how to correctly brush them. Lastly, we refill their water, make sure they have plenty of food, and give each of them some love before we part. I will definitely be riding her again very soon. The look Darien gives me tells me he wants to ride me *now*. He hoists me into his arms, takes me to his bed, and does just that.

Chapter 12

Darien

I'm face first in the grass. Gentle arms pick me up off the ground.

"Silly boy, you need to be more careful," my mother's sweet voice says before releasing me to continue playing with my soccer ball.

"Lydia, quit coddling the boy," my father growls, making mother stiffen. He used to frighten me too. Now it just makes me mad. My friend's dads don't talk to their mates that way. Their mamas aren't afraid of their mates. Maybe it's because my dad is an Alpha. Everyone seems to fear him.

"He's only six years old," mama finally speaks up as I continue to kick the ball around the yard.

"He's not going to be dominant enough to lead this pack if you continue to baby him and smother him with kisses," he huffs before going inside the house.

"Mama, I don't want to be an Alpha. They're mean," I say before she pulls me into a hug. I feel her tears run down onto my head.

Suddenly time fast forwards to twelve-year-old me. I'm in the kitchen cooking dinner, while mom reads a book at the kitchen table. Dad walks in when I'm just about done. I smile at him. He likes to eat, so I thought it would make him happy if I made a meal for him.

When he rips the book from my mother's hands and tears it in half, I realize that I made a terrible mistake.

"Why the hell is my son doing your job, woman?" he rages.

"It's not her fault. I wanted to cook for you," I try to intervene.

"I'll deal with you next," his cold glare snaps to me, before returning to my mother. He yanks her out of her seat while his other arm reaches back to strike her, but I shove him. I knock her loose from his grasp.

When his attention is turned back to me, my mother blocks his path to me. This time I'm not able to protect her from his fist. She falls to the floor with a cry and crawls away.

"We're gonna make an Alpha out of you, yet," my father smiles menacingly before his fist connects with my face, and all I see is darkness.

I jolt awake expecting to find blood pooled on the floor from the beating I received, but all I find is a soft, warm body.

Ari is still sleeping like the dead beside me. The sight of her calms my racing heart. With everything that has happened, and with the few things I've already revealed to her, thoughts of my past have returned to haunt me.

Now that I have my mate, I can't help but think about my parents and the relationship they had, or *didn't* have.

Aside from being a quiet constant at my father's side, my mother had spent every moment focusing on me. My father taught me how to fight, along with giving me lessons on how to be a leader; none of which I adopted from him of course.

Everything else came from my mother. As a child, she fed me, clothed me, and gave me an education.

My father didn't want me going to a public school so he had my mother home-school me. She also taught me how to cook when I showed an interest in it.

When I'd anger my father, she'd eventually step in to try and protect me. After a couple times of getting hurt, she stopped. I understood her not wanting to get hurt for my mistakes, but most of the time I didn't even know what I did wrong.

Once I turned twelve, I stopped spending so much time at home. In part because I didn't want to be the cause of my mother's pain, and partly because I was mad at her for letting my father beat me to a pulp for the stupidest shit. Staying away also got me out from under my father's thumb.

I spent my time hanging out with my pack mates and training with them. It was with them that I really learned how to fight, and what it meant to be a leader. Even way back then, I knew that Trent, Asher, and other pack mates would have my back. I envied the lives they had outside of my father's house and I wanted to protect that.

Without me being my mom's focus, I noticed too late that she was slowly starting to losing her mind. Everyone could see that there was no love between my parents, but they tolerated each other, until one day it seemed like a dark cloud of evil appeared in my home and it continued to grow day after day.

My mother wanted another baby, but my father said that he only needed one heir.

When I stopped being dependent on my mother, my father started to take more of an interest in me. He gave me more responsibilities in the pack, and after a couple years, he made me his enforcer. Whenever someone in the pack did something wrong, he sent me to deal with it. As a hormonal, testosterone-filled, dominant wolf, I actually enjoyed the hell out of it.

I was praised for the work I was doing. Even my father seemed to be in a better mood. He wasn't his typical ornery, edgy self around me. I'd felt powerful and respected. In those years as my father's enforcer, I had grown almost a foot, and my lean, teenager body puffed up to nearly three times the size.

My appetite had tripled too. The day I came home to find almost no food in the house, I snapped at my mother. She flinched away from me as if I was about to hit her. It was then that I realized that I hadn't gained any respect in my pack. I became feared. I had become my father.

Knowing that removing myself from the enforcer position would just anger my father, and that he would just replace me with a new puppet, I continued in my duties. Only this time around, I did things my way. I took it upon myself to get more involved in the lives of my pack mates. In doing so, I actually did start gaining respect, but I also took notice that there were some very wrong things going on in the pack, and it all traced back to my father.

My name on Ari's lips snap me back to the present. She's still asleep and apparently having much better dreams than I was having.

Even in her sleep she looks fierce. This woman would never let a man control or hurt her, nor would she stand by and let an innocent woman or child be hurt.

It's amazing how different our relationship is in comparison to what I witnessed between my parents growing up. Even though most haven't met her yet, I can sense that the pack is happier now somehow.

What's more is that when we became mates, my power over the pack seems to have amplified. I'm not sure if that's just what happens when an Alpha finds a mate, or if it's just because of her, but I'd be willing to bet that it's all because of Ari.

Pulling her tighter into my arms, I kiss the top of her head before closing my eyes. It's been a long time since me and the big guy upstairs have spoken, but I can't help thanking him for sending me my perfect woman.

Ari

The pack meeting is tonight. It is tradition to bring everyone, or at least those in the area, to meet any new pack member. The full moon comes in a couple days so there will be a more formal ritual then. Today's purpose is to make sure no one tries to kill the unfamiliar wolf on their territory, or so it was supposed to be.

Since Darien and I didn't take long to consummate the relationship, everyone will already know where I belong. They will sense that I am pack. Maybe it's just my nerves, but I feel like I'm being watched. Not many would dare to challenge the Alpha's mate, but I say 'bring it on'.

Night has fallen already. After being willingly assaulted this morning, we actually used the shower for its intended purposes.

For the remainder of the day, I just tried to keep myself busy while Darien focused on making arrangements for this evening.

Keeping busy is difficult at the moment. I don't really watch much TV other than select movies.

As much as I wanted to, I couldn't go off into the woods as I normally would, so I settled for loving on the horses and talking to them until it was time for me to get ready.

Instead of being inside greeting guests with him, I slipped outside to hide on the back porch. I am not hiding out of fear, but I'm not the type of person who is liked by many. I didn't fit into my old pack, so why would I fit here? Better to be scarce until Darien needs to introduce me so not to spoil the mood. It is a party after all.

The gaze that I have been sensing behind me grows closer. I assume it's one of Darien's wolves, but whether they are friend or foe is unknown.

For all I know it could be a jealous female or a traitor in the pack, though I don't think anyone would be dumb enough to attack at a house full of werewolves. Not unless the whole pack is in on it.

The possibilities have my blood boiling. Would I not be wanted here either?

Whoever is daring to sneak up behind me chose a good location to come at me from since the wind is blowing their scent away from my direction. However, they chose the wrong person to sneak up on because I know this game. I *own* this game.

I duck quickly and the whistle sound of a body sails over me. In the same second, I am up and moving. Before he makes it to the ground, I kick out, my foot succeeding in catching his. He tries to spin to face me, but I've effectively knocked him off balance. That's when I pounce.

My knee pins his chest as my left foot traps his wrist, and my hand grips his throat while the other is posed to strike. He smirks and raises his one free hand in surrender.

"Darien's going to have a blast with you," he laughs as I stand back and let him pick himself up off the ground. I glare at him just to keep myself from blushing. Just my mate's name said aloud seems to affect me. "I'm Jerek," he offers his hand out to me.

He is very tall and muscled but lankier than Darien. He has unusual strawberry blonde hair and sapphire blue eyes. He isn't Darien sexy, but he is a unique and a beautiful man nonetheless.

"Ari," I accept his hand, returning equal strength in his grip, causing more chuckling from him.

"So, what's the beautiful Alpha's mate doing sitting alone in the dark?" I'm thankful he doesn't start by accusing me of hiding. I sit on the porch swing, and he takes the empty space beside me even though I didn't offer it, but the company of just one person is much preferable to a whole roomful.

"I've just never really liked these kinds of things," I give the partial truth as I stare out into the darkness.

"Sure," he says skeptically, not buying it, "No one here will bite. At least not in their human forms, well, except maybe Darien, but you probably already know that." As he erupts into more laughs, I shake my head at his constant jokes.

"I'm not afraid," I say bluntly.

"Oh darling, I doubt much scares you, but I can't imagine what would keep you out here when there is a party inside just for you. You women usually love these sorts of shindigs. Doesn't look like you have any embarrassing defects to scare anyone away."

"I could ask why you are out here too, aside from trying to scare the shit out of the new girl," I choose to ignore his snide comments. They will all know soon I'm not a typical female.

"Touché," he chuckles some more before his thoughts seem to take him somewhere else. I can tell he is fighting his own inner battles so I decide to confess to him. Anything to take the tormented look off his face. I much preferred his light laughter.

"I don't exactly fit in anywhere. I am not a proper female Were. I do things I'm not supposed to. I fight the things expected of me. Although Darien is not what I expected, I feel like I am meant for more than to just be a pawn for gaining allies," his eyes meet mine on that last part, "but everyone continues to tell me to get over myself and stick to my duties."

He takes my hand in his and looks me straight in the eye with a knowing expression.

"Don't let anyone kill your spirit, Ari," he says sounding much older than he looks to be. "Once it's broken, it is hard to put it back together," and he seems to know the feeling. Though I just met him, I am sincerely worried for Jerek. Through his happy-go-lucky attitude, I can sense that there's something else in him. Something dangerous.

"Did someone kill your spirit, Jerek?" he ponders my question for a moment, lost in thought. Then suddenly, he smiles, breaking that haunting look in his eyes.

"Nah kid, I was just waiting for you to come into my life," he teases and ruffles my hair as if I am way younger than I am. I want to punch him, but I am just happy that he doesn't look so lost anymore. "What do you say we head into your party?" he extends his hand to me again. I stand on my own, earning another chuckle from him.

Darien catches my eye the moment I walk into the living room where everyone has gathered. The same living room him and I made sweet love in just last night. He looks suspiciously between Jerek and me, but I ignore his curiosity and move to his side.

"You been harassing my woman?" he shoots the question at Jerek.

"Hey, she's the one putting innocent bystanders in choke holds," he says matter-of-factly. My face burns red as Darien and everyone in the room erupts into laughter. Mom would have been scolding me by now, even if I had just been defending myself.

"Everyone," Darien calls the room into attention as he reaches for my hand, "meet Ari, my mate. If anyone messes with her, prepare to deal with, well, *her*." He laughs again and the rest of the room whistles and howls in welcome.

He continues to address them, and I watch their faces, amazed at how intently they listen. What's more, is how relaxed and happy everyone is, as if they feel safe here. Even my father's pack had the few edgy, annoyed, or just plain bored groups. Maybe it was the lack of sunshine we get there most months.

Throughout the night, everyone takes their turn to come greet me warmly and to get a sample of my scent, though I'm sure my scent is all over this place. I try not to ponder that thought too long before I lose my cool. A few males linger too long, mainly because of my increased hormones that they undoubtedly smell. Darien always came to the rescue though, keeping his aggression in check, but a few growls escaped when some pushed their luck.

Thank goodness we mated before the full moon. Senses and emotions are much stronger in wolf form, and an unmated female is fair game. Things would have been bloody.

A familiar face distracts me from my thoughts.

"Hey Ari," Alex greets me with a wink and a hug. We talk for a moment but she doesn't steal me away for too long. I am surprised at first to see her unmated to anyone, but then I remember she hasn't been here long.

I try to ignore Jerek's stare following me most of the night. He kept his distance from everyone and focused all of his attention on me so that people would leave him alone. I know, because I used to pull the same shit.

Darien noticed his eyes on me too, and he looked as puzzled as I felt. Hell, even Jerek himself looked confused about something.

I was finally relieved from his constant staring when Asher and Trace came over to redirect his attention, but as everyone was leaving, I caught his eye once again. His confused look had changed to one of determination. I smiled and waved as he left with the rest of the pack.

"What's his story?" I question Darien once everyone is gone. I didn't have to clarify whom I was asking about. He knew.

Darien

Jerek had been born into this pack a few years before me. He was always the goofy one, playing pranks and getting into mischief. He was strong though, and also a good guy with a nice girlfriend that he was head over heels for.

However, under my dad's rule, nothing stays good forever. My father didn't like Jerek, nor did a lot of the elders because of the trouble he always caused them. Not to mention that he is a dominant, and wasn't afraid to stand up to the older wolves when they were being shady bastards. He was young, but dominant enough to become a second.

When his girlfriend went missing, he went looking for her after the second day had gone by. Some wolves will take off for a day or two just to get some alone time with their wolf, but something apparently didn't feel right to Jerek. He said she wouldn't have left without telling him first.

It had snowed, so it took four days before he had found her body. He carried her home, accused my father of rape and murder. It wasn't clear if it was murder or suicide, but there were many scents mixed together on her body; one being his Alpha's distinct scent.

Jerek tried to fight him in his rage when he denied the accusations. My dad beat him almost to his death before setting the girl's body on fire in front of him. It broke him.

It took everything I had not to step in. The girl was already long dead. I had to be smart about it. If I had tried to kill him, the pack would have killed me. Nobody wants someone in the pack who would kill his own father. If he killed me, nothing would change, and no one would know the truth.

By this time, I had known the truth, but I needed to have evidence to show the pack. I'd been trying to find proof of my father's evilness for a while when that happened. I was also training, making myself stronger for the day that I would inevitably have to take down my own father.

It was shortly after that incident that I had found what I needed. It took me a while, but I'd figured out his password to his computer. I found emails to and from other Alpha's in nearby territories, containing pictures of women, female shifters from other packs. One was of Jerek's girlfriend.

After saving the emails to a thumb drive, I talked to a few of the women I knew were in my pack that were also in the photos. Most wouldn't talk to me, but I could see the fear and shame in their eyes.

Finally, one of them told me exactly what was happening. With that information, I gave the thumb drive to the people I trusted most, Trace and Asher, and then set out to kill the Alpha who was no longer my father.

His death, I think, is the only thing that kept Jerek from leaving the pack, although he resents me for not killing him sooner. I had even asked him to be my fourth in command, but he refused.

To be honest, I am surprised he is still here, and that he even showed up here tonight. I don't think he is trying to steal Ari from me, but he did appear to have an intense interest in her. Today I saw parts of the man he used to be rather than the cold, distant, lazy man he has been since that day.

I can understand now more than I ever have *why* he became this way. Feeling the way that I do for my mate, I know that if I were to ever lose Ari, I would blame myself for not protecting her. I would not be able to live with myself. The fact that Jerek hasn't gone rogue is even more astounding now, but I can tell that he has only been hanging on by a thread before today.

Ari seems just as concerned as me and questions me the moment everyone is gone. I reluctantly give her the gory details of his past. I also warn her to be careful because I don't know what he is capable of anymore. She's quiet as she processes every word. She knows few details of the pack's history and mine, and I'm afraid that the more she learns will send her running.

"Fuck your dad! Bring that bastard back to life so I can kill him myself!" She spits, and I am quickly retracting my last thought. A lot of female wolves are tough, but I don't think anyone but Ari would have been able to whoop my dad's ass without hesitation if he'd tried anything with her.

The thought of her anywhere near that monster sickens me though, and I instinctively reach out, pulling her into my embrace. She stiffens in surprise, but eventually settles into me.

Just her scent has me rock hard and throbbing.

"Everyone loves you, Ari," I whisper to her. I could tell that she was nervous earlier so I didn't push her to come inside. I knew she would come in when she was ready, but I hope she realizes now that she was worried for nothing. I don't know what it was like at her old pack, but here, she will be forced out of her shell.

She tilts her face up to me, looking unsure. We are connected by blood so I try something with her. I gently kiss her nose, and at the same time pour some of my power into her. Ari takes a sharp breath in, and then blinks up at me in surprise. I'd never tried this before, but it must have worked.

Ari

When Darien's lips gently touch my nose, I am suddenly filled with strength and power. His power.

I know that I am strong, but this was something else entirely.

It is warm and reassuring as it flows through me. With his energy I can feel the packs energy mingled in with his, and it's a comfortable feeling that I can't describe as anything other than *home.*

"You are my mate now, and the only one who can access this. Use it anytime you need it," Darien offers without the slightest hesitation, which is very generous considering Alpha's hate the drain on their energy and that it can affect the pack energy as well. I also heard, and know firsthand, that Alpha's can just be very stingy and controlling as well.

None of that mattered to me though. Unless absolutely necessary, I wouldn't take energy from him or the pack, but I am currently enjoying the feeling of being a true part of a pack. I can almost feel their thoughts, and his words appear to be true. They actually seem to like me.

Darien's actions are also gently telling me to stop being a baby.

I'm his mate. The soon-to-be wife of the leader of this pack. I don't have to be my mother, but I can be strong for my pack, and be there for them, along with showing support for Darien. I can't hide or run away anymore. Especially if I ever expect Darien to let me on the front lines or go on missions. I will need to be a team player.

Over the next couple days, following the pack meeting, Darien and I spend a lot of time getting to know each other better. Both in, and outside of the bedroom. He showed me around town some more, and drove me by his work, which happens to be a logging company.

At first, I thought it was odd for werewolves to be in that business, beings that our other half lives to run free in the woods, but it also made a lot of sense. After all, *someone* needs to do the job, and its way less risky for a werewolf than it is for a human.

Being the environmentalist that he is, Darien employs other members of the pack to go through and replant more trees once they've finished an area.

They also handle controlled burns to help prevent wildfires, and promote new, healthy growth for the future.

Of course, being the Alpha, Darien owns the company. Alpha's need to be in a dominant position or things can be challenging. They don't take orders from others well. Plus, being in charge is necessary since he needs be able to have more free time to take care of pack matters.

Trace, Asher, and another wolf by the name of Brendon, take turns managing the place when he is gone. Everyone is happy with the system because unlike me, wolves are usually very accepting of their roles and just content to be in a pack.

Darien and I also went grocery shopping, which was much more entertaining than I ever imagined it could be. It's almost comical watching this large, supermodel looking man doing something so menial and human.

My mother did all the shopping, though I tagged along sometimes just to make sure she got the things that I liked to eat as well since she liked to conveniently forget to pick up the items I'd ask for. Shopping with her was never fun, but I found myself really enjoying myself with my mate, and he was totally at ease.

Grocery shopping was most likely going to end up becoming a duty of mine though. I figure I will have to do the cooking too, which I don't necessarily mind, but I like that we have been taking turns when it comes to that so far. I enjoy his cooking, and he enjoys mine, so it's a good meal no matter who cooks it.

After the grocery store, he stopped at another store. Once he told me why we were there, I repeatedly told him that it wasn't necessary, but he ignored me and signed me up for my very own cell phone.

He insisted that he needed to be able to reach me somehow when he is at work or away for whatever reason. I guess shifting to communicate telepathically when at work is probably not the best way to go. Not to mention, we don't know how far our telepathy reaches.

I appreciate the phone and that he wants to keep in touch with me. It's just another thing he has had to spend money on. I have to admit though that it has been kind of fun learning something new, and I'll even be able to call my dad whenever I need or want to now.

Darien had the representative program all of his contacts into my phone so that I would have all of the pack's names and numbers. He then proceeded to send out a mass text, letting everyone else have my number. The next thing I know, my phone is "blowing up," as Darien called it, with welcoming texts and weird pictures called "emojis".

"I told you they love you," Darien had winked at me as we drove home. All I could think was 'Do I really have to reply individually to each and every one of these?' Later, Darien laughed at me and told me to just send back a "thumbs up" emoji and that everyone would see it since it's apparently a "group thread".

So now that I am educated in the ways of texting, I was able to figure out the rest on my own pretty easily. I love the camera feature most of all. I've already filled my photo library with photos of

Lightning and Royal, and the beautiful area around our home. I can also go online and apply for jobs, so that will definitely come in handy.

While Darien was busy with some work, I took the time to start applying for a few jobs that popped up. One was for a coffee stand, another for a waitress position, and the other for a receptionist at a dentist office. All nothing I could see myself doing. Maybe Darien will hire me at his logging company. Or maybe he will know someone else in the pack in need of a helping hand.

So aside from not having a job yet, I am pretty much set up and settled into my new life. All that was left now is to prepare for the full moon tonight.

Darien

When I got a call from a pack member that lives in Kalispell, Montana, I excused myself, telling Ari that I had a work call. Technically it wasn't a lie, but I felt bad all the same. Dave is one of many of my wolves that live close to Canada's border. Him and a few others run perimeter checks together, and he only calls when he finds something. It's a call I don't want Ari to worry about, but I know she wouldn't want to be kept in the dark.

Today has been such a good day, and I don't want to ruin it with worry about Canada making another move. After getting their asses handed to them, and going home empty-handed, I assumed they would lay low for a while. Alpha Flint is lucky to be alive. Instead of being grateful that we spared his life, he is apparently leaning more towards getting vengeance.

Dave confirms my fear when he tells me that the scent of Canada's wolves have been lingering way too close to the boundary line. Their scent didn't go very far East along our lines, but rather North, along Alaska's territory.

Now that we are united with them, Dave ran along some of the boundary lines of British Columbia, following their scent for a couple hours before finally turning around. Canada is definitely looking for a weak spot.

After thanking Dave for the information, I get Ari's father on the phone. I'm not going to wait to have one of the elders speak with him. He answers after a few rings.

"Hello?" his familiar voice says cautiously.

"Hello Alpha Wilder, do you have a moment?"

"Darien? This is...unorthodox."

"Sorry. It was a time sensitive matter, so I made the decision to call. I'll keep it brief," I say, not giving him the opportunity to refuse me, "I just received a call from my patrol in Montana. They found Canada's scent flirting with the boundary line, and they followed it up along part of your border in B.C. before calling it quits."

"I see. I will get more men on patrol." I'm about to end the call before he quickly asks, "How is my daughter?" I can tell that he is trying to hide the emotion in his voice, but I heard it all the same.

A million answers run through my head, but I finally decide on, "Amazing."

"I knew she would be. Take care, Darien," he says before the line goes dead.

Chapter 13

Ari

The night of the full moon is finally here. We all meet at a secret spot out of town away from most civilization but where there is a greater population of wildlife. Every pack member from the other night is present along with a few younger wolves, including children. Tonight, we hunt as a pack with the Alpha, and me, his mate. Together with his second and third flanking us, we will lead them.

When, whom I believe to be Trace, moves to take position on the other side of me, a wolf from the group growls and charges forward. Trace actually takes a step back and the other wolf stops right in front of me. I stand my ground.

His wolf towers over mine. He is almost as large as Darien. His strawberry blonde fur and glowing sapphire blue eyes tells me that it's Jerek before I can confirm his scent. There are even streaks of red in his fur and it's very different from most wolves' coats that

I have seen. He is definitely unique. I stare into his intense gaze.

Every set of eyes watches the scene, and I can feel the tension build as Darien and Jerek hold each other's gaze. Jerek's eyes shift away first, but he doesn't move away from me. Trace moving to flank me is what set him off. He's not trying to claim me, I realize, but trying to fill the position as my own personal second.

He waits for Darien's decision, but I growl, bringing Jerek's attention to me. His amber eyes jerk to mine in surprise. In fact, I can feel the shock of everyone around me, but my attention is given to Jerek alone. It will be *my* decision who I take as my second, not Darien's or anyone else's.

Who better to choose to fill that position than someone who chooses the role for themselves? I nod my head in acceptance of him, and he graciously bows his head before taking point beside me.

No one dares to question my decision, and I wonder if that's why Darien didn't step in sooner. Maybe he was waiting for me to decide, or maybe that is just wishful thinking. Either way, he didn't stop me, so he is at least okay with it.

We turn and take off into the darkness with every wolf following at our heels. It's not long before we come across the scent of an elk herd.

My heart sings and my stomach rumbles in anticipation.

Our movements become slower and quieter as we track the scent. As it grows stronger, the pack keeps their distance because too many bodies will give us away. Only me, Jerek, Darien, Trace, and Asher make our way closer to the herd.

As we approach a clearing, we stay down low in the tall grass and crawl forward to get a closer look at the grazing elk. Each wolf looks to me, granting me the first kill as per tradition. My eyes scope out the herd for my target. Never charge in without a specific target or a backup just in case plans go south.

The wind is in my favor as I stalk closer. I've trained myself to be as quiet as a mouse. Wolves hunt as a pack, but if I was going to go rogue, I needed to be able to provide for myself. Instead of using tricks and games that wolves tend to use, I taught myself how to go into stealth mode. Even when in a dead sprint I learned how to control my movements and breathing to make as little noise as possible.

As my eyes lock onto my prey, I take off full speed towards him. Before the large bull can get more than a couple strides in, my teeth close around his thick neck. My powerful jaw has a death grip on him that can't be easily broken.

Using the force of his momentum, I use all my strength to pull him down. He struggles against me as he falls, and I focus on avoiding his antlers before making my last move. One slash to his throat where I had already torn into with my teeth finishes the job.

Trace and Asher take down another bull together not far from where I made my kill. Darien and Jerek had been too busy keeping an eye on me and are now making up for lost time, still chasing down their prey. They end up taking down a young bull, and an older female at the edge of the clearing.

Now that all of the kills have been made, we howl in unison. The pack echo's our song as they run to join us. We share our kills with the pack. This is our bonding ritual. Not only me to Darien, but to the pack, signifying that we, together, promise to provide for them. Darien joins my group.

You just had to go for the largest male, didn't you? His disapproving voice enters my head. I flash him a bloody grin in response.

A small light brown wolf in our group also catches my eye, and the fact that her glowing teal eyes resemble mine, I know it must be Alex. Somehow, she even winks in wolf form, and my wolf huffs a quick laugh before we return to feasting.

Four large elk feeds our present pack of about twenty-five fairly well, but now it's the rest of the packs turn to hunt and provide for us. This is how the tradition works. It shows unity. There is a hierarchy to keep order, but it is also one big family. We don't feel as if one person's worth is less or more than the others.

Unfortunately, there are some Alpha's that do think they're above the rest, like Alpha Flint and Darien's father.

I used to feel unimportant, but in my short time here, my eyes have been opened. I felt it when Darien poured some of his power into me. We live, love, fight, and die for each other. Obviously not all packs are the same, but that is how Darien and this pack feels, and I am proud to be a part of it.

Under the light of the full moon, the pack hunts late into the night, while the rest of us wait patiently in the forest. To not wipe out all of our large wildlife in the area, they stick to smaller critters, like rabbits, a couple deer, and ducks.

The pack members present them to us, and we take what we want, leaving them with the rest. The higher ranks never take more than they need though, or at least *shouldn't*. A true Alpha makes sure his pack is taken care of first.

It is no surprise when Darien lets Trace, Asher, Jerek, and I make our selections first. I remain by Darien's side though, not needing more than what I've had. His wolf urges me to eat more, but I ignore him. Finally, he gives up before selecting a duck and dropping it in front of me for us to share.

My wolf would roll her eyes if she could, but this girl would never turn down perfectly good waterfowl. I guess it would be rude not to partake in what the pack provided for us.

As my wolf feeds with her mate I reflect on how much has changed. Up until a few days ago, I was practically a lone wolf.

Now I'm head over paws for a gorgeous, amazing man, surrounded by a pack that doesn't hate me, and I'm actually excited to get to know them. This is my life now, and I am finally happy and home.

Darien

Her grace and her beauty in both human and wolf form is astounding. Her strength was obvious from the very beginning, but she was also timid and unsure of herself. Now she is spreading her wings and taking on her new life in stride. Ari truly fits in perfectly and even earned herself her own personal bodyguard and friend, apart from myself.

Somehow in just a few short minutes, she changed the path of a lost man; a wolf I was sure would go rogue before the end of the year.

I remember the stories I had heard of the bride I was to take. Being on the other side of that coin, I did my best to ignore it all, and judge her by what I saw. According to those rumors though, my Ari was hotheaded, disobedient, and borderline crazy.

They also said she was wild and untamed, which that part I have seen with my own eyes, and I hope that never changes. However, I have been given the pleasure of knowing her story, the *real* story.

Since the moment I saw her standing in the cabin of that jet, greatly outnumbered, with fists up and holding her own, I couldn't believe someone hadn't snatched her up.

That thought triggers an involuntary growl. She tilts her pretty little head at me and I press my nose to her muzzle to reassure her. She licks my muzzle in return before laying her head back down on the forest floor. I stare down at her, feeling like the luckiest son of a bitch in the world.

Fate is a funny thing. Even the craziest, ugliest circumstances can lead you to something beautiful. Perfection like this doesn't last though. This is real life. Though they call us kings and queens, princes and princesses, this is no fairy tale. After all we are creatures of horror stories. I need to be ready for the storm that I know must be coming.

Aside from still needing to change this beautiful woman's last name, everything has been sorted out, so it's time to get back to work. For the next few moments though, I'm going to enjoy the calm serenity that's surrounding my pack, my family.

Ari

I wake up before Darien and take in the beautiful late morning. It was a long night; one I won't ever forget. Darien has literally saved my life. He has done so much for me and showed me a life I never dreamed possible.

I wanted to do something for him. Something I have never given or done for anyone.

I take advantage of him being asleep, and slowly slide down the bed and gently take him into my mouth.

His body tenses as I roll my tongue around his tip before taking him in deeper.

He tenses further and that's when I know he's finally awake. I also realize that I have no idea what I am doing.

When he moans my name in that sexy deep voice, I decide that I don't care, and resume stroking him with my mouth. His moans of pleasure encourage me, making me feel powerful, and I had no idea this could make me feel so much pleasure. I suck harder and deeper until he pulls me away and throws me on my back.

"Geez, was it that bad?" I tease, earning a growl in response.

I help him get my shorts and tank top off quickly, and once I'm free he instantly buries himself inside me, filling my need.

"Fuck, you feel amazing," he groans in that bone melting voice. He gives me a moment to adjust before moving inside of me. He thrusts into me deeper and harder every time, his huge length hitting as far as it can go.

All too soon, the world explodes around me. He bites my nipple, and I scream his name, bringing him along for the ride. Before I can catch my breath, his mouth is on mine.

I'm in his arms as he tenderly rubs and tickles my bare skin.

"So, what's the plan for today, Alpha?" I break the silence, and he growls before pinning me on the bed.

"Just Darien, or mate, Ari. None of that *Alpha* stuff," he says before nipping my neck. His scent fills me, and I am ready for the next round. He laughs and drags me off the bed with him. "You and I, *mate*, are going to enjoy a nice breakfast, then get dressed and go apply for our marriage license. Before the week is over, I'm going to change your last name to Arianna Shield."

My breath is caught in my throat. He waits for my reaction, and all I can do is stare into his fiery emerald eyes. This man has learned a lot about me over the past few days, and he still wants to marry me knowing what he knows.

"I love you," the words blurt out of my mouth before I can even think about stopping them.

"What did you just say?" he asks before looking at me in disbelief. It takes me a second to say it again, but the hopeful look on his face rips the words out of me again.

"I love you, Darien," and I'm suddenly in his arms. His lips take mine as he spins me around in triumph. I giggle and he sets me down, but doesn't let me go. He bends down to one knee and reaches under the bed. I can't believe my eyes when he pulls out a little black box. I mean sure, dad gave my mom a ring that has been passed down in their family, but this box is not a hand-me-down. I can smell the newness of it.

"I love you with every ounce of my being, Ari. Make me the luckiest bastard in the world and marry me," he says rather than asks as he opens the box to reveal a breathtaking diamond ring with smaller diamonds running down the band and interwoven with beautiful emeralds. Both of our birthstones intertwined together as a stunning compliment to one other. It's far more beautiful than anything I could have picked out.

"Only if you'll take me forever," I smile and he kisses my hand before sliding the ring on my finger. A perfect fit. He gathers me in his arms again.

"You had no choice in that matter. You are mine forever and always," he growls before claiming my lips again. "I have something else for you."

What the hell else could he possibly have for me? I wait as he goes to the closet and pulls out a hanger with—oh my God, what is that?

My mate and soon to be husband is holding a Steampunk wedding dress. The dress is about knee length, with lace, taffeta, and a brown leather underbust corset. And it's absolutely gorgeous.

"Do you hate it?" he asks uncomfortably. "I wasn't sure how you really felt about weddings or what you pictured, but this reminded me of you. I can take it back."

"Don't you dare return that! It rocks! Seriously, I love it," I practically squeal as I reach for it and touch all the different materials. "What shoes am I going to wear with it?" I ask to myself, but he answers for me.

"Alex actually found some. She is going to bring them by later. She's a photographer so she's going to take our pictures on our wedding day." He just pulled out all the stops, didn't he? And what do I have for him? Nothing, but an overdue "I love you".

Getting our license was shorter and much less exciting than I imagined it would be. Even Darien seemed bummed, but that's mainly because the lady at the counter said we needed to wait three days before we could marry. Strangely enough that had upset me too. I thought I was doomed to be a Wilder for life, but now I am anxious to be a Shield. Darien's mood brightens when we get back in the car.

"So now that we have a few days, where do you want to get married? There's a venue in town that I'm sure has openings but we can go farther for a bigger space. We can go look at caterers, do some cake testing, and pick out some decorations and floral arrangements. Whatever you want, we can..." the words keep flowing from his mouth and my head starts to spin.

"Whoa, whoa, whoa. Hold it. Why do we need all that?"

"Ari, it's a wedding. Every woman wants those things on their wedding day."

"Sounds expensive and unnecessary," I mutter. He's quiet now, unsure how to proceed. I'm not sure what else to say. I never went to pack weddings. I never imagined I'd have one of my own. Not one I willingly attended anyways. I didn't see the point. Maybe if I saw two wolves in love getting married, I would be more inclined, but I have never witnessed love like the way I feel for Darien, and the way he appears to feel about me.

"If this is about money, we can afford a nice wedding."

"No! It has nothing to do with money."

"So, what do you want, baby?" he asks softly, sending chills through me. I do believe that this is the first time he used a term of endearment for me, and I actually liked it. Thankfully he's smart enough not to call me "princess".

"I don't know, Darien. Can't we just get married like somewhere on your ranch? Just something simple?"

"That's not a bad idea. There are plenty of chairs and tables from pack meetings. A couple pack members own a restaurant in Spokane and maybe they can come out and cater. We still need to figure out flowers, though we won't need many if we do an outside wedding. I can have one of the guys get ordained to marry us, and that way, it will be all pack members. No worry about being uncomfortable around humans."

It still sounded a lot more complicated than I imagined, but Darien seems excited. I am being selfish. If Darien wants a real wedding then we can have a real wedding.

"I can take care of flowers," I offer and he grins at me, happy that we have a plan of action.

"Good. I'll talk to some people later and get the details worked out, but there is some other stuff we need to accomplish today," I laugh at his excitement, but when we pull up to a bank, I wonder what on earth we would be here for.

When he told the Teller that he was adding me to his account I almost choked.

The Teller seats us with a man wearing a nametag that reads "Brian". He pulls up Darien's account, and they ask for my info. It's a good thing that I didn't leave my bag at home. I hesitantly hand him a small envelope with everything he needs, though I want to run out of the building.

After a couple minutes of Brian punching stuff in, he glares at the screen, takes a breath full of anxiety as if he's about to give us terrible news.

"It appears that you have different last names," he muses.

"Yes, but that will change in a few days. I am adding her to my account now though," Darien says proudly and sternly.

"I see. That's wonderful. I hope it's a beautiful day. However, as a small community bank, it's our policy to recommend that you wait until then to add Miss Wilder to your account. You never know what could happen, and it could leave your account in danger. Of course, I can set up her own account today then easily add her on to yours at a later date," Brian says dismissively, unaware of the now enraged man sitting beside me.

When Brian realizes he hasn't gotten a response, he finally looks up at my mate.

Fear fills my nostrils, and I can see it clear as day on his face. I feel bad for him. Though I have never been on the receiving end of Darien's anger, I know his power is electrifying. And for a human, it is the stuff of nightmares. Darien reaches for my hand, and I realize he is trying to recover his control. I caress his hand in an attempt to soothe him.

"I. Said. Add her. To my account," Darien growls between gritted teeth.

"Yes, sir," the smart man gets back to work, "Is there anything else I can do for you?"

"A withdrawal please," Darien selects an amount but I'm lost in my own thoughts. I went from nothing to my name to instantly having God knows how much now, and I didn't even have to do anything to earn it.

I can't see myself ever feeling comfortable spending what isn't mine. I really need a job, and soon.

After our adventure at the bank we head home, and I thankfully avoid him having to spend more money on me. Once inside, Darien leads me towards the couch and pulls me down into his lap. The stress of earlier gets pushed to the back of my mind as he takes center stage. His scent and sweet nature towards me, soothes my soul. I relax into his body that I seem to fit perfectly against.

"I love you, Ari," he whispers in my ear, sending shivers through my body. I say it back, and he hugs me tighter to him as if someone might drag me away if he lets go. Only home for minutes and already the room is hot and steamy with need. His breathing grows harsh and I am right there with him before the doorbell rings, effectively snapping us out of what was about to happen right here on this couch.

Alex is at the door, and she smiles brightly at us, but her nose wrinkles the moment our scent reaches her.

"Sorry for interrupting," she says not really sounding sorry. She walks through the doorway and thrusts a box in my hand. Right. The shoes Darien said she picked up for me. I tentatively remove the lid and am beyond thrilled to reveal brown combat boots with buckles. They will go with the dress perfectly. Not to mention the rest of my outfits as well.

"Yes! I knew you'd love them!" Alex cheers.

"*You* knew?" Darien challenges.

"I'm the one who found them," she sticks her tongue out at her Alpha. Damn, where has this girl been all my life? Why was no one in Alaska like her? Would I have been able to ignore her too?

"Thank you. *Both* of you. You have gone far beyond anything I even hoped to imagine. This is truly awesome."

"What, you never thought about your wedding day?" Alex catches on, and I'm not sure what I should tell her. Apparently, the truth, as it spills out before I can stop it.

"Not really, no."

"I'll let you girls talk," Darien graciously gives us some space and goes off to do whatever he does when he's not doing me.

Alex is staring dumbfounded at me. I let out a breath of air and she follows me over to the couch. We take a seat and I prepare myself for my first ever "girl talk".

Before she can ask, I give her a few details of my life before I came here. Of course, she had some questions that I answered, but eventually I tried to change the topic to her. I wanted to know her story. Mine was sad and boring and besides, everything is good now. More than good even.

She reminds me that she was in the Northern California pack and that Darien took out her old Alpha for abusing women.

Apparently, she didn't stay in one spot too long so that's why she never had to deal with the Alpha. She is a photographer so she often moved around for work. She also spent a lot of time at parties, mingling with humans and taking pictures of celebrities to sell to magazines. She found gigs wherever she went.

I also learned that she's 28 and still single. Before I arrived, she was actually contemplating leaving again to travel, take pictures, and search for her mate.

She hesitantly confesses that she actually tried to put the moves on Darien, and my wolf stirs. She simmers down when Alex quickly tells me that Darien wasn't having any of it. And then I felt bad for her rejection. If only slightly anyways, but I truly hope that she finds a mate here.

Though I know her even less than I know my mate, I don't want to lose my first girlfriend.

After an hour or so she gets up to leave. I could talk with her all night, and once I get a job, I can see us shopping and having girl dates together which is something I never imagined enjoying before. I walk her out, but before she leaves, I have a question for her.

"Hey, you'll stand by me during the wedding ceremony, right?" I ask shyly, afraid she might turn me down. Instead she envelops me in her arms with a speed that even I was unprepared for. "I'll take that as a yes," I giggle and she joins my laughter.

"Of course, I will. Thank you, Ari," she beams at me before practically skipping down the steps to her car in the gravel lot. Darien walks up behind me and wraps his arms around me.

"Look at you two making fast friends," he says proudly.

"Yeah, with the girl who tried to put the moves on you," I fake my annoyance. He tenses at the comment.

"Hey now, nothing happened between me and her. You know you are the only one for me so don't let what she did bother you," he tries to calm me, but I surprise him by laughing,

"You mean how Charlie and Niko didn't bother you, and how Alpha Flint didn't bother you, and also how Jerek's relationship with me doesn't bother you?" I point out. He pales.

"You caught all that, huh? I forget how perceptive you are," he laughs.

When he kisses the top of my head, I turn to face him.

"Don't worry, I won't get between you and Jerek. I know it's irrational for me to think it's more than what it is, and I trust you to handle him if he tries anything more." His trust floors me. No one has ever trusted my judgment enough to give me so much freedom over my own life. Maybe it's because he knows I'll disappear if he doesn't give me freedom, but whatever reason it may be, I still appreciate it.

We made dinner together before he took me up to bed for dessert. We spent our remaining time enjoying every inch of each other, and every last moment together before our peace is disturbed. He goes back to work tomorrow so we no longer get to spend every second of the day together.

While I'm also excited to start job hunting and get on to our wedding, I have been enjoying getting to know the man I plan to spend the rest of my life with. It's comforting and pleasing to see that he's not eager to go back to normal life either.

Chapter 14

After Darien left for work, I spent the morning looking for any new job listings. There weren't many in this small town aside from some delivery jobs, which I can't do without a car. I most definitely won't be asking Darien for a car. I will purchase my own when I have enough money to do so.

Since job hunting was a bust, I start looking around the house for wedding stuff. With Darien gone, I've made it my job to make sure everything is ready to go for our wedding day. Really, I just want to say "I do" and move on rather than make a huge deal about it in front of a bunch of people, but it's what my mate wants. He's a typical Alpha male who wants to claim me in front of everyone.

He was right that there are lots of chairs. I found a ton in the barn, and it is a bonus to find that they are all wood fold-up chairs. They will hardly need any added touches to them since they are rustic and decorative on their own.

I also find a bunch of old wooden boxes and crates that I can definitely use as well, but the best thing I find are two old barn doors that were probably used before the barn was updated. Apparently, I am a lot more creative than I thought because I have an awesome idea for these.

Inside a storage room that I discovered, I found even more stuff to use as decoration. There are still other things I will need to make it all come together, so I am going to have to ask Darien for more money, but thankfully it's all stuff I can probably get from a dollar store if there is one around this little town.

In my searching I hear a truck pull into the driveway. I realize that it's Jerek as he gets closer. Just a couple nights ago, Jerek basically claimed himself as my bodyguard. Anyone else, I would have introduced to my wolf's teeth for trying to pull that shit. But, for the dangerous lonely wolf who has had a rough life, yet is still trying to hang on to a purpose, he has my respect.

That being said, I open the door, shift, and sprint towards his unsuspecting form walking up the driveway. He quickly shifts in a panic, and I lunge for his throat. I didn't say I was going to let him get away with what he did.

My wolf chases his retreating form into the coverage of the woods. A human's eyes wouldn't be able to see us from how far we sit from the road, but it's still safer just in case. He leaps onto a tree, using it to quickly change direction and face me.

I charge into him, and we tumble, a mess of claws and snapping jaws. Rolling onto my feet, I jump away from his reach. I let him charge me this time. When he does, instead of jumping away like he expects, I dive at his feet and slide beneath him, and rear up hard, sending him flying over me.

He stumbles, but he is agile and regains his footing quickly. Jerek faces me then and the confusion on his face is priceless, but he is even more concerned when I lay down. His wolf whines as he warily saunters closer. I'm showing him that I'm not actually a threat. I'm just trying to test his skills and strength.

Okay, so I may have enjoyed scaring him a little too much. I could have given him a heads up, but where's the fun in that?

Once he reaches me and looks me over for injury and finds none, I stand again. I give him a playful yip, and now that he understands, it's time for round two. I let him make the first move this time. We spar for another hour or so. He shows me his worth and determination, and I show him mine.

Bodyguards for the Alpha's mate are usually either appointed, or would just be one of the Alpha's guards as well. Typically, the guards are constantly changing, appointing whoever is available at the time.

I don't think I've ever heard of anyone volunteering for the position without even being asked. Especially to be a full-time guard. Only Alphas get that sort of treatment.

I don't need a guard, but since I've already accepted him as such, I need to know his strengths and weaknesses, and he needs to learn that he's not defending some amateur. If there is danger, I'll be right there by his side. From this moment on, we are partners and need to learn to fight as a unit.

With the little energy we have left, we sprint back to the house to get dressed. No one but Darien has seen me naked, and I don't plan on altering that fact. Once I'm fully clothed, I move to meet Jerek back downstairs. It appears that he found some clothes in one of the guest rooms. Werewolves always keep extra clothes around for all shapes and sizes in case of situations like today. Hopefully he wasn't too fond of the ones that got shredded.

Before my feet can touch the ground on the last step of the stairs, I am locked in an embrace with Jerek. His large form engulfs me. I should push away, but there is nothing inappropriate in his intention. The danger and sadness that I sensed in him before has morphed into something that is not quite happiness, but a feeling of contentment and purpose. He kisses the top of my head before finally releasing me.

"What was that for?" I ask a little bewildered.

"You know why," he returns, and I do know why, but I want to hear him say it. I want him to hear his own words said out loud to make it that much more real.

I raise a brow at him, and he sighs, but eventually he gives in.

"For giving me a reason to stay, and a reason to live. Thank you for taking a stranger seriously and not tiptoeing around me after I'm sure you heard my story. You just got here with your own demons to overcome, and I within only minutes of knowing you, found my purpose for being here," his words touch me more than I had expected them too.

"Well, I wouldn't go that far," I laugh nervously, but I'm glad you found your way. I'm proud of you."

"I'm serious, Ari. I was ready to go lone wolf, or worse, let the wolf take over. And you saw it in just seconds of talking to me. I also recognized myself in you, but I also felt a pull towards you. It was nice to feel something other than nothing all the time. I watched you that night, nervous and shy, but also strong. It finally clicked that what I saw in you was loneliness, but I wasn't lonely talking to you. I felt like I was supposed to be a part of your life, but you are Darien's," he says without any ounce of bitterness. I don't know what to say so I just continue to listen.

"I talked to Trace at the party and he told me what happened with Alpha Flint, and my blood boiled," he breathes, barely in control now, and I can understand why. My situation, I'm sure brought back the memories of his old girlfriend. "I don't know why it took me so long, but I realized that I wanted to be a protector, but not for just anyone. I want to be *your* protector. Reasons for that are unknown to me, but I don't care. I'm just relieved to have clear, focused thoughts for the first time in a long time."

The situation is getting a little too intense so I try to lighten the mood.

"Are you sure you are prepared to get your ass kicked by a girl every day?" I tease, earning a lighthearted chuckle.

"Bring it on," his sapphire blue eyes burn with determination.

Footsteps sound on the porch and we both look towards the door as Darien steps in. The noises he makes are a little too intentional for him. He must have heard the whole thing between Jerek and I.

Once he reaches my side, he sweeps me into an intimate hug and plants his lips on mine for a long second or three. When he pulls away, he stares deep into my eyes, smiles, then acknowledges our guest.

"Jerek," he smiles genuinely at him, "stay for dinner?"

"Depends, who's cooking. I'm not sure yet if this wild woman of yours knows how to cook a meal," he smirks, and I roll my eyes at him as Darien just chuckles.

"She makes a mean duck roast," he defends me.

"Well I guess I can stick around for a bit," he smirks.

"Good," Darien looks back to me, "I have a gift for you." And I am intrigued about what he could have for me when he pulls something small out of his back pocket and sets it in my hands.

I'm elated when I see that it's a deck of cards, and I practically leap for joy before kissing and thanking him. Then I remember that Jerek is still here, and I pry myself from my mate to look over at him.

"Rummy?" I wiggle my eyebrows at him.

"You're on."

Sitting down at the kitchen table with two men I have come to adore makes me think of the time spent with my uncles. Of course, I am in the lead with Jerek not far behind. Darien is holding up well, still confident he can catch up. That's the thing about rummy; you can be down for a long time but still make a comeback. It's all about strategy and risk. His comeback isn't happening here though. This game is all mine.

During the game, Darien asks Jerek about work, piquing my interest.

"Slow," Jerek confesses. Darien's lips pull to the side, but I speak before he can say anything more.

"What do you do?" I ask with perhaps a little too much interest.

"Wood carving," he smiles weakly at me. "It's a small town, and although we get lots of people traveling through in the summer, it's a tough business."

"Remember the carved table from our date the other night?" Darien asks me, and my head jerks towards Jerek.

"That was your work?" I ask incredulously. He nods with a brighter smile this time. "Are you looking for help at all?" The hopefulness and desperation in my voice is almost embarrassing. They both look at me with raised brows.

"Do you have experience carving wood?" he asks skeptically.

"No, but because there weren't many jobs available where I lived in Alaska, we had many manufacturers; people just making items by hand, so I have knowledge on how to increase your business based on what I learned watching them. And this way I'll be with a member of the pack, my personal guard, so neither of you has to worry about me." Darien growls and grabs me by the chin, tilting it up so that my eyes meet his fierce emeralds.

"I will always worry for you when I'm not around you, woman," he breathes before roughly claiming my lips. Message received.

Jerek's chuckles end our moment, and I blush in embarrassment, but Darien isn't fazed as he plays with my hair and continues to stare at me with those lustful green eyes.

"Alright, so let's hear your ideas," Jerek asks with complete interest. My smile beams at him, erasing the flush from my face.

"I'm still learning the whole social media thing, but I know that my pack had made a website, posted pictures of the merchandise, and even added in delivery for an extra fee." The two men in my life look at each other.

"Well, she's right," Darien shrugs.

"I know she's right, dammit. It's not like I haven't wanted to do those things for years, but it's hard to accomplish without help, and no one wants to be around me."

"*Wanted* you mean. Past tense. I want to be around you and help you succeed. Trust me, it will be worth it. And if things don't work out, you can just fire me," I wink at him. Apparently, Alex is rubbing off on me.

"Oh fine, of course you're hired. After all you are my Alpha's mate. You start tomorrow," he feigns annoyance, but I can tell he is secretly pleased with the idea of not being alone for eight hours of the day. Darien seems appeased with the plan as well. Everyone is happy.

"Rummy," I announce with a shit-eating grin as I place down three queens on the table and deposit my last card in the discard pile.

Jerek stayed for dinner that night and nobody died from my cooking. We made plans for him to pick me up on his way to work since it isn't far away. Of course, nothing is too far from anything in this town. Though everyone is spaced out, there's almost no traffic so it doesn't take long to get to wherever you're going.

I am actually excited for my first day of work. Darien was just happy that I was happy, and took full advantage of the situation by taking me upstairs to "celebrate" my first job. Of course, I didn't mind one bit.

In the morning I am waiting on the porch when Jerek pulls up in his red Ford F150.

I can tell right away that he isn't a morning person, but he still greets me with a warm smile nonetheless.

"You need some coffee, old man?"

"Nope. Your insults are just the refreshing cup of sunshine that I need," he says without missing a beat, and I chuckle. We're going to get along just fine.

His place of work is right off the main highway that goes in and out of town. The sign above the shop reads "Full Moon Furnishings". Clever. Technically his shop is more or less a fancy wood pole barn. First thing on the list will be to make the place a little more inviting.

Each and every one of his pieces is amazing though. There are lots of statues of various sizes, totem poles, tables, chairs, wall décor, and more. Every item is a masterpiece and high quality.

The only thing that might be an issue is how similar everything is, which isn't necessarily a problem, but every buyer has his or her own tastes.

"Do you have more wood to make more pieces?"

"Uh, not at the moment, no. There is no room for anything else," he motions towards the already jam-packed room.

"Don't worry about this stuff. It will be sold very soon, but how do you feel about custom orders?"

"What's wrong with these?" he bristles.

"Nothing is wrong with them! Geez, you're so sensitive when you're not the one picking on someone else. Not everyone wants the same pattern with the same finish. People want things to match the items they might already have in their homes."

"Fine," he sulks, "I guess I'm on board with it." I roll my eyes when he looks away.

"Great. Now how do we get more wood?" I guess the answer should have been obvious when he informs me that he gets it from Darien. Alphas provide for their pack. When Jerek needs wood, Darien delivers some, or lets him work a shift to come cut his own.

"Perfect. We will go cut some tomorrow."

"Hold on, *we*?" he sputters.

"Of course. I'm fully capable of helping."

"Darien and the others aren't going to allow the distraction of a female being there."

"Tough. Look, we can do this all day, but it's going to be the same outcome," I let him see that I am serious. I won't be kept out of anything anymore just because I don't have male parts.

"Yes sir," he gives in. At least he knows better than to call me princess.

Ignoring him, I get to work moving certain items outside for people to see from the road. I set up some of his prettier totem poles to flank the doorway, a bench on either side of them, and some end tables as well. He comes to see what I'm doing, and I feel a sense of pride when he smiles.

The rest of the day, I spend my time using my phone to take pictures, along with setting up a website while Jerek deals with customers. First, I have to research how to set up a website exactly.

Back home we just had dial-up Internet so researching is a breeze in comparison using Jerek's laptop that's connected to Wi-Fi. I'll probably buy one for myself once I've saved up enough of my own money.

Before the day is over, I make a sign that says, "Custom Orders Welcome," and even got one order put in for a wood bench with a fox and river scene that I quoted for almost twice the cost of his other benches. Jerek was very impressed then, and I guess I was proud too, but he is the one doing the real work. I am just glad to be a part of the process.

"I'm so smart for hiring you," he says in the truck on the way back to my place.

"Yeah, I hardly even had to twist your arm," I laugh and he joins me. When we arrive, Darien isn't home yet so Jerek stays to train with me rather than leave me alone in an empty house. We train in human form today. Having to go change is too much of a hassle, and it's a waste of money and good clothes to shred them in the shift.

After about half an hour of sparring, I'm surprised when Darien comes to partake in the action. He takes on Jerek first, and I watch every second of it, unable to take my eyes off of them.

Darien let Jerek attack first, but deflects it all with surprising speed and fluidness. Not a single movement is wasted.

Shit gets real when he switches to offense. Every advance he makes is lethal, but he pulls back at the last second each time he lands a hit. I continue to watch mesmerized, remembering every detail and learning each of their patterns.

I see the final moment come before Jerek does, and when he's knocked on his ass, I am already there, blocking and striking every opening I get, which is few and far between.

It takes every ounce of focus to fend him off, and I've never felt so exhilarated as he gives me his all.

My best chance is staying low and trying to knock him over, but I'd have a better shot at knocking over a brick wall.

When he makes a move towards me, I make the mistake of standing my ground. Simultaneously he snakes a foot behind my ankle and pushes me hard. I use the force of it to roll back away from him and into a crouching position. I'm thrilled to see him breathing almost as heavy as me.

He charges me when I make no move towards him, and I stay down low. Darien knows that I use others' size and weight against them, so he must have some plan to counter that as he comes at me. Now is my chance to show him that that's not all I can do.

At the last possible second, I spring up high from my crouched stance as he comes in low and I kick my leg down, aiming for the top of his left shoulder. The force takes him to a knee, but he's not down and out yet.

I spin and kick again, aiming for the same spot, but without even looking, his hands reach out and catch me by the foot, and he pulls me down to the ground. His strong arms crush me against him as his lips capture mine with an intense passion that sends shock waves to my core.

Clapping sounds snap us out of our fantasy world. My mate definitely doesn't hold back on claiming me in front of others. He stands, pulling me to my feet with him.

Darien catches his breath quicker than I can catch mine, but just barely. I can match him in speed and endurance, but his strength alone is greater than anyone I have faced.

"Impressive," Jerek approaches, and when I look around, I am surprised to see that our fight took us far away from where we originally started.

"How did today go?" Darien asks as he wraps his arm around me.

"Best day in a while," Jerek admits, "Ari has good ideas and good instincts." His praises make me blush, and Darien nods as he squeezes me tighter. "I'll see you lovebirds tomorrow," Jerek senses Darien's need for alone time with me. I want to hug him and thank him for today, but I don't want to rile up my mate any further.

"Bye, Jerek, thank you," is all I can get out before Darien swoops me up into his arms and carries me inside.

With the intensity burning through him, I expect him to throw me down and take me quick and rough.

When he sets me down gently, sits beside me, and starts rubbing my tight muscles, I'm in heaven. His gentleness after such heated sparring amazes me. Life, my life, was not supposed to be this good. Alpha males are not supposed to be this amazing. They aren't all like Alpha Flint, or Darien's father, but still, I never expected this man to be so perfect.

The following morning, Darien brushes his lips against mine, waking me briefly before he leaves for work. After all the events of yesterday, I forgot to mention that I would actually see him at work today. Maybe it's better this way though. Hopefully he doesn't mind my presence. I should probably text him to give him a heads up, but I'm stupidly afraid of the possibility of rejection. Why did Jerek have to make me so nervous about going?

How easily things can still be torn apart surprisingly scares me now, and I almost change my mind about going to avoid the possibility of a fight. Then I realize how stupid that is. I may be addicted to this man, but he won't break me.

With renewed determination, I throw on some durable clothes for manual labor and put my hair up. Since I have some time, I go downstairs and cook up some food to take with, and Jerek pulls up the driveway just in time. He looks nervous again, but I do my best to ignore his anxiety. When I hand him a plate of food, all his worry disappears with a genuine and hungry looking grin.

Darien, Trace, and Asher meet us at the truck when we arrive, and Jerek jumps out to greet them before they notice me.

"Jerek, I didn't know you were coming for a shift today. So then where is--," the sound of my door catches Darien's attention, and I catch his eye. He looks surprised and raises a brow at me, but he doesn't look mad like I had childishly worried over.

"Mmm, Ari you smell like bacon and blueberry muffins," Asher sniffs the air in my direction with his eyes closed. I reach into the cab of the truck and reveal a large tray of bacon and muffins that I made for everyone. Darien smirks knowingly at me while the others look at me like they have been starved for weeks. Suddenly there is a crowd coming out of the wood-works, literally, to greet me, but really just came for the food.

Before anyone can get their hands on any, Darien, being taller than everyone, though none of them are short, comes and lifts the tray out of their reach. Jerek is probably the only one who matches him in height.

Everyone protests as he stalks off with all the food. He turns back around though, walks back towards me, plants a kiss on my lips as he plasters me to his front with one arm, and carries me away with the food. I think it's safe to say that I was worried for nothing.

Darien finally quit fooling around and let them all come eat. I enjoyed his playfulness and acceptance of my being here to help Jerek. Helping turns out to be more of a challenge than I thought though since I have no idea how to use a chainsaw.

Rather than wasting anyone's time trying to teach me, I opt for moving logs and debris and assisting others when they need an extra hand with something.

Manual labor is easy work for us, but things still have to be done a certain way. A giant tree falling on a werewolf can still kill us. It's just less likely to happen with our reflexes.

Darien keeps his distance from me while we work. I haven't even seen him since I first arrived, so he could be up in the office for all I know. Either way, I think I am a distraction for him. I can't say it's not the same the for me, so I'm okay with the distance. Hopefully he doesn't change his mind on me being here.

Nearby, I hear Trace talking to someone, and I hear Jerek's name being used so I can't help but listen in. Though continuing to work, I slowly make my way towards their area so that I can see what's going on. Once they come into view, I see it's Braden, Darien's fourth, that Trace is apparently teasing. Typical Trace. I can also see that Braden is mad.

"I am not fifth to that jerk," Braden lifts his lip in disgust as he points to Jerek standing nearby with a chainsaw and clear protective glasses on. I'm taken aback at Braden's animosity towards him. Jerek looks unperturbed and focuses on his work.

"Well, you are since he is considered fourth now," Trace returns, making my eyebrows knit together. Since an Alpha's mate has never had a full-time guard before, I'm not sure how it works. Could it be true?

"No, I'm not," Jerek finally says matter-of-factly, "I am simply Ari's second."

"Oh please, you're nothing but the bitch's bodyguard," Braden says boldly without Darien in sight and not realizing I am in earshot. Or maybe he does know I am nearby but doesn't care. I raise my brow at his name-calling.

I can hear deep rumbles in the chests of pack members nearby. Their annoyance with Braden matches my own. I don't recall anyone talking like that in front of my mother. Maybe silently behind her back but not so openly like this.

Jerek shrugs in response, trying not to cause confrontation, but I can see that he is barely keeping his wolf in check. The tension in his shoulders grows with every passing second. Jerek is no submissive wolf. He is as dominant as they come. Even Trace and Asher may not stand a chance against him, or at least they for sure won't once I've trained with him a couple more times. What I don't understand is why Trace is goading Braden on like this.

"You can have whatever beef you want with me, but leave Ari out of this," Jerek says sternly.

"You don't get to tell me what to do," Braden stalks menacingly towards Jerek. In response to the threat, Jerek's expression shifts to anger and I know it's only a matter of time before he snaps.

"Hey!" I butt in, making my way closer before I can stop myself. It's not my battle, but my instincts are telling me that it is. I feel as if my judgment and role in this pack are being questioned.

I've never thought that Alpha's mates should automatically be given power, but we are, and I worked hard to become as strong as I am. If he wants to question my judgment, he will have to prove that he is better than me, or at least better than Jerek for that matter.

Braden flinches and turns to me, apparently unaware that I have heard the whole conversation and his blatant disrespect for me in front of everyone present.

"Pardon Miss Wilder, but this is between me and this asshole," he points to Jerek like an adolescent boy.

"You see, that's where I'm confused. You seem threatened for some reason, yet Jerek clearly is letting you keep your position even though he has every right to try and take it. But on top of that, you have called me a bitch in front of all of these pack members, and you seem to be questioning my acceptance of a personal guard. So please, tell me how this has nothing to do with me?"

His face reddens in anger, but also because he knows he fucked up. I'm sure he intended to fight with Jerek but got me instead.

"I'm not threatened. There's no way Jerek could match me in a fight."

"Oh yeah? I have been training with him, and he is quite the fighter."

"And you think that's going to scare me? You are just the Alpha's lover, not a fighter. Maybe you think you're strong, but you're just a little girl. Lydia knew her place and minded her own business. You and Jerek need to learn your place as well, princess."

Well, he sealed his fate now. "Princess" barely leaves his mouth before I appear in front of him and knock him on his ass. He is only surprised for a moment before he gets up. He doesn't hold back as he throws punches and kicks, one after the other. I deflect them all, and I understand his agitation now. Jerek is a much better fighter so he *should* feel threatened. He's strong and has more years of experience, but he's sloppy.

In his frustration, his fighting becomes dirty, but I expected that. Men don't want to lose to a woman so they do whatever they can to win. I can sense everyone around me wanting to stop the fight, but it's as if something is holding them all back. I even hear Jerek growling in pain as if something is physically keeping him from the fight. Hopefully he won't be mad at me for getting involved.

When a fist aims for my face, I duck out of the way, narrowly avoiding a broken nose. I spin away, using the momentum to deliver a swift kick to his stomach, and even *I* am surprised when he lands a couple yards away. Apparently, I've grown stronger since I have been here.

After failing to land a single hit, I expect him to give up, so I'm surprised when he starts stripping down and shifts. He is really taking this seriously. His large black wolf waits for me to do the same, but I am not getting naked in front of everyone. When I refuse, he growls in irritation, and charges, regardless of my human form.

Pack members' cries and growls have really amped up now, but I ignore whatever is going on with them. I can't afford to let them distract me.

The moment before Braden's wolf reaches me, I leap out of the way. His large teeth snap after me, but he's off-balance now. With as much strength as I can muster in the short second of time, I punch him in his snout. He's disoriented for a moment so I grab him by the scruff of the neck and flip him, throwing him down into the ground.

Belly up in surrender, I step back.

"I hope now you'll respect my decisions, and respect Jerek's role in this pack just has everyone else has," I start to walk away, but the balls on this guy. My ears pick up the sound of his movement. I turn to defend myself, but I don't have to.

Darien's menacingly large form is there with hands holding a death grip around Braden's throat. I can smell the fear rolling off of him as his life is still being decided by the angered Alpha.

Reluctantly, he releases him, but Braden is smart and doesn't make a move aside from trying to breathe air back into his lungs. Darien stands and addresses the present pack members, and even I'm shocked by what he has to say.

Darien

Working near Ari is a lot more distracting than I thought possible. Her scent, her hair pulled into a sexy ponytail, and those damn combat boots with jeans that hug her ass perfectly. All I want to do is throw her in my truck, take her home, and fuck her forwards, backwards, and sideways. Hell, I'd like to just take her in my truck rather than waste precious time driving when I could be inside her.

I entrust my pack to keep an eye on her while I work in a further location so that I can actually focus. When I can no longer hear the chainsaws going, I know something is wrong.

As I get closer, I hear Ari speaking to someone, and she doesn't sound happy. I about lose it when I hear that someone in my pack had called her a "bitch". That bothers me more than the fact that he dragged my mother's name into whatever the hell this is.

It doesn't take me long to reach the location of everyone, and I move to stand near Trace and Asher. My eyes quickly find Ari, and I am even more agitated than before when I find that Braden is the reason for her problem. My fourth dared to call my mate a bitch?

Trace and Asher give me a knowing look. This is not going to end well.

Ari is fierce as she confronts Braden. She really is a true and fearless leader.

I groan inwardly when Braden makes the mistake of calling her princess. My pack rushes in to stop the fight and protect my queen, but I use my power to stop them in their tracks.

They all look at me like I have lost my damn mind. I shrug in response and urge them to watch. See what this young woman is capable of. My mate can handle Braden, and I want to see what he does as well. This isn't the way I wanted things to come about, but it's something we have been waiting for.

Someone is tugging on my power, trying to escape my control. I find that it is Jerek trying to break free to protect Ari. While I am impressed with his determination to protect my mate, I reinforce my command. It takes everything I have to keep him in line. Is Ari teaching him how to break Alpha commands? Is that even possible to teach? He growls from the discomfort of it, or maybe he's just pissed at me. I hate having to use it, but everyone needs to see this. *I* need to see this through.

It takes everything I have not to laugh out loud when she kicks him, sending him flying as if he was merely a football. She seems to be getting even stronger from the couple days of training she has had. How has her strength increased so rapidly? Yesterday was the first time that I had taken her on seriously and if I hadn't, she would have gotten the best of me again.

I'm not surprised when Ari refuses to shift in front of all these people. Her body is reserved for my eyes only. Many eyes look to me to stop this now, but I'm not worried.

I could watch her do this all day long. However, I still don't feel comfortable bringing her to war or on risky missions with me if there ever are any. I don't think putting her in that much danger is something *I* can handle, even if *she* can. I can foresee the shit storm

I will have to deal with when I may have to tell her "no". That word is not in my woman's dictionary.

I stare in amazement along with everyone else when she picks up the 250-pound wolf and slams him down into the ground. I almost feel bad for him. Almost.

"I hope now, you'll respect my decisions, and respect Jerek's role in this pack just has everyone else has," she says, and now I understand why the fight commenced, and why Jerek was so adamant about trying to intervene. I'm not the least bit surprised that she stepped into a fight that wasn't entirely hers. She is a born fighter and protector.

Braden stands, and I can see the angry snarl on his face. I curse, and his throat is in my hands before he can touch her. I am at war with myself as to whether I should end his life now or later for his blatant disrespect. I need him for interrogations though. This turn of events shows me that he really is guilty, but I still need answers.

It's a struggle, but I release him moments before he would have suffocated to death. I step away slowly, and he doesn't dare make a move. I look around and call everyone to attention.

"For those of you who don't know, when I went to receive my mate, Ari had been intercepted by the Canadian Alpha who was posing as me. Thankfully she fought them off until we had arrived, but someone from either Alpha Wilder's pack or ours leaked information that could have destroyed us. Braden here is even more of a suspect now than he was before. If anyone has any other information or suspicions, I expect to hear it by the end of the day. The traitor will be found and dealt with.

Also, let this be a lesson to everyone. I consider Ari to be my equal in every way. I think she has more than proven her worth to this pack. Together we are one, and when I am away, it will be her and Jerek, and whoever else she may choose, that will be in charge."

I signal for Trace and Asher to take Braden back to my place and to the large cage under the barn. We can't have him running off before interrogating him. Based on the answers he gives will determine if he gets to live or die. Of course, I may still kill him anyways for how he treated my mate. His mention of my mother also wracks on my nerves.

Braden was a part of my original pack, and he followed me after I killed my father, but had he been active in my father's ways before I took over? He was closer to my father's age, and we have never discussed it before. In fact, he seemed just as disturbed by my father's dealings just as everyone else was, so I didn't think I had reason to worry. Maybe it was all an act, and I was the fool who bought it.

Ari's eyes meet mine, and I can see the storm raging inside them. She learned a lot today, and I assume I'll be getting an interrogation of my own this evening. Walking towards her I watch many different emotions play on her face, but she doesn't speak. She lets me pull her into my arms and run my fingers in circles on her back to soothe her. I can practically hear the wheels turning in her head.

Jerek stands nearby, waiting for his orders from his queen. She would hate that I call her that in my head, but no one is more deserving of the name.

"Can you give her a ride home?" I ask him, and he nods. Tucking her into my side, I walk her back to Jerek's truck and open her door for her. "Go home and take a hot shower. By the time you are out, I will be home," I squeeze Ari's hand and kiss her forehead before closing her door. I want to keep her with me and take her home myself, but she needs a few moments of space to process. I can only pray she is waiting for me when I get home to her.

Chapter 15

Ari

Jerek wouldn't elaborate. He said that Darien would fill me in on the rest, but felt that he needed to admit that to me, rather than risk someone else telling me. He stayed and waited in the living room on his own volition while I went upstairs to shower. I was too numb to care. I wanted to rewind to yesterday and let Jerek talk me out of going to help collect wood. I have always loved a good ass kicking, but normally it doesn't come with all the drama and secrets.

Whispering downstairs reaches my ears when I exit the shower. Darien must be home, and Jerek probably dropped the bomb on him that the cat's out of the bag. I get dressed and wait for him to come upstairs, which I don't have to wait long.

I barely get my top over my head when his core-stimulating scent fills me. I turn to face him, and his eyes are dark and clouded with worry. Something flickers in his gaze though, and I can feel his love pouring into me from across the room.

Before I can stop him, he has me in his arms. His mouth devours mine with intense need, and I am surprised to find myself matching that need. He removes my shorts and undoes his jeans without breaking our kiss.

Unable to wait any longer, he lifts me onto his harness, filling me completely, and tears burn my eyes. The emotional roller coaster of today has zapped the energy out of me. After everything, and knowing there is more to come, I need this. I need to feel his love to tell me that if nothing else, we still have us.

"I love you, Ari," he whispers the words that I need, and I moan with pleasure. The heightened emotions intensify every one of my senses. I feel like a time bomb, and every kiss, touch, and moan pushes me one step closer to exploding. He says it again as he thrusts into me, and I give him exactly what he wants. Detonating around him, I scream, as a single tear breaks free and runs down my face.

Using his free hand, he wipes the tear away, and plants sweet kisses on my cheeks, my eyes, my forehead, and everywhere else. He looks adoringly at me. His cock continues to swell inside me, but he is waiting for my permission to continue. I give him a small smile, and he doesn't waste time removing the remainder of our clothes.

The skin on skin contact alone has me begging for more of him. He pushes on the bed and surprises me by flipping me over onto my stomach. His arm reaches under me and lifts me to my hands and knees, pressing my back to his front. His large body encases mine as he pushes back into me.

I quiver and moan beneath him as the position angles him into me deeper than ever. Even he groans with pleasure in my ear. He bites into my neck from behind, and unable to control my reaction, I squeeze him tighter. He bites me harder in an attempt to muffle his moans.

His body pressed tightly to mine, and with my strength holding us up, he starts to move. Somehow, he feels thicker than ever as he impales me over and over, hitting nerves I have never felt before.

I'm moaning and screaming, not caring who hears as he fucks me roughly, filling me over and over again. I am a hot mess as he stretches me, holding me rigidly against him.

"I love you," I finally say the words back. His grip on me tightens and his movements become more erratic as he pounds deeper and faster, fucking me with even more passion than before.

"Fuck, Ari," he comes undone. His thrusts and his release into me cause an orgasm that goes on forever.

Darien's movements slow, but our breathing is ragged. He grabs my ass, and pushes deep into me, and the tingles that follow make me collapse on the bed. He falls with me.

"Dammit, Ari, how do you do this to me?" I don't respond since I should be asking him the same question. He turns me until my head rests on his chest. He looks down into my gaze and sighs. "What do you want to know?"

"Something I should have asked a long time ago. I want to know about your mother," I see a flicker of pain pass over his eyes just before they turn to ice.

"As you know, after I killed my father, other pack members came for my mother. I protected her and commanded that they leave her alone. In that moment I realized that I had become Alpha. Mom was granted a trial. From there, you know that we discovered she wasn't completely unaware of the things going on, yet she did nothing. She was too afraid to do anything. I didn't want to lose my mother, but she was begging for someone to take her life," he says with disgust.

"Being a young and naïve 17-year-old, I offered the kill to Jerek since he was one of the few who volunteered. I thought it would make him feel better, but for a long time, I think I made it worse," he breathes and I can feel the shame and anguish rolling off of him. I feel terrible for the awful choice he had to make at such a young age.

I reach out to him and touch his face. His eyes close as I gently glide my fingers across his skin. When they open again, it's his wolf eyes that greet me, showing me just how stressed he is. Darien blinks him away before giving me an apologetic look. His wolf doesn't frighten me though.

Darien would have probably fully shifted by now if we had gone straight into the heavy stuff, but the sex alleviated some of that stress.

"I'm sorry I didn't warn you about Braden, but I wasn't, and am still not sure. I also didn't expect you to show up at my work," he points out, gently reprimanding me for not giving him a heads up.

"I'm sorry too. It wasn't my intention to keep it from you at first, but then I got nervous."

"What on earth were you nervous about?"

"I don't know. I'm used to people always being mad at me for one thing or another, but I didn't want *you* to be mad," he raises his brow at me, "and Jerek made it seem like my presence would be a bad idea."

"Dammit Jerek!" he yells loud enough for him to hear, then softly says to me, "Baby, I would never have an issue with you coming to my work. You never have to be afraid of me," he runs his gentle hands through my hair.

"So then, I can come with you to interrogate Braden?" I ask slyly. His hand in my hair stops before he looks at me like I'm crazy.

"You don't want to see that, Ari," he warns, but he forgets who he is talking to.

"It's about me, so I think I have a right to be present."

"You have a point, but how about just being in hearing distance and I'll call you in if I need anything," he tries to compromise.

"Okay, I guess that's fair," he looks at me in complete shock. "What?" I ask as he stares open-mouthed at me like I have grown two heads. He clears his throat and tries to compose himself.

"Nothing. Just amazed by your ability to compromise," he admits, but hopefully he doesn't go too crazy over it. I'm not always so agreeable.

"Well, it's not an outrageous request. I already got my shots in," I smirk, "but I want to hear what he has to say."

"Yeah you did," he laughs, and I blush at the proud expression on his face. I wasn't sure when he'd arrived at the scene, but I guess he caught some, if not all of the fight. "Come on," he gets up and holds his hand out to me. I take it and let him pull me up off the bed. We get dressed again and I slide on flats so that I don't have to fuss with all the laces and buckles on my boots.

"Dammit, Ari," he uses what seems to be his favorite phrase for me, and I glare at him with a raised brow.

"What now?" I ask icily, but it's melted when I catch the molten emeralds in his eyes again.

"Why do you look so damn good in everything?"

I roll my eyes at him, but really, I could ask him the same darn question. Technically though, I have pretty much only seen him in jeans, t-shirts, and cowboy boots, but I can tell that he's one of those guys who can pull off just about any look.

"It's just jean shorts and a plain white tee," I laugh at his ridiculousness. At least he's easy to please.

"Yeah, but those legs! That ring on your finger. Those enchanting eyes," he steps forward and takes my mouth with his. "You are perfect," his lips claim mine again before I can argue, and I'm practically panting for more.

A giggle bubbles up when he lifts me by my ass and shifts me around to his large muscled back. I hold on tight as he giddily carries me piggyback style down the stairs.

Jerek gets up from his game of solitaire at the table, and trails behind us towards the barn.

As we get closer, I feel the tension resurface in Darien, and I slide down from his back. He lets me, but takes my hand in his.

When we reach our destination, he brushes his lips over my hand before leaving me with the horses. Jerek is torn on whether to follow him or stay with me. He decides to hang back with me, but Darien leaves the door to the basement open for us to hear. From this distance we will be able to hear even the slightest whisper if we focus.

Before the show starts, I give Royal and Lightning some love. Jerek joins me, and I can see that he is very fond of the horses just like everyone else. The horses can sense the stress of the situation, but I can feel them calm at our touch and presence.

I'm not surprised to smell Darien's two right-hand men present. I realize now that Trace was probably antagonizing Braden on purpose earlier. Had he intended to get me involved though? I couldn't see Darien being okay with something like that. Are there more wolves than just Braden betraying us?

"What the fuck is this?" Braden spits. I can just picture him tied to a chair and can even hear the clanking of chains rattle with every movement.

I flinch briefly at the sound of a fist against what I believe to be Braden's face.

"I'm asking the questions here. And that was for the stunt you pulled with my mate earlier," Braden groans in pain, but wisely keeps his mouth shut. "Now, tell me how the Canadian pack was able to intercept Ari."

"I don't know," he mumbles, and I hear movement before the fist comes again, but it wasn't Darien this time. He hadn't been the one to move, and I'm sure he is trying to maintain his composure to keep his wolf under control.

"So, your angst against my mate is just pure coincidence?" Darien asks in disbelief.

"My frustration is towards the guard dog at her feet. I was your father's third, and I'm constantly being demoted by *children!*" His words are bitter, and I can tell he is probably glaring at those *children* right this second.

Probably because you sound like a petty child, I say in my head. Even Jerek snickers next to me.

"Jerek's been a train wreck for a while now. He would have been out of our lives for good, but thanks to her, he is all of a sudden in a high position without even having to earn it? That's bullshit!"

"So, you're not happy about your pack mates revelation and his willingness to protect my mate, and you feel threatened?" Darien pauses and there is no response from Braden. Not verbally anyways. "Well you *should* feel threatened because your life hangs in the balance right now. Start telling me what I need to hear," Darien commands and the coldness in his voice sends shivers down my spine. This is the Darien Shield everyone else sees, and the only side of him I was aware of before meeting him.

For a few moments there is no response. I hear a muted crunch before screaming breaks the silence. If I'm not mistaken, someone just broke one of his limbs.

"Okay, okay!" he wails in desperation, "John Flint and your father were friends. He's the one Alpha you haven't taken out yet that I know of who was involved with sharing and exploiting women. As you know, I wasn't involved with it, nor did I know most of what was going on. However, I did know that Alpha Flint never messed with our pack. I wanted us to remain in their good graces, so I gave him a heads up that you were accepting a pact with Alaska. I never said anything about your mate, nor did I even know your exact arrangements for times and locations. I'm not the traitor."

Did he not just hear himself? I can feel Darien's anger from here.

"You. Almost. Cost. Me. My. Mate!" Darien growls back slowly and dangerously. "You almost ruined our pact with a strong ally. That alone makes you a traitor. Not to mention, you withheld information on Alpha Flint being involved in past crimes, and today you went off the rails."

"I didn't know Alpha Flint would do what he did. This is madness! I can't believe this is happening over some girl who has been here for only days. I get it, she's pretty, and I'm sure a good fuck, but she's changed you Darien. She is distracting you," he pauses suddenly. "What are you doing?" his demeaning tone has turned to absolute terror, "Please think about this Darien! I'm sorry...I will be loyal and do whatever you say. I won't—," his words are cut off, and the sounds that follow turn my stomach, which is not easy to do.

Braden was so paranoid that he could no longer see reason and apparently lost all sense of preservation until his last few seconds. Criticizing an already angry Alpha's mate was Darien's last straw. He had shifted, and based on the crunching and tearing of skin sounds, ripped Braden's head off with his teeth.

Jerek and I say nothing. Neither of us is shocked by the outcome. Traitors were killed, and he may not have been the main culprit, but he put things into motion, whether he intended to or not.

The moment he was decapitated, everyone in the pack felt his death. While the Alpha can't speak directly into our minds, we all sensed what he tried to get across. *Traitor.*

Darien climbs back up to us, still in his wolf skin. He steps in front of Jerek and stares into his eyes for a moment before Jerek turns to go downstairs to help Trace and Asher. The wolf tugs on my wrist, and I know exactly what he needs.

With no one else around, I strip out of my clothes and shift. Side by side, we tear off into the forest, running almost full tilt towards nothing and everything. I smell the scent of many different animals but there will be no hunting tonight. His wolf already made his kill.

Running quietly by his side, I let Darien feel my support that he deeply needs. However, I can't help but think that he wouldn't have had to deal with this if it wasn't for me. I've been a cause of stress for him ever since I arrived. Hell, I have been a source of stress for everyone almost my whole damn life.

Darien's wolf strikes mine and we tumble until he has me pinned beneath him. He stays down low though rather than standing high above me. I use my senses to search for danger around us.

'I can feel your stress and self-blaming. Stop it, Ari. This is no one's fault other than Braden's alone. He has brought war upon us. You on the other hand have brought love and a strength I have never known into my life. You are my mate, and you will never be anything less than precious to me.'

His words seep into my very soul and turn my insides to mush. How can he be so sweet right now? I'm the one who is supposed to be consoling *him*.

'I love you,' is all I say back, but I put every ounce of that love into my declaration. His wolf licks my muzzle and my wolf boldly licks the side of his face before bolting up and running.

He chases after me with a playful yip, and suddenly it is just the two of us in the world. Two people, two wolves, young and in love with no thoughts of war. No death, and no pack drama.

I wake to a nip at my ear. Darien's wolf is cleaning my face, and playfully nipping at me, and I then realize that we are still in the woods. The sun is starting to rise. Birds are chirping, and I can hear the sound of the river nearby. I want to go back to sleep, but we both have work. Was it really my idea to get a job? Damn. I could live out here in the woods with him for the rest of my life.

'Morning, beautiful,' Darien's words play in my head, and if I were in human form, I would have blushed. Instead my wolf's stomach growls as it always does at just the right times. Of course, it doesn't help that we ran all night with no food to replenish us.

Darien gives me a wolfish laugh, but stops as his own stomach roars in hunger.

'Who's laughing now,' I tease. We both stand and stretch before trotting back towards home. We should have taken the horses.

Still in our own little bubble, we make breakfast together in the nude, sneaking glances at each other, and flirting while we dance around the kitchen. After breakfast we shower together to save time, though I'm not sure we saved any at all.

When it was time for him to go, I could tell that he didn't want to, but his pack needs him today. He kisses me hard, leaving me breathless before he walks out the door.

Not twenty minutes later, Jerek is here to pick me up. We don't speak of last night, or much of anything at all.

Today I had made lots of sales after cutting some prices to make room for the new inventory Jerek has already been working on. Watching the man work is something else. It makes me want to learn how. Maybe I can get him to teach me someday.

He catches me staring and smiles before winking at me. Just like that, the tension between us melts away. From then on, we talk and laugh easily the rest of the day until Jerek pulls up the driveway to my home.

About a third of the pack is here, standing in the driveway and on the porch, waiting. Darien isn't here, and they know he doesn't get home for a while, so why the hell are they here?

Jerek growls beside me in the cab of the truck, sensing trouble. I share the feeling, but it eases when I spot Alexia. I jump out at the sight of her and Jerek follows, taking up position next to me. I didn't think so when I first met him, but behind his sarcasm and awkwardness, I can see that he truly is intimidating.

Alexia's smile at my presence erases any of the remaining panic in me. I look around to see that there are a few dominants here, but most are middle, to lower end of the pack. Alex, being the most comfortable with me, steps forward to speak.

"Hey Ari, Jerek," she tilts her head respectfully to him, "Can we train with you guys today?" Her question completely shocks me. Once I recover, I grin from ear to ear. It's been a while since anyone, aside from Jerek, has been willing to train with me.

"Hell yes, you can!" I shout with excitement, and everyone looks pumped that I have agreed. The more the merrier. Looking at Jerek I can see that he is as blown away as me, but there is excitement there too.

Apparently neither of us is shy about running a training course.

Together we lead everyone into the field where we would be extra shielded from the main road. Everyone looks to me for direction, and the feeling passing through me is foreign, but exhilarating at the same time.

"Okay," I address the crowd, "first off, we need to see what we're working with here. Everyone, pair up. Jerek and I will walk around to each pairing to observe and jump in at random. Don't hold back against us. Give us everything you've got and we will provide tips and may switch you around with who we see fit to pair you up with."

The words just flow out of me as if I was born to do this, and they all do as instructed. The less dominant wolves are a bit more hesitant to find a partner, but eventually everyone is paired up.

I walk up to Alex and her partner of choice first, with Jerek following behind. She chose a dominant male whose name I remember is Gabe. I sense that he is fairly high in the pack's rank. He looks unsure about fighting a girl, but they face each other regardless. I signal for them to begin.

Gabe delivers a barrage of attacks. Darien has trained him well, and Alex is blocking and defending each strike, but is unable to counter attack. As I watch, I can see her begin to tire. She can only take so many more hits.

Alex takes a chance to strike, but he blocks her hand before pushing her back. It's hard enough to have her stumbling backwards. He steps forward to deliver more, but I'm already in his path. Blocking, ducking, and punching, I push him back. His brows knit together in concentration and frustration. Right where I want him.

I sweep low to take his footing out, but he jumps back. That's why I always have a back-up plan. Before his feet touch the ground, I am up in a flash and deliver a kick to his chest, using his backwards movement to knock him onto his back. I'm above him in an instant, hands around his throat, and posed to strike, and it reminds me of my fight with Jerek when we first met.

Gabe isn't happy, but he can't hide that he's impressed as well. I back off and give him a hand up. My cheeks burn when everyone starts clapping and whistling. I signal Alex to stand beside me and have both her and Gabe bow like I have seen in karate movies. The clapping grows, but when I start to speak, they simmer down.

"Gabe is strong and surprisingly quick. Alex did an excellent job deflecting, but that drains your endurance. You must be smart, but swift. Take a risk. Endure a hit to deliver a stronger one. Give them a chance to make a mistake, and then use it against them," I say, and the determination in everyone's eyes reflects my own. I feel like a true leader.

The sparring continues as Jerek and I move from pair to pair, taking turns fighting and giving tips. After the first round, seeing everyone's strengths and weaknesses, we change up a few partners.

Before we begin the next round, I feel eyes on us.

Scanning the area, I find Darien watching me in surprised amusement. When the hell did he get here? I hadn't even heard his truck come up the driveway. I'm getting sloppy.

He comes closer once he knows I've spotted him. The pack looks nervous at his arrival. When they see the pride in their Alpha's eyes though, their determination is restored. Packs mostly train on their own or when their Alpha calls for it, which is typically only a few times a year. Usually it is to test out who is dominant, and determine everyone's order in the pack.

Is that why everyone is here? Are they all trying to step up their game and see who can move higher in rank now that Braden is dead? Or is it because of the imminent war that his stupidity instigated?

Darien joins our training, fighting and giving advice when needed. I catch his eye and he is genuinely smiling at me across the field. Through our bond, I can feel his pride in me.

Everyone is exhausted but smiling when it's over. Just one day of training and they are all several steps up from where they started. The three of us make a good training team.

"Same time tomorrow?" Gabe's question catches me off guard. He wants to come back? I look to the pack, my pack, and they are all giving me the same hopeful look.

"Same time. I'll even get all the guys from Shield logging here," Darien answers for me.

"Great job today everyone," I finish for him, doing my best to appear strong in front of them. They all nod and disperse, except Alex who comes and barrels into me.

"You are so awesome," she squeals, "I mean I heard from some of the guys about yesterday, but seeing you fight in person is something else." Her words flatter me.

Thanks to my uncles and hard work, I have always been confident in my skills, but it's not often that I, as a woman, am praised for my abilities. Maybe there was just something different about the women in the Alaska pack. Or maybe they just had an issue with me personally. Unfortunately, it's probably the latter. I won't make the mistake of being that selfish girl again.

Jerek walks up beside me, and I notice a faint flush on Alex's skin. I smile, but quickly hide it.

"Thanks, Alex. You know Jerek, right?" I try not to be too obvious, but I've never played matchmaker before. Alex nods, looking up at him as if it's the first time that she is really seeing him.

"You did well today," Jerek says a little shyly, and hope blooms in my heart for these two. She nods in thanks, and attempts to hide her reddening cheeks. Jerek looks pretty clueless though since he hasn't talked to another woman, other than me, in who knows how long. This is going to take some work.

"Hey Alex, can I ask you a favor?" I ask as an idea comes to me, and I try to mask my excitement. "I'm working with Jerek and trying to post pictures of his inventory on the website I created for him. My phone pictures hardly cut it, but since you know your way around a camera better, would you mind coming by to help out?"

"Not at all," she beams at me, "I can come by tomorrow."

Jerek gives me a sideways glance when she waves and walks away, but I ignore him. I haven't known Alexia long, but I never expected to see a shy side of her. Jerek is a special case though, so she is most likely trying to tread carefully. He pats me on the back, and I smile up at him before he leaves with the rest of the pack.

"Well that was new," Darien's voice purrs behind me.

"Yeah, I guess they all sense that there is a war coming, or they must want a higher position in the pack," I say absentmindedly, but Darien spins me to face him. The sudden motion has me in a daze for a moment. He smirks down at me in his arms.

"That might be part of it, but you earned their respect. They didn't come here to train and learn from *me*," he points out. "What's more is you did an excellent job. In just one day, they are twice the fighters they were before today. You were born for this, Ari. I'm putting you in charge of training," he declares, and my eyes all but pop out of my head. Trainers were usually the Alpha himself or his seconds.

"Are you serious?" I ask, and he smiles in confirmation. "Trace is gonna be so pissed!" and I can't hold back a chuckle. Maybe he'd pick a fight with me over it. That would be awesome going head to head with Darien's second.

Unaware of my insane thoughts, Darien laughs with me. He would kill Trace before he let him pick a fight with me. He wanted to kill Asher the first day in the hotel room when he tried to make a move. I'd saved his life by flipping him on his ass.

"Does this mean you'll let me go on missions and into battle?" his laughter dissipates immediately.

"No Ari," I open my mouth to respond, but he cuts me off, "You are MINE, and I won't put you at risk." His possessiveness seems to have grown over the short time we've been together. That's unfortunate for me.

"But you can put *yourself* at risk?" I protest. "You know that I can protect myself and the other members of this pack."

"Ari," he says sharply, making me flinch. I know that it's not really allowed and that I'm pushing him, but I thought he understood.

Once again, my immaturity shines through as I shift and run off, ignoring his desperate pleas behind me.

It's not fair. Him, and any male, can go off and risk their lives, but I'm supposed to wait at home when I could be watching my mate's back.

I never imagined I'd find my true mate, but I should have known it wouldn't change anything. I'm still female. I'm the mate of an Alpha; a cherished member of the pack to be protected. Not sent out into danger, even if they have been training to do just that for most of their lives.

It may not be everything I want, but I have to admit that it is generous enough that Darien is giving me full charge of training. Why can't I be satisfied with that?

Gunfire rings out not far from me. I hit the ground mid-stride and stay down low, unsure of where the shots are coming from. I'm so stupid coming out here alone during hunting season on wolves. How did I miss their scent?

Putting my nose to work I smell beer, smoke, and sweaty human. Their scent is far away, which is why I didn't smell them sooner.

I'm too far for the human eye to see, so I quickly realize that I'm not the object of their fire. I stay low and creep over the hillside. Bile rises in my throat at the scene I come upon.

A gray wolf, a real one is caught in a trap. Blood seeps out of her from buck or birdshot that has sprayed into her.

My blood boils as their laughter meets my ears. They shoot all around and at her feet, making her flinch and dodge in her weakened state.

Before I can stop myself, my paws pound against the earth. I will myself to be quiet just like when I hunt, but the wolf has only moments left before they tire of their sick game.

Humans aren't supposed to see us. We just look like wolves, but larger, especially the males. Hopefully they will just think I'm just a very large, strange colored wolf. I won't just sit by and watch this happen. Not when I have the power to stop it.

Darien must have heard the gunshots and sensed the adrenaline coursing through me.

'Ari! Where are you?' his voice booms into my head, and I'm not sure how, but I know he's running. I can't respond though because they've seen me now.

The three humans turn and the one with the shotgun takes aim at me. I dodge at the last second as I watch his finger pull the trigger, then leap onto him, using my teeth to rip the gun from his hands. I head-butt him, knocking him unconscious before turning just in time to see one of the men pull a pistol on me.

Pain rips into my hind leg, but it would have been my head if I hadn't moved as quick as I did.

'Ari!' I can hear the distress in his voice, and I feel bad for the worry I'm causing him. On top of being a part of the pack, I am his true mate so he can sense and feel my pain when something happens to me.

His howl follows my lack of response. I'm too focused on not getting killed as the guy with the gun keeps firing, but I'm too quick. I've never had to dodge bullets before, but I knew I didn't want to get shot again so my adrenaline gives me the ability to stay a step ahead.

When he runs out of ammo, I pounce. The fear on their faces makes me smile. Now they know what it feels like when the hunter becomes the hunted, except I'm giving them a justice they don't deserve. Hunting is a part of life, but torture is something dark and twisted. These assholes should be wiped from this earth.

Knocking over the human with the pistol, he screams in terror, and the other guy takes off running. I quickly knock the first one out and chase after the other. Causing a little head trauma will help make their stories invalid. I take the coward down and he begs me for mercy. Tears stream down his face as my jaw hovers over his throat. I watch his eyes roll back, but I hit him over the head for good measure.

'I'm fine,' I send a quick message through the bond as I make my way back to the wolf, slowing my pace as I near her frazzled form. She holds my gaze, unsure of what to think of me.

Stopping in front of her, I shift into human form. She flinches back, growling and trying to get away, but I don't move a muscle towards her. When her eyes finally come back to mine, I stare her down, showing her who is in charge, and that I'm not going to hurt her. I'm not like the others.

She whines when I urge her to lie down, but eventually she gives in and lies back on her good side.

Slowly, I move toward her broken form. She whines, but I quickly get to work pulling shot out of her as best I can. Her whining settles as she begins to trust me, but her body still jerks at the pain from my fingers digging into her.

Once I get out as much as I can, I shift back. My wolf starts licking over her wounds. Animal's wounds can heal with their own saliva usually, but werewolf saliva speeds up the healing process. I wasn't sure how it would work on anyone or anything other than a werewolf, but the wounds look better already.

I take the trap that holds her paw in my jaws and shatter it into a million pieces. The poor girl is lucky her leg isn't broken, but it is pretty mangled. Though she wants to run, she stays still a few moments longer to let me heal the wound on her leg. She will be limping for a while, but she should make a full recovery.

Backing off to let her stand, she rises weakly. Her legs shake in exhaustion after the ordeal she has been through. She holds my gaze, but not in a challenging way. Her eyes look over my shoulder, and I follow her gaze to find Darien's wolf walking towards me. When I turn back, she is already limping away.

Darien's anger thunders into me as he takes in the scene around us.

Three unconscious humans, bullets and shotgun shells litter the ground. It must be quite a sight to find your mate in the center of. I can tell that he wants to yell at me. He holds his tongue though, knowing he would have done the same thing. Besides, I kept it clean, saved a wolf, and I'm fine.

'You're bleeding,' he growls. Okay so I'm *mostly* fine. Luckily it seems the bullet went straight through due to the close-range shot. As I did for the other wolf, Darien licks my wound, and it's healing faster than anything I have seen before. Must be crazy Alpha mojo.

It's time to go before these assholes wake up. Hopefully they won't be hunting again any time soon. I'm sure I at least scared them enough to never pull that bullshit again.

My limp is slight, but Darien makes us walk slowly. Moving too fast with an open wound could make a wolf bleed out, but it's basically already closed.

The walk back is quiet. I can feel the tornado of emotions swirling through him, but I am still upset with him as well. Even though I made him worry, that wolf would be dead now if I hadn't done what I did. We can't have people coming around torturing and killing wolves so close to home.

Once we are inside the comfort of our home, we shift back to humans. My body sways from all the shifting I've done. Darien catches me before I can fall over.

I try to tell him that I'm fine, but I'm in his strong arms before I can finish the sentence.

He carries me upstairs and draws a bath for me before looking over my almost fully healed bullet wound. In truth, I actually was a little freaked out since this is my first time ever being shot at, but I don't tell him that. He would be even more concerned than he is now. I need to act like I don't care, and show him that one little bullet won't change my mind.

I'm submerged in water now, and Darien sits on the edge of the tub. I just stare at him, waiting for him to yell at me for running off, and tell me how I'll never be able to go on missions.

"You scared me," his voice holds true fear and sadness. My stomach drops at his admission. Regardless of my selfish needs and wants, he is my mate, and I don't like seeing him upset like this.

"I'm sorry. I had to act fast," I defend myself, but he holds his hand up to stop me.

"I just got you, Ari. I had no idea I would ever feel this way, and part of me wants to give you what you want, but a bigger part of me wants to lock you away and keep you safe. I heard those gunshots and..." his words refuse to form. He just shakes his head trying to rid the tortured look from his face, but I already saw it.

I remain quiet, giving him time to rein in his emotions.

"Now that I know you, I can't live without you. You're it for me. I'm not ready to just throw you in to danger just because I know you can face anything and overcome it. Something bad could still happen, *even to you*, and I would be the one to blame. Maybe someday I'll get on your fearless level, but not now," his hand holds my chin as he stares down into my eyes.

He isn't saying *never*, just *not now*. I'll still fight my way into the first potential mission, but the fact that he is saying he might be willing someday, is good enough to make me forgive him.

Water splashes everywhere as I pull his large form into the tub with me. Our lips find each other's, and our hands glide over skin, finding comfort in one another after a tense day.

Chapter 16

The next day at work, Alex came by just as she promised. She decided that we needed some props, and Jerek let me go with her because I needed to pick up some items for the wedding as well.

Shopping with Alex is easy. She knew just what she wanted, got it, and got out. On top of that, she helped me pick out my own stuff, and was very honest and straightforward about her opinions. For someone like me who is so new to this, it was very helpful to have the help of an expert photographer.

Together we set up the props for the pictures, and once they are all done and loaded onto the laptop, we call Jerek over to take a look. Alex looks nervous as he inspects them, but Jerek is speechless. Not even one of his sarcastic remarks.

These pictures would sell the inventory in no time. The pieces are gorgeous themselves, but with the props, you can really picture them in your home.

After viewing them, Jerek looks at Alex with an intense gaze.

Many emotions cross his features, but in the end, he just nods and walks away. Alex tries to act like she's not hurt, but the sting is evident in the way her shoulders pull together.

I follow him out back while Alex gathers her things.

"What the hell was that?" I snap at him, though I try to keep my voice low so that werewolf ears can't overhear.

"What do you mean?" he plays dumb.

"You like her, and it's obvious she likes you, not to mention did an awesome job for you, and you give her the cold shoulder?" I scold him.

"I can't go down that road," he sighs, and I watch his shoulders slump.

"Bull shit you can't! You don't have to do anything crazy right now, but you can at least treat her like a normal human being, or human-werewolf being." He stares off into space, no doubt thinking of his late girlfriend. "I know you feel it's wrong, but *she* wasn't your mate," he knows who I mean, "I know you loved her, but if it were the other way around, would you want her moping around remaining lonely the rest of her life?"

He ponders my words for a moment then gets up from his seat. Finally. Alex looks up when we reenter the room. I hang back to give them space.

"Thanks, Alexia. I'll call you when I have some more projects done," my palm smacks into my face. What the hell is wrong with him? Getting them together is not going to be easy.

"Sure, I'll be here. I can't wait to see more. Your work is stunning," Alex puts herself back out there, taking the risk Jerek is struggling with. He smiles shyly in return. This Jerek is so different from the one I know him as.

"Thanks, I'll get you some money for the pictures and props you bought," he turns to leave, but she stops him.

"That's not necessary. I'm just helping out," she states, and Jerek frowns. Then he perks up just the slightest bit seeming to have an idea of some kind.

"Fine, what's your favorite animal?"

"Falcons," she says hesitantly. Jerek sticks me with accusing eyes.

"What?" I glare right back at him.

"You told her my favorite animal?"

"How the hell would I know your favorite animal?" I say at the same time Alex asks, "You like falcons too?"

Jerek turns to her with wide eyes and they start gushing over the bird. I leave them to talk while I deal with customers. Maybe this won't be so hard after all. They are made for each other.

Almost the whole pack is at our property after work. Even some of the kids in the pack are here as well to observe. Thankfully, my leg is back to 100%, and nobody even knows what happened yesterday. Today we start by getting everyone pumped up with a wolf on wolf fight between Jerek and me. I asked Darien, but he said he didn't want to hurt me in front of everyone. He is regretting those words right now.

I told him he wouldn't be getting lucky tonight.

Everyone howls in excitement when I pin Jerek in our demonstration. They all shift and begin sparring with the partners we placed them with yesterday.

Our wolf forms have better instincts, therefore are typically better fighters compared to our human side. However, when you strengthen the human part, the wolf is a force to be reckoned with.

I can feel the frustrations in the pack as they fight. After just a single day, a select few are moving up in pack rank. You can gage each another's dominance just by looking in the other's eyes. Sometimes you can just feel the power and dominance just rolling off of them.

Being in a pack, everyone in that pack just seems to know where each stand in superiority through the bonds. Gabe, Alexia, and two others, Benjamin and Mindy, are all standing a little higher today. Even Jerek could be second now if he wanted that position.

They may be upset now, but the pack as a whole will be stronger when all is said and done.

During the training, Jerek watches Alexia with pride. I smile at the both of them and wonder if Jerek will still be my guard if him and Alex end up together. Of course, I couldn't blame him if he didn't. Maybe then he would take point as Darien's second and that would be that. As if sensing my thoughts, he looks over at me with furrowed brows.

Ignoring him, I go back to observing my pack. Their movements are a blur of colors and clashing of teeth. Each of their efforts is thrilling, and I want to join in the fray. So, I do.

Shifting quickly, I leap out to the center of the field and howl, calling my mate and guard to me. Trace and Asher follow Darien, and it's five of us against at least twenty. Adrenaline pumps through my veins from the excitement and anticipation.

Unfortunately, it's a high possibility that if we go to war with Canada, we may be severely outnumbered so this is a great training exercise. Plus, I have always wanted to try this. If all goes well, we can keep doing it to really watch everyone grow.

I can sense that Darien isn't thrilled, but he lets me do my thing. Probably trying to get back in my good graces...aka, my pants.

My roar sounding begins the battle.

The pack rushes us, and my group dodges and counters. With how many wolves we're up against, I expect more action, but my damn mate and guard won't let anyone through. Together they furiously defend me, and while I'm touched and impressed by their skill, it's unnecessary.

Mindy, Ben, and Gabe make a move towards Darien who already has his hands full. I take the opportunity to leap over him and tackle the strongest of the group, Benjamin. Luckily, I caught him off guard, but he recovers quickly, just like I taught him yesterday. Mindy and Gabe come at me from the sides, hoping to confuse me.

Smiling inwardly, I run towards Mindy, and I know they have no clue what to do at the turn of events. I control the situation. Because she is lighter, I slide at her feet, then use my own to kick her up and over my head, aiming for Gabe's wolf charging me. I hit my mark and don't waste time, making a b-line for Ben.

Like all the other males, he is bigger than me, but he has learned well not to leave me an opening. He is a strong opponent. We trade blow for blow, testing each other out.

Even though I am the Alpha's mate, he doesn't go easy on me, and I respect him for that. I think we found Braden's replacement. Ben is no Darien though. I soon overpower him and get my jaws around his throat. That ends our battle, and he stands down.

Two more wolves charge me, but before I can react, Darien and Jerek take them down. One is Alexia, and Jerek faces off with her. She fights well, but it's not long before he gently nips her neck. Darien and Asher make quick work of their last opponents.

We are the remaining four. Only one casualty, but I don't feel like I was much help in the process since they all tried to keep me out of it. Is this really how it would be in real battle? Everyone would be trying to protect me rather than fight *with* me? What if that would keep us from having no casualties?

There is a mix of emotions written on each wolf's face; excitement and determination to get stronger, anger and disappointment that only one dominant was taken out, while some were simply proud of the progress they have made. I try to hide my own storm of emotions and focus on my pack.

I howl, pouring all my pride and strength into my song to cheer everyone up. Darien is the first to join in, adding in his own power. One by one they all join in focusing on the same goal, to get stronger together.

Darien spends the rest of the evening contacting other pack members from different cities and states. He wants a select few from every state or big city coming to train with us, take what they learn, and teach it to any wolf that is willing to learn back home.

When war is a possibility, it's not unheard of for these steps to be taken. No one wants a war, but Canada is itching to make a move. They want everything for themselves, and who better to start with than us? Especially since dad, and technically Darien now too, controls part of Canada. That fact alone must irritate them most.

A single Alpha can't control the whole werewolf population. My guess is that Alpha Flint plans to split it with his son, the son he apparently thought he would *gift* me to when he tried to kidnap me. They basically share control of their piece of Canada already. Of course, they have to remain on opposite ends of the country to avoid a possible challenge.

I guess if both Alpha's have the same, shared goal, and keep their distance, it's possible to run a territory together.

I've never met his son obviously, but his father must be pretty confident in his abilities to rule over all the other Alphas in the world. I shudder to think of the fact that Flint was going to force me to be his bride. I know nothing about him, but if he's anything like his father, I'd be just fine if I never met him, unless it's his cold, dead, corpse.

I'm half asleep when Darien comes to bed. We're getting married in a day and a half so we both have tomorrow free to make sure everything is ready.

Now I'm just waiting for someone to pull the rug out from under my feet. There's no way someone like me can have it all. Nothing is perfect, but my life has become damn near close to it.

At that thought, Darien's arms pull me in tight against his strong chest, and I soon drift off to sleep.

Darien

My mate proves to me every day that she deserves to be one of my top fighters. Hell, she is my top fighter, but I can't tell her that. I can't bring myself to allow it.

Just the thought of her facing a real threat causes a rage in my wolf, stronger than I've ever felt before. My human side almost feels bad for the fools that would ever try to harm her, but I also don't know what I'd do if anyone ever did hurt her. My perfect control would shatter. How Jerek stuck around after what happened to his girlfriend amazes me more now than ever before.

Two short days and she has my pack pumped up and ten times the fighters they were when she arrived here. My mate is the damn God of War herself. Is this her power? Is it just her strong blood that draws people to her? They must sense her strength, and she can train them in a way I've never been able to.

As an Alpha, we just take those who are already strong, make them battle ready, and call it good. We don't concern ourselves with much training. We expect them to train on their own time. I've lost a lot of wolves in my quest for taking out the Alphas that have abused their power.

No one has ever stepped up to train the pack. Dominant wolves typically don't have the patience or skill set to teach. Ari fills that role perfectly, and I'm 100% on board with it. Jerek's support of her gives him the ability to help train without any issue. This method of training could save a lot of lives.

I need to get the rest of the pack from our other territories in on this. I'm waiting on finalized lists of how many wolves we have all together, but so far, we are guessing around 1200. However, about 200 of them are just teens or younger. Also, another 200 of them are women, so in all actuality, we have maybe 800 fighters, and I would guess that Alaska alone doubles us in fighters as well. I'm hoping that we have more than it seems.

Alpha Flint alone has his hands full with the number of wolves he has. Canada has at least twice the amount of wolves than mine and the Alaska packs wolves combined. It's a shock that Canada hasn't taken over already, but an Alpha can only control so many wolves at once.

When his son became of age, instead of sending him out to another pack, he gifted half of Canada to him, and together they share the territory. The whole thing was an experiment for something much bigger though. Once they learned that they could share, they also realized that they could increase their territory. And where is a better place to start other than the bordering territories?

Other packs along their borders have joined forces as well, but if even one territory is taken out, we are all doomed. I've never feared death. I have always assumed my end would come quickly, which is why I have gotten where I am so fast, I didn't want to die before my mission was complete.

Now that I have my mate, my reason for existing, it's going to take one hell of an army to put me in the ground. No one is taking us from each other without a fight, and we don't go down easy. Maybe it's selfish, but increasing the pack's power will also serve in helping protect Ari. My woman is strong, but she's not invincible, yet she insists on putting herself in danger.

She's asleep when I crawl into bed with her. Snuggling up beside her, I breathe her in. That cool mountain air and wild berry scent fills my nose, and I am instantly at peace. Watching over her while she sleeps is one of my favorite things to do. Listening to her breathing and her strong heartbeat calms me. There's something about her allowing herself to be so vulnerable with me that gives me more pleasure than I ever thought possible.

The need to protect my pack has always been fierce, but protecting Ari is something else entirely. Something tells me that if anything ever happened to her, I wouldn't survive, nor would I want to without her.

My wolf growls at my thoughts. The wolf half thinks some things differently from the human half. Wolves don't typically have negative thoughts, or at least dominant wolves don't. In his eyes, we are invincible, and no one can take or hurt what's ours. Sure, it makes us selfish and egotistical, but it's also what makes us strong. It's how we survive in a world where humans grossly outnumber us. The only greater risk than war with wolves is exposure.

The few who are mated to one of us know of our existence, but they are sworn to secrecy. Some humans can handle the truth, but the majority would either hate or fear us, which would lead to riots, death, and most likely experimentations. We would be wiped out, or be forced into hiding at the very least. Thankfully the world is currently oblivious to us, and hopefully that will continue to be the case.

Drifting off to sleep, I dream of my wedding. My mate is beautiful as always. She is happy and so am I, along with everyone else in the pack.

In the next scene of the dream, Ari is mad at me and looks at me with disappointment in her eyes. My happy dream turns into a nightmare when I smell Ari's blood, but she is nowhere to be found. As I search for her, I find my pack. My men, women, and children all slaughtered, and somehow, I get the feeling that it's my fault.

Something hits me, and my eyes open to darkness. Ari's voice shouts my name. I let my wolf peer out so that I can see her better in the dark. I need the reassurance that she's really here with me.

"What's wrong Darien? You were starting to shift," the panic is obvious in her sleepy, but alarmed eyes. She must have been trying to wake me for a while. I wish she had gotten through to me sooner.

"Sorry for waking you. It was just a bad dream," I say, not sure if I am trying to reassure her or myself as I caress her face.

"Do you want to talk about it?" Fuck no, I don't want to talk about it! I could never repeat what I saw aloud. I pray those images don't haunt my vision ever again.

"No, it's fine," I lie, "Let's get some sleep, baby. We have a big day tomorrow." I pull her in tight and kiss the top of her head. She snuggles into me, trailing her fingers over my bare skin. After the nightmare I'd just had, I was prepared to not get any sleep the rest of the night, but Ari's soft and sweet touch makes my eyelids heavy.

The next thing I know, the sun is shining through the window, and my arms are empty.

I try to reach for Ari, but the bed is empty. Terror shoots through me, and like lightning, I am down the stairs in a flash.

Bacon and other familiar scents tell me that she is in the kitchen, but I'm not believing anything until I see it with my own eyes. When I find her, I pinch myself to see if I'm still dreaming.

There's a beautiful girl wearing my t-shirt, and making breakfast in my kitchen. My shirt reaches to almost halfway down her gorgeous thighs. The beauty spins and glares at me.

"No fair! I was going to surprise you!" she gripes at me and I can't hold back the laughter that bubbles up. Yep, this beautiful spitfire is definitely my woman.

I cross the kitchen towards her, lift her up by her ass onto the counter, and take her mouth with mine. She wraps her arms around me, and moans as my hard length presses against her.

My name, a whisper on her lips, calls me forward. I slide inside of her and raw emotion consumes me.

She throws her head back as I pound wildly into her, not bothering with gentle and slow. I need this woman like I have never needed anything before.

Though it was only a nightmare, I had felt the loss of her all the same.

Buried inside her, I hold her tight to the point that I wouldn't doubt that I'm leaving bruises. I'm not one to be into causing pain, but the thought of marking her brings me to my release. She screams in ecstasy, and her muscles clench around me as her orgasm consumes her. I love that I can make her feel this way and that my coming undone is her undoing as well.

We pant against each other, and I hold her to me, not ready to let go. I kiss her head and breathe in her intoxicating, reassuring scent.

When she pulls back, I look her over.

Shame falls upon me when I see that I really did leave bruises on her beautiful skin. The quickie was fucking fantastic, but at what cost? What will she think when she finds what I did?

I wince as her teeth bite into my chest, drawing the tiniest bit of blood. I throb inside of her and it almost brings me to my knees. What in the fuck was that for? I give her an incredulous look.

"Did you feel more pleasure or pain?" she asks smugly, and it dawns on me why she did what she did. She must have sensed my shame or saw me staring at the marks on her. I just smile and nod in understanding and place a quick kiss on her pouting lips.

My sulking had ruined the moment for her, but she quickly forgives me. I should know better that my girl can handle a little pain. Though I don't like the reminder, she had even taken a bullet like a champ.

Pulling out of her, I help her off the counter. She giggles at her shaky legs, and the precious sound centers me. The stress from my nightmare recedes a bit.

Now my hunger is at the forefront of my brain, which is slowly getting blood flow back.

Ari sets to work making me a plate of food, and I realize that she recreated our first meal together; bacon, egg, and cheese croissants and hot chocolates. My sweet Ari. The toughest person I know, but has a pure heart of gold.

Chapter 17

My bride to be has a vision of what she wants our big day to look like. She has been firing out orders all day, and I have to say that I am very impressed with her ideas. It had been her great idea to hold the ceremony out in the yard. There are two trees that sit about 10 feet from each other, and she plans to make that arbor area.

As per her request, Jerek and I get to work, building a double doorframe for the two barn doors that she found. It turns out just as she wanted, and it's what everyone will walk through as they make their way down the aisle. When I spoke to the out of town members about training, I also invited whoever wanted to come to the wedding, so who knows how many guests we will have.

Together, Ari and I set up chairs, and on the end of each row down the aisle, Ari places a wooden box and or crate upside down.

When I think she's lost me, she puts lacey mats, old style lanterns, and small mason jars filled with fake flowers on each one. It looks beautiful.

She then takes the extra boxes and crates and stacks them around the trees that will become the arbor. Using two larger carriage lamps that she took from the barn, she places one on each side, and then fills in the rest of the scenery with more mason jars. No flowers this time. She tells me that she wants real ones for those, and plans to pick wild ones in the morning.

I help her hang lights from tree to tree to tie it all together. The finished product is something out of a fairy tale. I might just leave it like this all year round. All of the pack members could have their weddings here if they wanted to.

While Ari makes some finishing touches, I carve our initials onto the tree next to the arbor. And with that, the ceremony area is complete.

As for the reception, a few of our pack members are catering and bringing tables with linens as well. Ari has a box ready to go of candles and other little trinkets to use as centerpieces. What impressed me most was that she found most of the items here on the property, and the rest she got from discount stores.

Of course, I told her that money was no object when it came to our wedding, but she is keen on not taking more than she needs.

The set up took a lot less time than we thought it would so we decide to take the horses for a run. We then spend the rest of our time relaxing and talking. Trace and Asher are taking me out tonight, and then we are staying in the large guest room in the barn. Silly human traditions. This is going to be the longest 24 hours of my life.

Since Benjamin appears to be the most promising to fill Braden's role, I had him get ordained and am giving him the privilege to marry Ari and I. We don't bother with a rehearsal. Werewolf weddings aren't as stressful as human weddings. They are similar, but a lot more laid back. More like a party, I would say.

"Should I be worried about your last night out on the town?" Ari feigns insecurity. With my arm wrapped around her on the porch swing, I pinch her side. She looks up at me with a silly grin.

"Ari, most of the pack has seen you fight. No one would dare cross you by making a pass at me," I grab her by the chin, forcing her to look into my eyes, "and there will never be anyone or anything I want more than I want you."

Our mouths mold together, but Trace and Asher riding up the driveway together in Asher's GMC Sierra, halts our passionate kiss. They honk obnoxiously, knowing they are interrupting our moment.

I could kill them.

You'd think the two men closest to me in this pack would know not to push my buttons. Growing up together as children must have affected the typical relationship between Alpha and his seconds.

"Hey you two," Trace drawls out the window. Ari flips him off, earning chuckles from both of them. That's my woman and my soon to be wife.

"Get in. It's time to get our party on," I glare at Asher's command toward me, and he quickly raises his hands in surrender.

Giving my attention back to my mate, we stand together and I turn her into me before I press my lips to hers, kissing her like no one's watching. Pulling back, I look at her, taking in every gorgeous inch, and I don't want to leave. Her eyes even beg me to stay, but she blinks the look away and steps back.

"Go have fun. Enjoy your last night as a single man, because once you say 'I do', you are all mine," she smiles wickedly.

"Baby, I have been all yours since the moment I watched you kick an Alpha in the face," I growl before claiming another kiss from her. Her chuckle vibrates against my lips.

It pains me, and I have to physically tear myself away from her. The sooner I leave and get this over with, the sooner I will have her back in my arms.

I kiss her hand that wears my ring before running to the truck like a lovesick teenager. Her gaze trails after us until we are out of sight.

Ari

Darien gets to have his bachelor party, so I'm having my bachelorette party, though only Alex, Mindy, and Jerek are here. Inviting anyone else would have felt weird. Even having Mindy here was a little awkward, but since we started training, I sensed that we just might be able to get along.

Over alcohol, pizza, and cards, we chat about various things. Jerek wasn't happy about babysitting three girls, but after some beer and shots, he relaxes and becomes his normal goofy self that he is with me. As he flirts and jokes around, I can tell that he was quite the ladies' man before his girlfriend had been taken from him. With just a few drinks to numb his pain, he becomes the life of the party.

Alexia and him are really starting to hit it off. Alcohol makes everything better. Until the next day of course. This is actually only my second time drinking.

Last year, when I turned 21, Niko and Charlie came over with a whole truckload of alcohol to celebrate. Technically, I didn't have to wait until then to drink since alcohol doesn't affect us nearly as hard, or as long as it would a human. It also has no long-term effects on us, so we don't have many restrictions on it.

Due to the fact that I had chosen to wait, they just had to make a big deal out of it. The whole night we had played games outside by the bonfire, and we drank way too much.

Then after they liquored me up, they challenged me to a fight, and me being me, I couldn't turn it down. Getting my drunken ass kicked by both of them made me swear off alcohol around them, afraid that they would take advantage of the situation again. Hopefully Jerek doesn't decide to challenge me tonight.

Focusing back on our conversation, I come to find out why Mindy is such a strong fighter. She is a healer. Though she remains in the back, she gets to go to war in order to help the wounded in battle. The job is still very risky, and there are targets on the healer's back, so she has to be a good fighter.

I'm surprisingly jealous of her, and contemplating becoming a medic, if that's what it is going to take for me to get what I want. The medics of the pack usually come from the same family and are trained from children. Apparently, it takes special training to be a werewolf doctor, and there are only a few in each pack.

We also end up learning that Mindy has a crush on Ben, but his father was Darien's fathers second, whom of which apparently took advantage of Mindy's mother. Ben and her had been only kids, but he keeps his distance even though Darien had killed him to get to his father. Both his father and Ben's were equally guilty.

I feel bad for Mindy, and hope that things end up working out for them. Now that she had mentioned all this, I remember the way Ben had watched her during the training; proud, but also protective.

Life had seemed a lot simpler in Alaska. If there was all this pack drama back home, I hadn't heard about any of it. My father is a good leader though. As far as I knew, the males cherished and protected the women, not abused them.

It's upsetting to learn how wrong I was. I thought I had it bad, not being able to fight and choose my life for myself, but at least I didn't have to fear for my life, or be paranoid about someone trying to sexually and, or, physically assault me at any moment. Once again, I am reminded that the first 20 years of my life could have been much happier if only I had let it be so.

Tonight, is my last night as an unmarried woman. Tomorrow I will stand before my pack, in a badass dress, and marry the leader of this pack. In just one short week here, I have made a solid handful of friends, and somehow earned myself the position as head trainer. It has been quite the ride so far. Tomorrow I will no longer be a Wilder, but a Shield.

My laid-back but fun evening makes me think of what Darien must be doing right now. Most males would be fall-on-your-face drunk, and crying or panicking over the fact that they will be stuck with the same damn woman for the rest of their lives.

Darien is too reserved for that though. I've never seen him drink, but he looks like a man who can hold his liquor, and I'm not worried about him shacking up with anyone.

Somehow, I won the key to his heart and have the only pass to what's beneath his pants.

He reserved it all for me; the girl who had planned to kill him from the moment I learned we were to marry.

My turn comes around, and I make my move. I waited for them to get bored of my games, but they all seem to be enjoying them as much as me, even the ones they didn't know that I had to teach them. We play Rummy, Golf, Black Jack, and Crazy Eights, while my favorite movie, *300*, plays in the background. At some point we take a break to make banana splits, making my night complete.

Darien

My one and only bachelor party that I'll ever have, and I spend most of my night thinking about what Ari is doing. I have to remind myself that she has only been here a short time, and though she has bonded with a few pack mates, it's still all so new. She belongs here, and I want her to feel that way every damn day of the rest of her life. Ari is mine, and I am hers no matter how many girls try to give me that *"come hither"* look, or try to approach me.

The few that tried, I sent steely gazes that say *not happening*, turning them right back where they came from. I have no ring on my finger, so they have no idea that I am taken, but I'm not the least bit concerned that I've hurt their feelings.

If Ari were here, they would have fared a lot worse, just as any man would have if they ever dared to hit on my mate in front of me.

Trace and Asher try to get me to lighten up, but she's the only one I can be relaxed around. I feel like my younger self when I am with her. When she is not getting into trouble at least.

Benjamin and Gabe and a few other guys meet up with us at the bar in town. Since my father's rule ended and my mission began, we haven't really been able to do stuff like this, and the awkward silence makes it obvious that it has been too long.

"You're marrying quite a woman tomorrow," Gabe breaks the ice, instantly bringing a smile to my lips. Everyone erupts with their own agreement. I don't need their approval on who I mate and wed, but I can't deny that their acceptance of Ari makes me damn pleased. Most royals don't give a damn if you like them or not, as long as everyone pretends to, but Ari truly wants people to like her for who she is, whether she believes that or not.

"She is something else," I agree, starting up a conversation on how awesome it has been training with her and how good she is for our pack.

It's not typical bachelor party talk, but it's made my night. The rest of the evening flows easily, with good drinks, good food, good conversation, and typical boy rowdiness. This will be the beginning of a happier, healthier, and stronger pack.

After Ben and Gabe leave, Asher drives us back to my house. There is a large King size bed and a pull-out couch in the barn. I let them have the bed and take the couch for myself. I don't want to share a bed with anyone but my mate right now.

As I lay in the darkness, I can't help but think of the storm must be coming soon. Someone or something is going to pull the rug out from under me at any moment.

My wolf rises to the surface, ready to take on any threat.

Able to see better in the dark with my wolf's eyesight, I find mine and the groomsmen's suits hanging in the open closet. I'm getting married tomorrow. No one is going to stop me from marrying the woman of my dreams, and no one is going to take us away from each other. Ever. With that thought, sleep comes easy.

Morning comes, and I feel well-rested as sun-rays stream through openings in the curtains. I check the clock on the wall, seeing that it's already after ten, and the boys are still snoozing. Ari had planned to get up early to pick fresh flowers. If the others helped, they are probably already done by now. I want to go to her, but I'm not allowed to see her until the ceremony.

We aren't superstitious beings, but for us, it's more for the intensity of the moment. Women want to see our reaction when seeing the bride in her dress for the first time, even though I was the one who picked out the dress.

Tires roll up the driveway, and I smell food so I know it must be the caterers. I wake the boys and we dress quickly before meeting them outside.

It's a beautiful morning, and I smile brightly at my pack members, unable to contain my excitement for the day. My sunshine attitude must have caught them off guard based on the shock in their eyes as we shake hands.

They have brought fold-up tables, and we get to work setting them up and putting on the tablecloths while they go into the main house to start working on the food. The fresh flowers for the ceremony are already set up, and they look perfect.

Mindy brings out a box full of various vases, jars, and canisters filled with fresh flower arrangements. They must be with the centerpieces for the tables. We give her a hand, placing them where we think they should go. Ari isn't too picky when it comes to this stuff and has kept everything simple thus far.

The ceremony, the arbor, the reception area; it all looks like something out of a movie. Everything, aside from me and my men, are ready.

"Go get ready, boys. Alex and I are going to come by in an hour to take a few pictures," Mindy says. Ari had invited her last minute to attend her bachelorette party, and then Alex had the bright idea to have her help take photos when needed. Pack members are family, and always ready to help whenever needed.

"Yes ma'am," Trace drawls when I shoot her a 'thank you,' and a smile. I've known Mindy for a long time, and Ari has great taste in friends. She is surrounded in love and what will very likely be strong friendships.

Less than an hour later, we are showered and dressed in our suits. To match Ari, we wear dark brown pin-stripe pants with a matching vest over a cream collared shirt, and western tie. The vest has more buttons than there typically are, and we wear our boots to match Ari's dress the best that we can.

Before we went out last night, the boys and I stopped at the barbers to get a fresh cut and a clean shave. My hair is a bit shorter now, and I have it gelled down in a sleek look.

I smell Alex and Mindy before their knock sounds at the door.

"Wow, Darien, lookin' good," Alex looks me up and down, and I only hope I can get the same reaction from my woman. I show her my full set of teeth in return.

She takes our pictures while at the same time showing Mindy how to use the camera. We only spend a few minutes posing in the barn with the horses and then a few outside. After that she gives us strict orders to go back to our suite and to not look outside while she is taking Ari's pictures. It's almost showtime.

Not more than thirty minutes later, I hear the guests arriving. Given the all-clear, we make our way out to start greeting everyone, and try to lead everyone to their seats. Most want to talk and visit, but I want to get this show on the roll.

The music is all set to go with Gabe, the packs electrician in charge of it.

Ben is at the alter with everything he needs at the ready.

I take position at the front. Trace and Asher stand to my left, and finally the last few people take their seats.

Suddenly I'm nervous with everyone's eyes on me, their Alpha, the ruthless man who has taken territory after territory while never showing affection for anyone, and now I'm taking a bride.

There are a lot more werewolves here than I anticipated. They are all curious about the girl who is tying the knot with the Alpha after barely only one week of knowing one another. I have to admit that it does sound crazy, but it doesn't feel crazy. It feels exactly right.

As if on cue, the music begins. "Turning Page," by Sleeping At Last, plays in the speakers as Alex, in a knee-length teal dress and combat boots, walks down the aisle. Her hair is mostly up, but a few curly pieces hang free. She looks stunning, which makes me that much more excited to see my bride. Alexia now stands a few feet from the opposite side of the arbor, and she winks at me.

The tempo of the song starts to rise, and that's when she comes into view. Everyone stands, but my eyes are for her alone.

My breath hitches as she and Jerek, arm in arm, step through the doorway.

The dress on her is more beautiful and sexier than I could have ever imagined. I want to take her upstairs and peel it off her this very instant. The only thing holding me in place, is the need to claim her further. After today she will be even more than just my mate. Ari will be my wife.

She smiles knowingly at me as my eyes rake over her calf-length combat boots and her sexy legs that are only partially hidden by the dress.

Ari isn't one to wear much makeup, but Alex and Mindy must have talked her into more for the day. Other than just her typical mascara, she has added a touch of eyeliner with light browns and gold eye shadow to bring out her beautiful hazel eyes.

Her smile is breathtaking as she walks towards me with a bouquet of flowers in her hand.

Her hair has been curled, but loosely pulled into a messy, beautiful braid that wraps around her slender neck, and rests down the side of her chest. A white ribbon has been braided into her hair, and it is stunning and unique, just like her.

I can tell that she is nervous with the amount of people surrounding her, but she keeps her eyes on me as she walks down the aisle like the badass that she is.

The love in her eyes melts my insides, and when Jerek hands her off to me, I release a breath that I must have been holding since I let her go yesterday. Now I have her back, and I'm never letting go.

Ari

Walking down the aisle towards the man I never thought I would find is surreal. I never even dared to imagine a day like this. I stopped reading fairy tales when I was seven. Now I'm living one, and the man waiting for me is ruggedly handsome with a new haircut, and a suit that I can't wait to remove.

I'm shocked by the amount of people here, but with the heated look Darien is giving me, I focus on him. I walk towards him with purpose, practically dragging Jerek. He chuckles beside me, but picks up his pace so not to get hurt by me. Darien's bright whites show, all for me.

Once we reach the end, Jerek releases me to Darien whose hand reaches out for me. When my hand touches his, everything in the world is right again.

He gives me what I want and pulls me in close. His scent fills me, drowning me in his essence.

Ben's voice pulls me out of the emerald sea that was holding me captive. He continues speaking, but I don't hear most of it until he asks Darien if he will take me as his wife, to cherish and love, until death parts us.

"Hell yes. Every single day of the rest of our lives," He growls, making me shiver. The crowd laughs at his intensity, not seeing the dangerous look in his eyes that I saw at the mention of death. Ben then asks me the same question.

"I do, and death doesn't know who he is dealing with when crossing us," my mate raises a brow, but smiles at my declaration, easing some of his tension. Ben gets a bit thrown off by our unconventional responses, but quickly snaps out of it.

"Okay, do we have the rings?" he looks over to Trace, who brings forward my ring that I had to hand over last night. Darien places it on my finger with a possessive grin, and I don't even mind, cause I'm about to do the same damn thing.

Jerek steps forward, and both of Darien's brows rise this time. I wanted to surprise him, so Jerek gave me an advance so that I could get Darien a ring.

He hands the ring to me before I slide it onto my mate's third finger. Darien inspects the gunmetal band with awe. A wolf outline with one blue diamond eye and one emerald eye stares back at him, showing him that we are one. Equal in every way that counts.

"You may now kiss your bride," Ben announces, and I barely have enough time to look up from Darien's hand before his lips claim mine in front of everyone. I'm hoisted up into his arms as he deepens the kiss.

Everyone cheers, and in this instant, my heart is full. We did it. We are officially tied together in every way possible.

After the ceremony, everything goes by in a blur. Mindy takes our pictures, we eat, make our rounds greeting everyone, and Darien introduces me to pack members from all over our territory. Everyone is very welcoming, and together we laugh, dance, and party the night away.

It all feels like a distant dream when I'm in Darien's arms in our bed. He makes love to me wildly, kissing and marking me all over, claiming me, body and soul. I can't help but join his enthusiasm as he makes me fall apart multiple times before he gives me what I really want; his own release pumping into me.

"I love you, wife," he whispers as we cuddle, and the feeling that follows his words is unexplainable.

"Right back at you, husband." Hands down, this has been the best day of my life. Knowing that I'll have this wonderful man at my side, I know that there will be even better days than this to come. The excitement of topping this perfect day is the last thought on my mind before sleep takes me.

Chapter 18

We've been married a week. I have been waiting for someone to pull the rug out from under me, and I knew someone was about to when my ears pick up Darien talking on the phone. On the other line, I hear a familiar voice, and I know just who it belongs to. My father.

By the time I am dressed and down the stairs, he is clicking the call off. My husband lets me snuggle into him, but I can feel the anger building. He doesn't have to tell me anything. I already know.

The war is about to start.

That is exactly the reason I spent the first couple days of marriage training the pack, right along with the wolves from out of town. In those two days, I worked them until they could barely stand, teaching them everything I know. Darien says I left quite an impression on them. Let's just hope they had enough time to get the others trained.

Darien spends the next hour calling each leader of different parts of our territory.

Everyone able to fight has been ordered to get here, now. A few others will come too; mostly female fighters if called for back-up, but some just follow to be somewhere safe. Since we are so close to the border of those we are going to war with, it's not exactly safe, but Darien is happy to have more pack together than apart in times like these.

While he takes care of the phone calls, I send out a mass text to everyone.

"TRAINING SESSION. NOW."

They respond by promptly showing up. We don't waste time getting started. I split the group in half, trying to make each side as even in skill as possible. They all shift and I spray one group with white paint on their back and front before releasing them on each other. There is a different energy today compared to previous trainings. They are all serious and ready to put their life on the line for our pack and territory, just as I wish to do the same.

From the sidelines I bark orders, yelling tips, and correcting errors. Jerek does the same. I tell him to get in on the action with them, but I'm caught off guard when he refuses. I raise a brow at him, waiting for an explanation.

"I'm not going with them," is all he gives me. Suddenly, I feel Darien's eyes on us. Watching *us* now instead of the pack. Listening from afar.

"Why the hell not?" I ask. Is he planning to go rogue after all? Did I push too much with Alexia? They had seemed to be getting along fine. He looks at me as if I have lost *my* mind, which confuses me even further.

"I'm not leaving you," he says like it's obvious, "I'm your second, so if you're not going, neither am I."

"But they need you. You have to go," I argue before Darien's voice reaches me.

"I agree with Jerek. He *would* be a valuable asset, but I'd rather he stayed with you," he says from his place on the porch. Many emotions run through me in that moment, but I just tear my eyes away, and focus on the wolves in need of my attention.

Hours pass before the fighting ends. A few of them stop to chat and thank me for the training before they leave, but one comment in particular has my every nerve going crazy.

"I sure wish you would be there to cover our butts," Gabe had said, and the honesty in those words stun me. He isn't someone who likes to be outdone by a woman, so the fact that he is admitting something like this, shows me that I really have earned his respect.

I know that Darien heard so I turn and find him with his back turned and shaking his head as he disappears inside. You can run, but you can't hide.

Gripping Gabe's upper arm, I meet his gaze. I'm not giving up just yet, but with my own stare, I try to instill as much confidence in him as possible. He smiles and nods with determination. With that, I take off after my husband.

"It's not happening, Ari," Darien's voice booms the second I enter our home. Bastard isn't even in the room. I follow his scent. He is in the kitchen pulling out food to cook for dinner. The sight of it actually makes my stomach rumble, but I'm here for business.

"Why do you insist on keeping me out? They want me out there."

"They may *want* you, but they don't *need* you there, Ari. You gave them everything they need. You made them ready, and they are. We would have never been this prepared without you. I completely agree that you could be a great asset, just like Jerek would be, but I am not willing to sacrifice you."

"I won't die!" I scream not knowing if the words could possibly be true, but I know that I wouldn't let death come easy. He knows he needs me and that the pack wants me to be there, so why does he still fight me?

"Unless I had absolute proof, I can't risk it. I told you *someday*, Ari. That's all I can give you. I love you too much to lose you." His words are sweet, but firm. He is not going to be budged. It's not fair. It's cruel keeping me out when I have spent my whole life training to fight. My pack members could die. Darien could die. Emotions erupt in me, and I have lost all my hard-earned control. I won't run this time though. I can't keep running away if I'm going to prove to him that I'm not weak.

"I need to go. I can protect you. You don't want to risk *me*, but what about *you*? You can't die! I won't allow it!" I know I sound like a child but I can't stop the words or the sudden burst of tears that flow freely down my cheeks. So much for not looking weak.

Through my blurred vision I can see the look of absolute fear and shock on Darien's face. I haven't cried in front of anyone since I was a little kid. I especially never wanted *him* to see me cry. I'm a complete train wreck right now.

His body molds to mine, and he pulls me into his arms, taking us to the couch where he holds me like a little kid. I've soaked his shirt in my tears but he doesn't care. He rocks us back and forth as I continue to cry and scream into his chest, sounding nothing like the warrior I wanted to come off as.

Tomorrow night he will be leaving me, and I'll be wondering what's going on and praying the whole time that I don't feel the loss of a loved one through the pack bond.

"Shh, baby. I got you. Everything is going to be fine. I promise," he coos, but I'm inconsolable right now.

Darien

I was firm. I was prepared to do whatever it took to keep her out of this fight. The army we will be facing is the greatest battle we will ever go up against. Keeping her, my wife, my mate, safe is my top priority.

When the tears started streaming down her cheeks, I wanted to give her everything she demanded just to wipe the distraught look off her face. My strong, beautiful woman was falling apart at the seams, and it was my fault. Never have I seen her cry, and I never expected the storm it would cause in me. All I can do is hold her, take her hits and screams, and carry her to bed when sleep finally claims her.

After cleaning up the food I pulled out, but was unable to make, I join her in bed and hold her. Streaks remain on her cheeks from the tears, and her eyes are swollen. Guilt eats away at me but I can't give in. I need to stay strong and do right by her. Her stomach growls in her sleep, and I want to wake her to eat, but I am afraid of what will happen if I do. She needs sleep as much as she needs food.

My wolves are on their way here. Some from nearby cities like Spokane, Coeur d'Alene, Seattle area, and Missoula have already arrived. Most are staying with other pack members that they are friends with or related to. Some were supposed to stay with me, and I set up a couple in the barn, but sent the other ones to other pack members that had the space.

Ari wouldn't want anyone to see her in her state. Everyone else should be here in the morning, and in the afternoon, we will leave.

I don't get much sleep as I think about Ari, and the fact that I'll be leaving her behind. Though I want Jerek to come, I'll feel better leaving him at Ari's side. His skills match hers the closest with all the training they have done together.

I wouldn't be surprised in the least if he could take Asher now, but I know that he has no intention of being anyone's second other than hers.

It's early when I hear pack members arriving. Ari stirs as well. I kiss her cheek, and she looks bleary eyed up at me. Her eyes are still red and slightly swollen, but she looks better. She looks embarrassed, but I let her see the love in my eyes. She smiles weakly, but I will take what I get.

"Everyone is showing up. I need to go meet them. You should take a relaxing shower, and come down when you are ready." She nods at my request and heads for the bathroom as I make my way downstairs.

Her stomach growling is what actually woke me this morning, so first things first is cooking up some breakfast. I make all the bacon, sausage, and eggs in the house, cut up some fruit, and made some toast for whoever might be hungry.

The sound of the shower cuts off once I'm finished. Leaving the food for her to find, it's time to go outside to greet my men and women of war. Of course, the women, aside from Mindy, my healer, will mostly be our back up, but a few have been approved for war. Someday I will keep my promise to my mate, but not this time or anytime soon.

An hour later, Ari and the pack have eaten, and not a crumb is left. The house looks like a car lot with all the vehicles parked outside.

Ari is pleasant, but I can tell that she has crawled back into herself. My strong, confident Ari is shaken and unsure. There will be hell to pay when I get back.

Everyone has been gathered. We have a plan. In total there are about 600 wolves heading to war with me. There are 45 extra wolves, 39 of them are women, and 6 are the kids who travelled with them to stay with my mate and the remaining few that live here. Five of them are women from town, and all but one of them has a child.

Ari has never hosted so many people before by herself, but I instruct Jerek and Alex to give her a hand. They don't refuse, but the worry on their face is obvious. Looking around, I find many of my wolves sneaking glances at my woman sitting on the porch swing, lost in her thoughts.

Her lost look is affecting my wolves' confidence. They look to her more than me. She truly has an effect on them just as she has one on me. From across the lawn she feels my gaze on her and looks up at me. I look around at everyone outside with me, trying to show her what I see, and she follows my gaze.

Her eyes shoot up, bringing life back to them before she stands.

I expect her to smile reassuringly at them when they all look to her, but she surprises me by speaking out instead.

"I want to be there with you all," she begins and I start walking towards her with purpose. She can't do this in front of everyone. "And I *will* be there. Who trained you?" she asks with a growl, stopping me in my tracks.

"You did!" the majority shouts with a fire only Ari can ignite.

"Damn right I did! Use what you learned. Do whatever it takes to survive and protect your pack mates. Protect your Alpha, and make me proud!" She roars, and every single person in the crowd roars their excitement. Upset and enraged at me, she is still a fierce woman. She is a modern age God of war.

She goes inside, and I can see her crumble from the distance. I follow her and find her in the bedroom hunched over the toilet. I rush to her side, and she quickly flushes the toilet.

"Sorry, I ate too much and got a little worked up," she says weakly, and a little flushed. I help her up to the counter. She grabs a glass to fill with water and rinses out her mouth. I run my fingers through her hair and down her back.

"That was quite a speech," I smile at her. In the mirror, I see her slight smile before her eyebrows knit together. She turns back to me with a fire in her eyes.

"Please reconsider Darien. I'm ready. We can fight together," she pleads, but I'm not listening anymore. She isn't going to quit.

I didn't want to have to do this, but I think it's the only way to save her.

"ARIANNA ATHENA SHIELD YOU ARE FORBIDDEN TO JOIN THE WAR OR FOLLOW US WITHOUT MY SAY SO," I pour every ounce of my power into my command. She staggers back in shock. "I need you here baby. I need you to be here for the women and children while I'm away. You will forgive me one day."

She turns away from me, and her rejection is the worst thing I've ever felt, but it needed to be done.

"I'm sorry, Ari. I love you," I say hoping that she will look at me, but she never does. I kiss her forehead then walk out the bathroom door.

After everyone says their goodbyes, much sweeter than my parting with Ari, we squeeze into about 100 large vehicles and make our way to the Spokane airport.

Our pack mate in Seattle, Gray Fuller, is sending two large planes to bring us to him. We will be meeting up with him, along with almost 300 more of our wolves that reside in the area. From there we will rest, then those same planes, plus another, will be dropping us off in Canada near Kluane National Park. From there we will travel in wolf form, hopefully sneaking up on the group Alpha Wilder's men came across preparing for battle near Alaska's border.

Ari never comes down, but I find Ari watching out the window from our bedroom upstairs. Women, children, and Jerek wave us on. I can't think about the mess I'll be coming home to. Focus is what I need so that I can make it home.

Ari

He left. Darien took my freedom of choice away, and he got in a car and left me behind. I knew that everything in my life was going too perfect. It's like the last few weeks never happened, and I am still back in Alaska with no life and no real choices of my own.

"Hey," I jump and turn to see Jerek standing in the doorway. My self-pity is clouding my senses.

"What's up?"

"I know you're mad and upset with Dar—"

"Don't!" I snap. "Do not defend him. Not right now."

"I'm sorry, I won't mention him again, but we have a shit ton of people downstairs to take care of," he says, and I can sense the stress in his voice. He's right. No matter how upset I am, I won't let it destroy me. I am still the Alpha's mate and wife, and I have a job to do.

Together we head downstairs and find everyone sitting around chatting. I expected sadness and stress in the group, but they all seem relaxed and confident. Maybe I should feel the same, but I feel anything but calm.

Alexia's eye catches mine, and I make my way to her. She seems unfazed just like everyone else here. Of course, the guy *she* likes is still here, safe and sound while the love of my life is in danger. Why does no one here care? Why do I have this need to fight, while so many others are content with the way things are?

Every eye in the room openly stares at me, sensing the storm of emotions coursing through me.

My problems shouldn't be made theirs though, so I try to rein them in.

First, we need to figure out where everyone is staying. Alex can stay with me, and Jerek offers to take the couch, so we need to figure out who gets the remaining six bedrooms. It's like picking battle partners. I can do this.

With my friends help, we assign two females and each of their children to the king suite in the barn. For the four remaining children, I give them the last king size bedroom since they can all fit in the one bed together.

That leaves six women to split the remaining three queen size rooms. That leaves 18 under my care, plus Jerek and Alex, and a remaining 27 that need to find a place to stay.

The last four other women that live in town are here, and offer their space for them, but I don't want to spread us out too thin.

I have trained some of these women, and they are good fighters, but when all the men leave, we are vulnerable to other attacks. If other packs get word of battle, they will try and steal the women left behind.

So, maybe keeping them rounded up would be counterproductive, but I'm hoping strength in numbers is key.

After the details are taken care of, the women have gone to their arranged homes, and I sit alone outside, trying to calm my nerves. I can't help wondering if they have made safe passage so far. They only planned to fly into Seattle tonight to meet with the rest of the pack before flying into Canada. They could easily have wolves working in the airport though, and they would easily sniff out hundreds of foreign wolves. Our only hope is that their resources there have been pulled for the attack on Alaska's pack.

We predict that they are trying to take back British Columbia first. Even though there is a dense population of wolves there, taking them out or getting them to switch to their side would be a huge hit for us.

Footsteps and laughter erupt as the front door opens, and the children come running out of the house. Though they are all different ages, they play together easily without a care in the world. They wrestle on the lawn in front of me, and watching them is a nice distraction.

Only a few minutes go by before I can't sit still anymore. I want to join in on the fun.

As I approach, they look at me, and it saddens me to see fear in their eyes. I guess my actions in the past few hours have been less than impressive.

"Want to learn how to really fight?" I smile, and their eyes widen in excitement. They all scream, so I take that as a "yes". That's all that I need for me to switch into training mode.

In this moment, there is no war. My husband isn't gone. I am just a trainer doing what I know best.

Training the kids takes much more patience than my other pack mates, but it's also more fun, as it isn't nearly as serious. Someday I may be *really* training these youngsters for battle. Maybe by then I will be able to fight alongside them.

I show them how to fight in their human forms, how to work together as a team, and most of all, how to defend themselves against a stronger opponent. When I assume that they have had enough, they tell me that they want to learn to fight in wolf form too. Who am I to turn down kids that want to learn? I smile and shift, shaking my clothes off, and they follow suit.

Suddenly, Jerek's wolf is beside me. I smile, and we do a mini demonstration, keeping our pace slow so that they can track our movements and learn.

Together we turn our attacks on the children and it's three against one for both of us.

Their wolves are beautiful and spunky, but all six of them together wouldn't be able to take one of us down. Not yet anyways, but two of them stand out from the rest; the only girl, Madilyn, and a boy named Cole.

When we are all tired, I look up to find everyone watching us from the porch.

The tension they felt towards me earlier seems to have dissipated, and the rest of the evening is easier to bear.

My stomach burns with hunger so I go inside to shift and change before making my way to the kitchen. Feeding twenty people is a first for me, so I make a giant pot of potato cheese soup, rolls, and a large salad with all the fixings.

Together we eat, and I find myself surrounded by kids. They all gush excitedly about my wolf and my fighting skills. Each one of them is pumped to learn more and begin more training. I thought they would get a good night's sleep after everything today, but I forget that werewolf pups are full of unlimited energy. I have to admit that they are a blast, but I'm going to have to hide the sugar from them.

I didn't have to worry though. Right after their tummies are full, exhaustion seeps in. Their mothers smile gratefully at me before taking them to bed.

After three helpings of dinner, I'm tired as well, and I look to Jerek to ask him to tuck me into bed.

"Not a chance," he says before the words can even leave my mouth, and Alex laughs as I pout.

We all hang out in the living room chatting, but I find it hard to keep my eyes open. I try my best to get to know everyone, and I am genuinely interested in their conversations about the kids that Jerek and I trained and played with today, but it's not long before I fall into nothingness.

Chapter 19

Waking in my bed next to Alexia, I realize Jerek must have had to carry me to bed after all. The thought makes me laugh, but a pain in my stomach cuts it short. I run to the bathroom, barely making it in time to release part of my dinner into the toilet bowl.

Worry for my mate consumes me. Is something happening to him, and it's affecting me? I brush my teeth and wash my clammy face.

Alex is gone when I come back into the room. I must have grossed her out, or she wanted to find a bathroom not being contaminated by me. I crawl back into bed, dizzy from losing contents in my stomach. Half an hour later, I hear a car pull up and get up to look out the window. It's Alex. Where the hell did she go so early this morning without telling me?

Someone is making breakfast downstairs, and I am surprisingly hungry now. I change into clean clothes and am about to go meet everyone before Alex comes back through my bedroom door.

"Hey, where did you run off to this morning?" I ask, and she watches me warily. My already shot nerves spike at her shadiness. Using all my senses, I tune into her, watching her every movement. Time stands still as I wait for her to do whatever she came up here for.

For the first time, I realize that she is holding a little black plastic bag. Hesitantly, she lifts it and pulls something out. I tense for whatever it may be but it looks harmless enough, until she turns it for me to see what it says. My breath catches in my throat.

"Have you and Jerek been having sex?" I ask in alarm.

"What?" her eyebrows raise before she shakes her head, "No!"

"Then why do you have a pregnancy test?" my own brows pull together in confusion, and she looks at me like I am an idiot.

"For you, Ari. I think you are pregnant," she says gently as if she is trying not to spook a timid animal.

"What? Why on earth would you think that?"

"Come on, Ari. The mood swings. Puking two mornings in a row. I slept beside you last night, and I can smell your hormones starting to intensify. It could just be all the stress, but I think you should at least take a test to be sure."

I stare at her for what feels like forever. Can I really be pregnant? Well of course I can. Darien and I have been having unprotected sex for weeks, but most female werewolves don't get pregnant this early on. There has to be another explanation. Werewolves have shorter pregnancies, and therefore we get symptoms sooner, but if I'm already showing signs, that would mean we would have conceived in one of our first couple times.

I'll take the test and prove her wrong. She needs to see that it's just not possible to get pregnant this easily. Taking it from her, I head to the bathroom.

Not three minutes later I'm staring at a stick that has a stupid plus sign on it. It's clear as day, but I still can't believe it.

Alexia comes in without even asking and looks at the stick in my hand. She puts a reassuring hand on my shoulder. I can feel the giddiness in her, but I personally don't know what to think.

I'm pregnant with Darien's child. I never imagined having my own kids. I'd never imagined finding a mate, and I didn't want my kids to grow up in a world with no choices, so I never even entertained the idea. Why the hell didn't I insist on using protection?

Darien and I had talked about kids once before, and in that moment, I was actually excited about the idea. We haven't discussed it since though, and I assumed that I had time to consider the possibility. How could I have been so wrong? Even my mother took over a full year to become pregnant, then another three before she had me.

"Hey, is everything okay up here?" Jerek's voice cuts into my thoughts. "Something smells different," he wrinkles his nose before glancing at what I'm holding, "Whoa, are you pregnant?"

The fact that he scents something off in me as well, confirms it for me. I'm truly pregnant. There's no denying it anymore. My hand goes to my belly. A little piece of Darien and me is growing inside. And he left us. I go back to the bedroom and stare out the window.

With a "Congratulations", and "We're here if you need anything," Alex and Jerek leave me with my thoughts.

I slide the window open for some fresh air.

Darien is heading into war with no guarantee of returning to me, and he has no idea of the condition he has left me in. I won't raise this baby without him, or under the rule of another leader. He needs to come home to us.

Without even having to think about it, I leap out the window. When I land, something holds me in place. Darien's stupid command. I can feel the power he put into it, and it's stronger than anything my father has thrown at me. He really wants me to stay put.

Too bad.

For my third time ever trying, I break the command with ease. In the next second, I'm a wolf, running west into Washington.

I can get to Spokane and fly straight from there to Canada and probably get there close to when they arrive. Whatever it takes, I'll do it.

My senses are in high gear, and I know I'm being chased.

I smell Jerek first, but I sense another further behind. I can outrun them, but I don't want to push my body too hard when I am with child. It will be easier to take out my pursuers first. I'm posed to attack when Jerek comes into view.

He blows right passed me, then turns to look back, wondering why I've stopped.

Just as I thought, Alex's scent reaches me next, and it's not long before she finds us. They both look at me, waiting for direction. I forget that I am in charge when Darien is away. They know I shouldn't be doing this, but three is better than one. Do I really want to put my two best friends in danger? No. But if we can make it there in one piece, the three of us could make a difference.

My decision is made.

They flank me as I take the lead, but before I get up to speed, another scent catches my nose. This must be what they call "pregnancy nose". It's a familiar smell, but it's too far away to tell so I follow it. Once I'm closer to the fresher scent, I know with certainty exactly what it is. I stop in my tracks, and my heart sinks into my stomach.

Alpha Flint is here.

Jerek and Alex whine as the scent of foreign wolves meets their noses. Together we realize exactly what's going on.

The army gathered outside of the Alaskan border was a ruse to leave our packs women and children unprotected. John Flint and his men could be hiding nearby, or already on their way towards the women and kids that I left behind.

We need to get to a phone to call Darien, *now.* I start sprinting back towards home with my wolves on my heels. I can feel their urgency to return as well.

Suddenly, I am reminded of my telepathic communication with my mate. We've never tried to use our ability at a distance though, and if he isn't in wolf form then I am screwed. All I can do is try.

Unfortunately, we are probably going to be screwed no matter what. They will never make it back to us in time.

Darien! I focus on him, our love, our connection, and pray that he can hear me.

Darien

We quickly make it into Seattle. I call Alpha Wilder for an update. His men are at the ready, but so far there has been no movement. Are they giving us time to get there and get organized? Something doesn't seem quite right. My gut hasn't steered me wrong so far, so I listen to it, and even though we are all ready to change plans and go ahead with the next step, something is telling me not to go any farther.

There are lots of forests in the area so I order everyone that doesn't have anywhere to stay to go to the woods to hunt and rest before we leave in the morning. We park our cars in a visitor parking lot, which is typically used by hikers and off-site campers. Technically we fit the bill.

Hiking into the woods, we deposit our clothes somewhere safe and shift. It's not often we get to run with basically the whole pack nor hunt together. In fact, I don't think we have ever had so many wolves together like this. There's excitement in the pack, and we run, hunt, and even play together. Life like this is so much simpler.

In the morning, a surge in my power wakes me. Ari's emotions have been going haywire since yesterday so maybe she needed a pull of power to settle down. I don't have time to dwell on it though. We need to get moving. Everyone else is still asleep so I gently start waking everyone. Waking nearly a thousand wolves takes a while. Maybe I should have just commanded them awake, but that would set a bad tone for the day.

Once everyone is awake, we go in hunt of our stashed clothes, wallets, and cell phones. Apparently, we ran pretty far into the woods last night because it takes over half an hour to reach my items.

I am mid-shift when Ari's terror laced voice brings me to my knees. My wolves whine around me as I stop my shift.

Darien! I've never heard such fear in her voice before.

Ari? What's wrong? Where are you? How am I able to hear her when she is supposed to be hundreds of miles away?

Oh, thank God! I was coming after you, but I didn't get very far.

Dammit Ari, how did you break that command? I had put everything I had into that.

Not important right now, Darien! THEY ARE HERE! She screams at me through our connection, sounding nothing like my strong woman, and her words shoot ice into my veins.

Who, Ari?

Alpha Flint! And God knows how many of his wolves. My gut clenches at her statement, and I puke every bit out. I'm such a fool. I played right into their hands, and left my woman in danger. My nightmare from the other night is coming true.

Jerek, Alex, and I are heading back to protect the women and children now. I'm so sorry that I left them.

No Ari! RUN AWAY! Find safety until we get back. We will try to contact the others and let them know to do the same. You three need to save yourselves. That's an order.

Do what you have to do Darien. Give the women a heads up, but I'm not going to hide. Just as you told me before, I need to be there for the women and children. It's my duty to protect them.

I'm already running out of the woods to a car, not giving a fuck if anyone sees my wolf. However, I stuffed all of my clothes and other items in my mouth so that I would have them when I needed them. I feel the pack following, and I know they sense that something is wrong, but my focus is on my mate.

Ari, be serious. You are strong, but you can't take on a whole army by yourself. For my sake, please, go somewhere safe. I will find you.

Maybe I was a runner once, but the woman you married is different. I won't leave them behind. I will get them and myself to safety if I can. She says stubbornly, even though she is scared out of her mind.

My woman isn't dumb. She knows it could be a suicide mission, but she won't give up without a fight. I want to argue further, but it's pointless. A command can't hold her and she won't change her mind.

Fine! I'm coming, Ari. Please get to safety or hold them off until I get there. DO NOT DIE! YOU HEAR ME? YOU ARE NOT ALLOWED TO DIE!

I love you too, she whispers, and it breaks my heart.

I love you, baby, and I will tell you in person soon. I need to shift now, I tell her as I reach the edge of the woods. Since it's now broad daylight, I need to be human and get to a vehicle.

Wait, I need to tell you something.

Can't you tell me when I get there? Though I'm curious, I want to hear that she has hope. I want to know that she is going to be strong for me until I can get to her.

No, I think it's important to tell you now, she says but it doesn't sound like she actually believes that or not.

Okay, tell me quick, baby.

I'm pregnant.

A howl rips from my throat, and the next thing I know, I'm in a car. The fastest car in our fleet; a BMW X5.

I don't know how I got here, or when I changed back into my human form and put clothes on. I'm not even sure how Trace, Asher and Ben got in the car with me in time before I peeled out of the parking lot. I've never been one to drive fast, but I'm pushing 120mph towards the airport.

I reach for my phone and quickly dial Gray's number.

"I need the fastest plane you have ready to go. Now!" I scream into the phone as soon as I hear his line pick up.

Hanging up on him, I hit the gas pedal harder.

Vaguely I notice that other vehicles I recognize are following, but struggling to keep my pace. I can't wait for them.

My mate, my beautiful wife is pregnant with our child, and I left her unprotected. Any fucker who dares to touch her is going to die a slow and painful death.

"Darien, what is going on?" Trace asks sternly. Shit, I forgot that no one could hear my conversation with Ari.

"Call my house and the others. The women are in danger. Ari found Alpha Flint's scent in the woods, along with his wolves. I don't know how many, but it will be more than they can handle. Tell them to run and hide if they haven't already been found," I bark out. There is a collective gasp, but they do as I say, each one pulling out a phone and calling everyone.

"No one is answering at your house, but everyone else is safe. They went straight to their cars and are leaving town," Trace informs me.

"Get someone from my house on the phone," I growl. Unsure of who exactly is staying at my place, they just start calling random numbers, hoping that one of them is there and picks up their phone.

"Hello?" I can hear a female's voice answer, and I recognize it as one of my men's mate.

"This is Asher. Are you at the Alpha's house?"

"Yes, what's going on?" Asher switched the phone to speaker.

"Danielle, this is Darien. Try not to get everyone into a panic. Ari found the scent of the Canadian Alpha while out running in the woods. We are on our way to you, but you need to get everyone out and to somewhere safe."

"All of the vehicles are gone, sir. Only Jerek's truck, and Alexia's sedan remain and they aren't here right now. There are 18 of us here, minus Jerek, Alex, and your mate," she says in a panic. Dammit!

They could just run in wolf form but their scent will be harder to track in a vehicle. Plus, if they get somewhere populated, they wouldn't dare attack without the cover of night.

"I'll get the other pack members to come pick you all up. Ari and the others should be there soon. You need to get out fast!"

"Yes sir," she says before the line goes dead.

Without me having to ask, Asher contacts the other pack members about going to pick up the wolves from my house. I pray I'm not leading them to their death.

Gray gets to keep his life when we arrive at the airport, and he has a large jet ready to go. There's only enough room for maybe twenty of my wolves, so I take everyone who was in the car with me, plus Gabe, and fifteen of my strongest that Ari personally trained when they came for the wedding.

With Gray that makes 21 of us in total. I send the rest to follow through with our original plan just in case. I may be dooming us all, but if there really is an army outside of Alaska, I would bet that the larger threat is there.

"How quickly can we get there?" I ask Gray as he prepares us for take-off.

"If the wind is with us, about an hour and fifteen minutes."

"Make it an hour," I growl.

Ari

Everyone is on high alert when we reach home. Darien said he was going to tell everyone to get out of town, but my group had no way to leave except by wolf, and that's too risky in the daylight. The whole pack is here now, with enough vehicles and space for everyone.

It's too late though.

My strengthened nose can smell them, and we can all hear a large number of vehicles in the distance moving closer to our location.

The pack has clothes waiting for me, and I quickly shift, not caring who sees me naked for once.

"We are out of time. We need to get the kids in the basement. Moms can stay with the kids," I bark orders at them. I'm not okay with separating families, and who's going to protect a child better than their own mother? "The rest of you, prepare for battle!"

Heading inside, I go to the trap door that Darien showed me on my first day, and open it up for them. My breath whooshes out of me when ten kids pile into me. They are afraid. For me, and for themselves. I kneel down and look each one of them in the eye, though I have no right to. Without hesitation, I had left them here. I should have expected something like this.

"Hey. I'm a fighter. I will do everything I can to keep them from finding you. Do you remember what I taught you?" I ask, and they all nod. "Good. Believe in me just like I believe in you. If someone dares to get passed me, be ready to give them hell."

The look of determination on their little faces makes my heart swell with pride. I hurry them down the stairs.

Each mother places a hand on my shoulder for a moment on their way down, instilling strength in me. When they are all safe, I command everyone to shift and direct half to the barn while the other half waits in the house. I have a special task for a select few though.

Trucks, SUV's, and large moving vans come speeding up the driveway and through the trees. My heart is in my throat. They must have nearly one hundred and fifty wolves, while we have less than fifty. Unconsciously my hand drops to my belly, giving me surprising strength, and I smile.

They won't be leaving with that many.

Chapter 20

With as much inner strength as I can muster, I step out into the opening between the house and the barn to greet our unwelcome guests. Jerek, refusing to leave my side, follows at my heels. The cars stop a short distance away.

As expected, Alpha Flint, and another who I assume is his son, exit separate vehicles. They sniff the air in amusement as they approach us. I also recognize Garrett and Ryan from the night he helped kidnap me. Flint's son appears to have his second with him as well. His third must be with the wolves in Canada, leading the attack in British Columbia.

"Ari, my dear, how nice to see you again. Is it you I have to thank for rounding everyone up for us?" Flint drawls with a sadistic grin. I just stare him down, not letting him get to me, but I can't help my glare when he sniffs in my direction.

"Wow! You're pregnant already! Congrats! Meet the new and improved father of your child, my son, James."

James looks me over appreciatively as he sniffs me as well. He looks to be around the same age as

Darien. Just as large as well, but has short dark hair with pale blue eyes that rub me the wrong way. He smiles when he catches me looking, and if I had anything left in my stomach, I'd puke.

"What's the matter, boy? They leave you behind because you can't fight?" Flint laughs, but Jerek smirks dangerously in response. When he says nothing else, Flint glares before turning his icy blue eyes back to me. "We're not here to hurt anyone. This can be very civilized if everyone cooperates. Just tell everyone to behave and get into the trucks. Everyone will be well taken care of when we get home."

I pin him with an annoyed glare.

"Why do you think everyone is gathered here?" I ask, and he gives me a stupid look before I answer for him. "I discovered your scent. My mate is on his way home now. We're not here to hurt anyone," I repeat his words, "This can be very civilized if you and your son get back on your way, and get the fuck off our territory."

I know it's a long shot to believe that Darien and reinforcements will get here, but the more I stall, the better chance we have.

"Nice try, but your pack just left on a plane for Canada," he spits angrily.

"Oh yeah? All of them? Are you willing to bet on that?" I laugh when his confidence sways, and his anger flares.

"You have made a fool of me for the last time, girl," he looks to his son, "If you want this bitch, grab her and let's go. If not, I am killing her right now," James smiles and moves towards me.

I step back and take a defensive pose, but Jerek intercepts him before he can get to me.

Before I can even exhale, James Flint's body is unconscious on the ground. Holy shit! Jerek is scary when he is serious. I'm starting to get the feeling that he has been holding back against me.

"Last chance," I recover quickly from the shock, and try to pull John Flint's attention back to me when he steps towards Jerek with murder in his eyes. He glares absolute hatred at me. I know he is finally done trying to take me. He wants me dead.

Lifting his son into his arms, he backs away. His hand flashes towards his men, and they come flooding out of the vehicles. They move toward us and start their shift as car engines start up inside the barn. The barn doors are torn open.

For a second, Flint's men are sitting ducks as my girls partake in a little demolition derby. When this is all over, I'm going to be working off a lot of debt. I'll owe Jerek and a few others some new vehicles. I don't think anyone's insurance company covers werewolf damage.

My plan is working. There is blood and guts everywhere. It can only last so long though as the cars quit, or are physically stopped by our enemies.

Right on cue, the rest of my women, in their wolf form, sprint out from the house and the barn, attacking Flint's men from both sides. We are still outnumbered, but we are strong. We have to be. I can't let Darien come home to see that we failed. We can't fail him.

I shift into wolf form and hear John Flint yell out to his wolves.

"Try not to kill them all. Knock them unconscious if you can. I want those two wolves dead though!" He screams as he points to Jerek and I. His wolf growls beside me.

Many wolves turn to us, thirsty for our blood after the slaughter of their comrades. At least twenty dead, with equal amounts injured in under a minute has to be some kind of record for werewolf battles. They would have fared better if they had been in their wolf skin. Lucky for us, they weren't.

The wolves descend upon us, getting passed my women with ease. Their numbers are too great, but the fact that Flint wants them alive is a blessing. It's one thing if *I* die, but I can't stomach leading my whole present pack members to their deaths.

In my last few seconds, I watch them. I didn't get to train them personally, but I can see that they have learned a few of my moves. Each and every one of them is fighting with everything they have. Even Alex, with all the training we went through together, is a true warrior now.

Watching them in those few moments, I know that if by some miracle I lived through this, I am going to change things. These women deserve more. They deserve a choice to be a part of something bigger. They deserve to fight, to go on missions, and to be truly seen as high-ranking members of the pack if their skills prove worthy. That is my vow to them.

With that, I snap the neck of the first wolf that dared come near me. Jerek, my guard, fights valiantly, taking on multiple opponents like a force of nature. It's just like we practiced. Not a single move is wasted.

I try to keep track of everyone around me, but the surrounding wolves demand my attention. I dodge left and right, clawing, tackling, and sinking my teeth into fur and flesh, every opening I get. Bodies begin to pile up all around us.

"WHAT IS WRONG WITH YOU FOOLS? THEY ARE JUST WOMEN!" Alpha Flint is passed his breaking point. I can feel his eyes burning into me, waiting eagerly for someone to take me out. It only fuels my desire to disappoint him.

Alexia's whine distracts me, and a wolf takes the opening, biting into my shoulder. I reach around, grab him by the neck with my teeth, and flip him over onto his back before slicing his throat open with my sharp claws. I keep my guard up, but I also catch Jerek glancing over to Alex as well. He wants to help her, but he doesn't want to leave me.

Go! I try to urge him with my mind. I'm surprised as hell when he shakes his head, refusing my command that he shouldn't have even been able to feel. Somehow, he sensed me even though I'm not an Alpha. Alex yips in pain again. No one is able to help her. *GO!* I steal a little of Darien's power this time to make the command stronger, and he obeys instantly.

Jerek's departure leaves me with ten wolves surrounding me. I have never taken on this many by myself before, but I have always wanted to try. No one can keep me out of this fight, so now is my chance. It's me and you little pup. Let's see what your mama can do.

Speed is my best advantage. No one can match me in that category, so before they get to me, I choose my victim and sprint right towards him. I use my signature move and slide under his taller frame. He yelps as I grab him by the leg and do something I have never done before.

With his back leg in my mouth I use all my strength to spin, using him as a weapon to hit multiple targets in my proximity at once before launching him into one of the wolves. As I anticipated, none are dead from the blow, but two are out cold, and at least half are injured.

I don't hesitate to choose my next victim, sprinting at them again, but this time leaping over him as he moves low, assuming I'm making the same attack.

Before he can turn around, I tackle him from behind, knocking him to the ground before snapping his neck.

A wolf sneaks up behind me and catches my shoulder, narrowly missing my neck. I had dodged just in time, but after taking two bites now, my shoulder is mangled. My speed suffers from the damage, but I face off with my attacker, blocking and dodging the brunt of his attacks while watching my back at the same time.

Finally, I get my opening and rip his throat out before a great pain and sadness fills my heart. One of my pack has been killed.

Rage fills me, and I lash out at one of the wolves before I'm hit from behind and thrown through the air like a soccer ball. Fuck. My body screams at me, and my thoughts go to the little pup growing inside me. That thought alone gives me the strength to get up.

Facing my attacker, I find a huge gray wolf, and he's pissed. I almost think it's Alpha Flint, but the pale blue eyes tell me that it's his son. James recovered quickly. His coat is lighter than his fathers, but somehow, he looks more intimidating. He's fully healed while I am bleeding and aching all over.

Though I hate having to do it, I pull a little bit more strength from Darien. I'm going to need it right now.

With a roar, the gray wolf charges. I hold my ground and let him come to me.

At the very last second, I decide to dodge right and use every bit of force in my body to hit him from the side. As intended, it throws him off balance, and I pounce. He pushes me off with ease, but not before I take his ear. James howls in pain, and I'm surprised at the thrill that courses through me. It must be the high of Darien's power inside me.

James charges me again, and I meet him head on. I don't have the capacity to dodge anymore. We fight tooth and nail, trading blow for blow. He's a worthy opponent, but if I wasn't weakened from all the hits I've taken, I might have been able to win.

The snapping of teeth, the scent of blood and death, the sadness, pain, and anger I feel, all consume my senses.

This is it. This is the end of my story. Though most of my life was pathetic and shameful, my last few weeks were magical. I wish I were leaving this world with a better legacy, but I don't deserve it after today. My only hope is that Darien gets here and stops the enemy before Jerek is killed, and before all of our women are taken.

Making a risky move, I slide tackle James, and sink my teeth into his neck, but I don't get a tight enough grip.

He growls and throws me off. Before I can get away, he has me pinned. With some effort, I could probably get away, but I felt and scented Alpha Flint nearby.

In my state, there is no way I can take out two Alphas. My time is up, but I'm going to take Alpha Flint's son with me. James' wolf stands over me, ready to rip my head off.

I'm sorry Darien. I love you.

A howl nearby causes goose bumps along my skin. The raw power and emotion in that howl steals my breath. It also catches the Alphas off guard for a moment. A moment that I was going to take advantage of.

Using my back leg, I kick James off, slicing his belly open at the same time. He roars in pain before his father lunges for me with bared teeth, but I have just enough space to slide away.

John knows he is screwed now that Darien is almost here, and he gets sloppy. He leaps towards me, swiping his sharp claws at me.

Somehow, I dodge before clamping my teeth down on his front paw. I yank him forward, sending him head first into the dirt.

His face crunches against the ground, leaving him disoriented, and I don't hesitate to use teeth and claws to try and tear his head off.

James throws me off, but it's too late. I killed the bastard. I killed his father. I killed an Alpha.

Tumbling away, unable to catch my balance, he bounds after me.

Every last bit of my strength is gone, and the enraged gray wolf is poised to strike, but a large mass of fur barrels into him.

In an instant, James' head is no longer attached to his body. I used everything I had and couldn't even get John Flint's head all the way off, but this wolf tore it off as if he was taking a bite out of a muffin.

Darien. The sight of his massive wolf has never been so reassuring. He made it in the nick of time, along with a small army of wolves.

Bounding over to me, his wolf looks over mine. Seeing all the blood and my weakened state makes his eyes glow fiercely.

The baby? He asks gently, despite his anger.

I can't know for sure.

I didn't know what else to say. I couldn't lie to my mate.

With that, he howls again and leaps into the fight with his men.

Now that the Alphas are dead, these men don't have to be slaughtered if they give up, but they came here to steal and force women and children into situations that they should never be forced into.

Darien doesn't make deals with men like that. Regardless of their attempts to surrender, they are all dead men.

My girls did well. They took on an army three times the size of ours, and we only have one casualty. However, it is a loss that will haunt me forever. Someone has lost a loved one when they shouldn't have.

Looking around, I see my fierce warriors. Some have taken quite a beating, but there is a change among many of them; a fierceness they didn't realize they had in them. Most of these women, including I, have killed for the first time today. A small part of me thought it would be difficult taking another's life, but knowing that these men were here to take these women and children gave me the strength to take that step without pause.

Jerek tends to Alex, licking her wounds to help heal them, but I can see that he has some wounds of his own. Neither of them or anyone else appears to have their life in danger, so I try to relax.

Darien's presence by my side soothes my soul, and suddenly I am exhausted. His tongue laps at my wounds. It's painful yet blissful at the same time as I begin to heal. When he's satisfied, he goes inside, and I'm suddenly hurt that he just left me lying here. I'm too tired to follow after him so I stay put with all my wolves surrounding me.

Darien returns in human form, dressed, and with a blanket in his hands.

Damn, has he always been that sexy? I laugh at myself. Of course, he has. My mind apparently goes to the gutter when it's been run through the ringer.

He throws the blanket over me and through our bond, I feel him gently urge me to shift. He has learned not to command me to do anything. It doesn't have the wanted results. I do as he asks though.

He keeps me wrapped in the blanket as he lifts and carries me into our home.

"Women and kids are locked in the basement," I say through the fog that seems to thicken with every passing second.

"I smell them. I'll let them out after I put you to bed, baby," he gently lays me in our bed, pulling the covers over me, "You did good, love." And with those words I plunge into nothingness.

Darien

I'm sorry, Darien. I love you.

Those words. The pain in her voice. Every nerve in my body exploded at that statement. I was so close. I could smell the blood and death from where we landed.

In wolf form, I bolted out the emergency exit and had already started running before we touched the ground. I pushed myself faster than I ever have before.

When her words hit me, a howl with intense power and emotion rips from my wolf's throat. I'm right here, baby! Fight just a little more. I don't send the words to her so that I don't distract her, and I sure as hell am not going to say goodbye.

When they come into view, I see that Ari had been pinned by Flint's wolf, and another who I assume is his son. In the same second I spot her, she gets away.

She needs me.

My legs carry me even faster. With amazing skill and strength, I watch as she kills John Flint before I can reach her. She killed an Alpha.

Flint's son charges after her in a rage, but I slam into him. He stands no chance against my bloodthirsty wolf. His head is mine.

Ari is my first concern, along with my unborn child. When she says she is okay, I take in the wreckage behind me. The others have arrived, and I join in on taking out the remaining few men. Some try to surrender, but my wolf wants their blood. No one comes onto our territory, injures my mate and pack, and gets to live.

The gory scene displayed in front of me is unbelievable. Nearly 150 bodies litter my lawn.

Cars are wrecked and covered in blood and gore like a scene from a zombie movie. A few women had been knocked unconscious and thrown into trucks, while many others are injured, but they are all alive. All except for one.

Everyone gives me room as I make my way to Jamie's body. She was an older woman and was a nanny to a lot of the children in the pack over the years. The devastation I feel through the bond is almost crippling, and I can feel them waiting for an update. I send them all a message through our pack bond, letting them know that it's all over as I kiss Jamie's hand. She is with her husband now who had lost his life in one of our raids.

Walking to get a blanket for Ari, I notice Jerek sweetly tending to Alex's wounds, and I smile. My mate has sneakily been trying to set them up for weeks, and it looks like they have finally figured it out. They both deserve to be happy, and I have to agree with my mate. They are a great match.

Hurrying back to my mate, dressed and in my human skin, she eyes me strangely. I ask her to shift, not daring to *command* her. She does as I ask, and I scoop her up before taking her inside. Her rambling is cute as I take her up to bed. She is asleep the moment her head hits the pillows.

I want nothing more than to crawl in beside her, to hold her tight, and reassure her. This beautiful woman is carrying my child. Even underneath the scent of blood and death, I can smell the change in her. I feel like an ass for not noticing before.

It's true that I don't deserve this Goddess, but no one is taking her away from me. I'll become a God myself if that's what it takes to keep her.

Holding her hand, I realize how exhausted I am from all the stress. My mate handled the *real* hard work. Now it's my turn to take over and do what needs to be done.

I kiss her lips, tasting blood from the wolves that dared to challenge her. Putting my hand over her belly, I shake my head in amazement before I leave her to rest.

Hours have passed. While the women rested, the men and I loaded bodies upon bodies into the trucks. Jerek wanted to come, but I made him stay behind as me and a few others drive the trucks to Shield Logging. There we have a giant pit where we burn rotted wood and various other things. Together, we push the trucks filled with bodies into the pit and light them up like a funeral pyre.

Though I feel terrible for doing it, I leave them behind to bury it once it's all burned to ash. We will make a new pit somewhere else later, but I need to be with my pregnant wife.

I hurry home to her, and I am surprised to find her awake. Not only that, she is showered, dressed, and in the kitchen helping a few of the other women cook dinner for everyone. Some women are still cleaning up or resting, but everyone is surprisingly calm.

Our eyes meet the moment that I walk in. I don't hesitate to go to her. Wrapping her in my arms, I take in her intoxicating scent, not giving a damn who might be watching.

I'm so desperate for her that I'd take her right now, except my shy mate would kill me on the spot. However, when she whispers, "Take me upstairs," into my ear, it about takes me to my knees before I swoop her off her feet and do just what she commands.

Holding back is a struggle, but I make love to her slowly and sweetly. She has had enough roughness today, and I won't put our baby in any more danger. In fact, I might just retire early so that Ari and our little pup will always be at my side. I've never been one to stay out of a fight, but I've never had reason to. Now I have two reasons.

When I have taken care of our needs, I kiss her belly. We have only been together a month, and she's already pregnant. Before, I had never imagined kids, and you would think since our relationship is so new, that we would want to have more time together as lovers rather than parents, but I am out-of-my-mind ecstatic. A baby won't change my lust for my wife. Not in a million years.

Ari smiles sadly at me, and my stomach drops with worry.

"Is everything okay? Is something wrong with the baby?" I stiffen, waiting for the ball to drop. This day had turned out much better than it could have, but maybe not so well after all.

"Shh," her finger moves to my lips, "The baby seems to be fine. I'm sorry for ruining the moment. Let's go back downstairs." She tries to distract me, and moves to get up, but I pin her back down.

"Ari," I warn, "tell me what's going on." Defiance shines in her eyes, but then it's replaced by something that I never want to see on her face ever again; shame.

Something inside me snaps, and I'm no longer the tough Alpha as I cup her face in my hands. I'm sure she can see my weakness as fear overcomes me. Tears pool in her eyes, but they don't fall.

"I'm so sorry, Darien. I disobeyed. I left everyone, and then they waited on me to return. It was all my fault that we didn't get out in time!" Her voice is hoarse with unshed tears as she looks away from me. I drop my hands to my lap, unsure of how to proceed.

My wolf rears its head then, with an intense power, and my strength returns tenfold. I can feel the power in the pack, and I know they will all agree with what I say, and she needs to hear it.

"Arianna," she looks up at my sharp tone, "you would be dead right now if you hadn't broken my command. What's worse, is that every single one of you would have been taken, and I wouldn't have known until after the fact. They could have left, but they chose to stay and fight with you, not because you are the Alpha's wife, but because they love you."

She tries to process it all, but all she can see in her mind is that she abandoned everyone, that she held them back, and that she couldn't protect them all. She has more compassion and sense for what's right and wrong, more than anyone I have, or will ever meet.

Her eyes avoid mine, not believing, or perhaps not wanting to believe. Though she has plenty of reason to boast, and is confident in herself most of the time, she is also very humble. She doesn't want to believe that she did a good job when she also feels guilt. It's my fault that she feels that way.

I tilt her chin back up again, forcing her eyes to meet mine.

"I was wrong, Ari. Commanding you to stay was wrong of me. I don't always know what's best, and it was a stroke of luck that you did what you did and discovered John Flint's scent. You saved my ass. If you hadn't tried to follow me, it would have been *my fault*, not yours. You have this amazing gift to defy Alphas, and because you are such a strong fighter and trainer, and taught our pack how to fight, we survived. You, Ari, are the real reason that we are sitting here having this conversation."

The tears fall freely now, and I'm not scared of them like I was before. I know the reasons why now. Pulling her into my chest, holding her tight, I rock her until she cries it all out.

She recovers quicker than expected, and she goes to the bathroom to clean up. Her face is clear when she returns. She starts dressing, making me wonder what the hell she is doing, and she looks up at my confused expression.

"Baby's hungry," she says simply, and that's all the answer I need. I'm up dressing right along with her, and we make our way downstairs. Everyone watches us descend, and the way everyone looks at my mate is not lost on me. They have all become fierce warriors; ready to do battle for the woman I love. She is just as much their Alpha as I am.

All of the younger pup's pounce on Ari before I can stop them. She laughs and picks some up to hug them. I can see how happy she is that they are safe. Only gone a day, and they all absolutely adore her. Seeing that fills my heart, and I can't wait to bring our own child into our home. I will be the father mine never was, and I already know that Ari is going to be the best mother in the world.

After loving on the kids, she makes a plate of food that she had been helping make earlier. I join her, and we all sit together. Though there is a collective sadness for Jamie, everyone is in high spirits. Women have always been made to appear weak, and while I knew that wasn't true, their strength is far greater than I ever imagined.

While I still don't feel comfortable putting our women at risk, I can't deny them anymore. After what they proved today, we need their skills.

For now, though, I am going to enjoy the rest of my night, chatting, laughing, and watching my beautiful mate capture everyone's heart, just like she has captured mine.

Chapter 21

Ari

Darien's phone going off wakes me early in the morning. He answers, and I roll away from him. That was a mistake. I run to the bathroom, clutching my hands over my mouth before throwing up dinner into the toilet. Thank God werewolf pregnancies are much shorter than a normal human's pregnancy. My morning sickness should only last maybe a week or two.

I'm startled when a hand starts rubbing my back, but realize it's just my mate. He helps me up, and I rinse and brush my teeth before going back into the bedroom.

"Time to deal with Canada?" I ask him. He nods in return. "So, what's our plan?" I wait for him to tell me again that I can't go with him. I'm not sure I have the strength to fight him on it again. After yesterday, I still feel guilt heavy on my heart, but at the same time, Darien's words were true. I should be happy about the outcome of yesterday's events.

"You're pregnant, Ari," here we go, "I am a fool to bring you, but I would be an even bigger fool to leave your side again. I try to learn from my mistakes." Wait, what? Our eyes meet. Is he serious?

"You mean you're not just nice to look at?" I tease, making him laugh softly.

"Everyone is coming. We are going to meet at the border with your father's pack and the rest of our pack to figure out what to do from here." There is no humor in his voice, so he must be telling the truth. He's not going to leave us again.

I leap into his arms, and he catches me with ease. Our lips meet, and it's as if all my confidence has been restored. Without even a fight, I am making good on my promise to myself and to the women of my pack. We won't be left behind and will never be without a choice.

As I get dressed and pack a couple items in a small bag, Darien goes to tell everyone the game plan and to get ready to move. Gray already has a plane ready for all of us.

It didn't take us long to get organized. Together with our remaining vehicles, we headed to the airport and boarded our plane.

Darien held my hand the entire time and kept trying to talk about baby names, but I haven't quite gotten that far with everything that has been going on. Our flight is short, and when we land, I realize that I am excited to see everyone.

We land in Alaska not too far from the border of Canada. We aren't far from the pack so we decide to shift and run with our belongings in our mouths or strapped to us. Darien and I take the lead while everyone else follows closely behind us.

I feel at home again, recognizing certain smells and even catch the scent of some old pack mates.

When we aren't far, we shift and change back into humans before getting dressed. Without having to ask, Darien shields my body as I change. I didn't care much yesterday since it was just the women and Jerek, and I am surprised to find that I don't really care today either, but I would rather be covered than not.

The sound of people coming alerts us before they come into view. Even from afar, I recognize dad, Charles, and Niko at the head of an army of people. My group stops a short distance away, but I close the distance to my father. He engulfs me in his arms with a huge grin plastered on his face. I hear him sniff me, so I lean away to look at his face.

"Ari! You're pregnant? Already?" he asks in disbelief. I guess Darien didn't fill him in during any of their conversations. I nod at him with a smile, and he looks so happy for a few moments before he frowns, "And you *fought* yesterday in this condition?" *And Darien brought you here to yet more danger*, he says with his eyes as he glares at my mate over my head.

"Well she needed some kind of handicap to make it fair," Niko laughs, making me grin.

"And she still handed their asses to them," Charlie adds in, and suddenly everyone around us joins in the laughter.

Despite his anger at Darien, he looks proudly at me, and I know he can see the changes in me. I'm not his disgruntled little girl anymore. I'm happy and strong in a way I wasn't before. Darien steps forward to shake my dad's hand as I take turns hugging my uncles.

Backing away to stand beside my mate, he tucks me into his side a little possessively. He still doesn't like other males touching me.

They all see his display and smirk, but I could care less. As long as he doesn't take it too far that is. I am his, and he is mine after all.

"Let's go somewhere where we can sit down and discuss things comfortably," dad suggests and starts to lead the way with Charlie and Niko flanking him. Our pack leaves to intermingle with theirs, and I know the women must be tracking down their mates. I follow my mate of course, and Jerek follows me, along with Trace, Asher, and Ben.

We go into a large tent with tables and chairs. Dad frowns when he turns to see how many people followed us. Darien dismisses them, and everyone moves to wait outside. That is, everyone but Jerek. Darien looks at him, but lets him stay. As if he could make him leave anyways. Jerek is a huge part of the reason I'm still here, so my mate wouldn't dare send him away.

My dad and uncles look between the three of us, but say nothing.

"There's still an army waiting on the other side of the border. Since both of their corrupt Alphas have been terminated, they are confused on what they should do. There is no point in unnecessary bloodshed, so I suggested a temporary truce and a meeting between Alphas.

"That's reasonable," Darien remarks from deep in his thoughts, thinking of how to proceed. "We will give them a chance and see what they have to say. I'd like to be the one to do most of the talking."

It's quiet for a moment. Darien didn't ask for permission, but he doesn't demand it either. This is why Alphas shouldn't be in the same room together, or have conversations at all.

"What do you plan to say?" my father finally speaks.

"Not sure yet. I'm just going to wing it and see what happens. Unless you have come up with a better plan?" he questions my father, stunning him for a moment. I can see that he doesn't have a plan either. No plan is unfortunately the best we have.

"Very well then. Choose three people to take with, and I will take these two with me as well. We agreed on seven each."

He tried to leave me behind with the rest of the pack. I wasn't having any of that, no matter what he threw at me. Bullshit about not wanting to upset my father, and that I shouldn't push so much in my state. Whether I go with or stay with the pack, I could die, so I am going with, and so is Jerek. Trace fills spot number three, and we make it to our meeting place.

Our pack isn't far behind, and neither is theirs. We can smell the large number of foreign wolves, and I flash back to when I came across the same scent yesterday. This could all still go down as a war that would most likely wipe us all out being that we are a not even half the size of Canada's army. We had the same odds against Flint and his men though, so who knows.

Our meeting place is in one of the free territories on Canada's side, that way no one feels the extra threat of an enemy on their territory.

We arrive first to a field in the middle of nowhere, surrounded by trees, but there is a small cabin on the edge of the forest. Apparently, a wolf and his mate vacation here for peace and quiet, but no one is here today.

Seven foreign wolves enter on the other side of the clearing as we wait near a picnic bench by the house.

They move timidly, watching their surroundings. None of them have been in power before and their weakness is showing. Some look angry while others look slightly lost.

I look to the men in my life. Even in this shit storm situation, they each have masks of ease. Showing your emotions to your enemy can get you killed. What are they teaching them over here?

Two wolves stand in front of their group, and I assume one is James's third, while the other was John's fourth being that their predecessors were killed on my property. My mate and my father take the lead in our group, but I stay just behind Darien. I'm prepared to protect him just as much as he is ready to protect me, along with his child that I am carrying.

My father speaks first, introducing himself again, and his son-in-law, Alpha Darien Shield. The two at the front stiffly introduce themselves as Patrick and Henri. They both glare openly at my husband. A couple others look disgruntled as well, but there are two in their group that appear unconcerned about their fallen Alpha's, one of which keeps staring at me.

"You killed our Alphas!" Patrick shouts at Darien, unable to keep his emotions in check. Darien laughs darkly at his statement.

"Your Alphas tried to kidnap, rape, and force my wife into marriage. When they failed, they entered *my* territory. Attacked and killed *my* women and children like cowards," only one woman was actually killed, and all the children were safe, but he knows not to rub it in their faces about how badly they failed, "and you expect them not to pay the price?"

Patrick growls, but Henri hushes him before he speaks.

"Even if they did, what is there to stop us from retaliating?"

"To give you a chance, son," my father speaks calmly, trying to divert attention away from Darien, "We don't have to have war. We can all just live peacefully."

"Oh yeah, is that why you teamed up? To live *peacefully* beside us?" Patrick spits.

The crap John Flint and his son have been feeding his men is poisonous. How can we reach an agreement if they truly see us as enemies?

"Believe what you want," Darien chimes in again, "but our agreement is only to deter threat from outsiders. We're only here to help you. Canada is a large area with a lot of wolves to control."

"Fuck you! We don't need your help. We do have a lot of wolves. Plenty enough to eliminate both of your packs!" Patrick is asking for death, and I step in to speak, but I keep my voice calm. Dad tries to stop me, but Darien silences him.

"You don't think you will have a huge loss on your side? Maybe you could wipe us out, but how many of your wolves have trained for war? With the amount of wolves that you have, no one would dare try to invade your land unless everyone in the US packs joined to take you out, which you are asking for if you insist on war. My pack is trained for this. We may not win, but we are much stronger than you think."

"Why is there a woman here?" the one that has been staring at me finally asks at the same time Henri asks, "Why would the US packs join forces to take us out?" I choose to answer Henri, but Darien growls quietly at the other man's comment.

"Because by attacking us, you threaten everyone. Greediness is what killed your leaders, and by continuing this war, you are asking for the same fate."

"Who is she? Why did you bring a female?" the stupid man asks again. Jerek moves a little closer to me, and I can feel the annoyance in my group. No one dares to speak for me, and I love them all for it.

"I am Arianna Shield, and I am here because I choose and deserve to be," I say confidently. He stares at me, unsure of what to say, and they all watch me now, wondering why Darien would bring his pregnant wife along.

"But you're a woman and pregnant at that. Why did you bring your mate, Darien? I don't understand," the man asks, and Darien smiles as he tries to hide his anger. He doesn't have to answer the fool, but he is trying to keep peace.

"My pregnant mate is the one who killed Alpha John Flint. She is a skilled fighter, and so are the rest of the men and women in my pack. The world is changing, boys," he remarks, and some of them look fearful and angry, but others are in a state of disbelief.

They assume that I had help, and that there's no way I could have killed an Alpha on my own. Young women like me aren't allowed to go to war so they don't believe we have an army of men and women waiting to fight.

To be honest, I can hardly believe it myself. I just hope we don't all die today.

"Prove it," he challenges.

Both Darien and my father bristle at the comment, losing composure, and the other guy chuckles darkly.

"Prove she is strong enough to take on an Alpha on her own. She can take on our strongest fighter, and winner gets to decide what happens next."

Something changes in his expression, and I realize that we have misjudged this group.

"By the way, I am Simon, the current Alpha. Patrick and Henri are my seconds."

"No! We can make peace another way," Darien refuses venomously.

"What's wrong? No faith in her? What a joke. Your lies will prevent us from ever becoming allies," Simon growls.

My group struggles to keep their calm. His offer is tempting, but no one wants to risk me. If we turn him down, we risk an all-out war. Darien ponders silently. He tries to hide it, but I can see the internal war is breaking him.

"Darien! You can't seriously let this happen," my father shouts at him.

My mate ignores him and looks at me. His dark emerald eyes bore into mine searching for the answer. I stare right back into his, unwavering. I've never had so much at stake, but Simon made a mistake by seeing me as the weakest one here, and he made an offer we can't refuse. Darien's eyes shift to my belly. My mate wants to refuse more than he wants to give in, but letting me fight may save us all.

Finally, he nods, and I smile at him with all the love I have.

"No!" my father shouts again, but he knows he can't stop me. He has never been able to before. I look around me at everyone else. Charlie and Niko smile and give me a thumbs-up, Trace smirks with arms crossed over his chest, and Jerek looks as confident as he always does, but I can see the tightness of his jaw. Jerek wants to take my place, but knows he can't.

"We accept the offer. Whoever wins gets to decide on who gets what territory. Agreed?" Darien looks at each wolf's face, waiting for each to nod. They reluctantly do. None of them believe I can win, except one who looks a little unsure.

Simon strips out of his clothes to shift. Darien covers me even though my men divert their eyes. Some of the other men stare openly at me as I strip behind the cover of my mate and shift.

When I am fully in wolf form, my mate pinches my tail. I turn to find him smiling at me. He doesn't say anything. This is not the end. He believes I will come out the victor, or at least that's what he is showing me, and hides how he really feels.

Simon's wolf is light gray with a white chest and white paws. His eyes are pale blue like James's, and I wonder if they are related at all. He sizes me up as everyone gives us space.

A sudden wave of nausea comes over me from shifting multiple times today and being pregnant of course. Unable to hold back, I puke in front of everyone. I should have eaten before we came out here. My pregnant body needs more food to keep up with this new lifestyle.

I can feel the worry in my men nearby, and I see Simon's wolf's lips rise into an evil smile. He takes the opportunity to charge as I move away from my own vomit.

His wolf leaps into the air as I dart away and get a quick shot from behind with my sharp claws.

Growling menacingly, he quickly turns his body to snap at me, narrowly missing my face. His agility, even when off balance, reminds me of my own fighting style.

We tumble, but both recover quickly. I try to get away, but he catches me by the leg. He pulls me towards him, and I let him, surprising his wolf with my front paw across his face. It causes him to release me, but I'm fine right where I am.

Using our close proximity, I swipe and snap at him, releasing my anger and frustrations upon him, fighting more like a lioness than a wolf.

He becomes a bloody mess, but catches my upper front leg with his teeth. I howl with pain and he throws me, making me land awkwardly on my injured front leg. I'm able to stand when he charges me with fury, and I should leap away, but with my injury, staying low is my best option until I know exactly how bad I'm hurt.

I take a pull from Darien's power to heal quicker.

Simon smiles when I charge him, and just like the first time I fought with Jerek, I slide under his legs, and use my shoulders to send him sailing. When I did the same thing to Jerek, he had recovered quickly, but Simon is disoriented.

Before I can charge, he stands and turns to me. His eyes glow with anger, but he looks wary now. He finally realizes this isn't as easy a task as he thought. Did he not understand that when my own mate allowed me to fight?

Frustrated, he finally comes for me again. I expect him to come in low so that I don't pull the same trick again, but he stays level. His goal is to overpower me with his size, leaving me only one option, one shot to execute, or I could be dead.

He is only feet away as I rise up on my haunches like a bear. The move leaves my vulnerable underside exposed, but the instant before he makes contact, I slam all my weight down on to his face, shoving him into the ground. Simon struggles against me as I slash at his throat. His claws slash at me to get me away, but this needs to end now.

Taking a few scratches, my teeth latch on to his throat, and I shake him with every bit of strength I have, breaking his neck. As his life seeps away, the painfully familiar sound of gunshots rings out.

No!

My ears ring as my senses tell me to hit the ground. With nothing to hide behind, I make myself as small as possible. Werewolves hate guns. Only cowards use them. I can only hope their aim is poor.

Time seems to slow down as I frantically search for my men.

I'm frozen in place as a strange force takes over my body. Only a second passes when my eyes land on my father's crumpled form. Ice runs through my veins at the sight. The ice shatters a breath later when the guns point towards Darien.

Before I can do a thing, my amped up senses alert me to the sound of the trigger pulling. My mate goes down. Trace is sprawled out on top of him with a bullet wound in his shoulder that is bleeding profusely.

Jerek rushes to shield me, while the rest of my little family ducks for cover, but there's nowhere to go.

Only two of the men hold guns, while the other two appear shocked as they start to back away.

My furious mate slides out from under Trace's body. His eyes find me first to make sure that I'm unharmed before redirecting his attention to the men holding the guns.

Still locked in place by some unseen power, my heart stops as he charges the gunmen taking aim at him.

Stop! I shout with a roar, grabbing a hold of the power filling me. It's all I can do because I won't be able to help him in time.

Something freezes the gunmen. Their fingers continue to hover over the triggers, but they don't pull it as the enraged Alpha tears toward them.

My body trembles with the foreign power as I look around to see what the hell is going on, but find nothing out of the ordinary.

An idea hits me.

DROP YOUR WEAPONS! I command.

When they do just that, I just stare in shock.

Chapter 22

The world is changing, Darien's words from earlier repeat in my head. Did he see something like this happening? Those words couldn't be more true right now if I just became an Alpha.

Darien's wolf sprints across my vision. In the next second the gunman, Patrick and Henri are dead. I feel the loss of them through this new strange bond. I couldn't have stopped Darien even if I wanted to, which I didn't. In his rage, he leaps for the other two wolves from Canada's pack, and I can't let innocent lives be lost.

Darien! Stop! And he does, but he doesn't take his eyes off the others as they cower back from his ferocity.

Why the hell are you telling me to stop? He growls at me.

This is going to sound crazy, but I think I'm their new Alpha. He doesn't respond for a while.

Are you sure?

Hell no, but he didn't pull the trigger again, did he? His silence is answer enough. I want to go to my father, but I can't until I figure out what's going on.

Moving to join Darien, I look at each of them. Every single one of them drops their eyes.

Holy shit, Darien speaks the words I was thinking, *you* are *their Alpha. But how, and why don't I feel threatened by you?* That last question I can answer.

Because we're true mates.

Another wolf comes into the clearing, and I recognize Mindy's amber coat. Darien must have called her to us through the bond. She shifts, and though naked, she goes straight to checking on Trace and my father. I don't watch. I don't want confirmation that they're dead.

Jerek brings my clothes to me so that I can shift and talk to my pack. Him and Darien do their best to shield me, and I dress quickly. I'm coated in blood, Simon's and my own, but my injuries heal quicker than they ever have before. It must be because of the pack energy flowing into me as their Alpha. I look at the remaining four men, and get right to the big question.

"Am I your Alpha? Is that what your wolf is telling you just as mine is telling me?"

"Yes," one of them steps forward, "you both actually feel like Alpha, but I feel you more than your mate right now. His presence seems to be slowly growing through the bond." He comes forward to kneel at my feet, and he takes my hand, "I can feel something in you that I have never felt before. I sensed it before you became Alpha. I thought maybe it was just the pregnancy."

"Okay," is the only thing I can form right now.

"My name is Macen by the way, and I will be a strong and loyal second to you."

Jerek snorts.

"Don't bet on it," he takes position next to me with a *'don't fuck with me'* sneer. Macen glares at him, but backs off. Poor guy has probably never been a second in his life.

"Well, stay here," I order them. "I'm going to go check on my people who were shot," then I sprint back to my father.

Mindy is covered in his blood, but at least she is wearing Niko's shirt now. My tears start to well up, seeing my father lying there helpless as she pulls a second bullet out of his chest. I can see that he is breathing, but just barely. Charlie shifts and comes forward to lick his wounds closed. Recovering from a bullet, multiple bullets, is one thing, but all the blood loss can kill a wolf.

Mindy, Jerek and Darien start helping Trace so that I can focus on my father.

"Ari," his weak voice calls to me. Taking his hand, I kneel beside him. He smiles before speaking again, "I hereby name Arianna Athena Shield the new Alpha of the Alaskan—

"No, father, you can't! You're going to be fine. Don't do this," I beg of him.

"Baby girl, even if I don't die, someone will challenge me for my position in this weakened state. And I know you don't want to put your uncle's at risk either. Let me do this. You can give it back to me later if you want to." He's right. If anyone tries to take Alpha, Charlie and Niko would lay down their lives to try and protect him.

"But I'm the Canadian pack's Alpha now. I don't think I can control so many at once," I try to think of another solution.

"Do you hear yourself, Ari? You are an Alpha of the largest pack in America, maybe the whole world, so what's a few more?" he laughs, and it makes me smile through my tears. "Your ability to break my control and your own mate's control isn't some magical ability. It's because you are dominant. More dominant than anyone I have ever met. This is your destiny."

"Fine, I will take over for now, but you are going to get healthy, and when you are healed, I'm giving it back." He smiles, and finishes his declaration this time. I am officially the Alpha of Canada and Alaska. The first ever, female Alpha.

I can feel all the lives under my command, but most of all, my protection. It's a heavy weight to bear, but it feels right.

I hear Trace come around. From my distance, I can see that he has lost a lot of blood, but the bullet has been removed from his stomach, and his wound is being licked closed by Darien himself. It's time to get them out of here, and I need to go deal with my new pack. At least, one of them, anyways.

Pulling out my phone, I call a ride for my men and tell them to have enough space for Trace and my father to be able to lie down. Asher offers to steal an ambulance, making me laugh, but he will probably do just that.

Darien and Jerek come with me, and together we follow the four men. Macen and I chat a bit on the walk. He definitely wants to get in my good graces, or maybe he is just that nice.

There's too much on my mind to concentrate. First, I'm still bewildered about the fact that I am pregnant, I killed an Alpha, well two actually, and now I'm an Alpha for not one, but two packs. I guess technically it's all one big pack, but one is just temporary.

The army awaiting us blows my mind, and I can see that my mate and Jerek are in awe as well. Thousands of people gathered in the woods.

Many different expressions greet me; anger, amusement, excitement, confusion, and respect. What surprises me most is the happiness and adoration that conquers them all. It gives me the strength to speak.

"So, I guess I'm your new Alpha," I begin, and most laugh along with me. "This is my mate, Darien Shield, and my second, Jerek Carver. I know you came here for a war started by John and James Flint, but there will be no such war, or any future wars unless someone decides to come take our land. My goal is to *grow* our population of wolves, not destroy it. If anyone has a disagreement with that goal, please search for another pack."

After a few tense moments, they all cheer. Once they have calmed down, I ask for questions and answer each and every one before I send them on their way. I told them about how we are all connected with Alaska and the PNW pack and that they can now move wherever they want in those territories.

Darien speaks as well, and they all accept him as their Alpha too, but there is something there that's different. This is all so new, that no one really knows what to think.

With excited energy, we shift and run back to our pack. Everyone greets us warmly, relieved that we are no longer going to war. Everyone is staying the night and celebrating, and I use the opportunity to speak with my old, yet new, pack that I now control.

Some are hesitant to accept me at first based on the past I have with them, but hopefully they can see the new me that I have become. The person Darien and his pack have helped me become. Even though it's only for a short time, I want to use this time to repair the damage between us.

Later that evening, Carrie Wilder struts into our camp. Holy hell. She makes a b-line for the tent my father, her husband, is resting in. I move to intercept her. Dad doesn't need the stress and anger she is about to lay on him.

"Mom," I call to her.

"Ari," she looks at me nervously, and her eyes avoid mine. Surprising her and myself, I hug her. As expected, she hesitates, but finally hugs me back, and it's the warmest interaction we have had since I was just a little kid. We pull back from each other, and she looks me over. "You look good sweetie," I ignore that part for once, "and are you really pregnant?"

"I am," my hand unconsciously moves to my belly.

"Well that Darien sure doesn't waste time, does he?" we laugh together. It's quite a moment, but I break the silence.

"I'm sorry I was such a brat growing up," the words just spill out. It must be this whole 'becoming a mother' thing. While I'm not sorry for *all* of it, I do regret that our relationship was so cold, and that I could have tried harder to get along with her.

She just stares at me for a while, and I watch all the disbelief, pain, and regret flash across her normally serene features.

"I'm sorry too, Ari. I should have tried harder as well. But look at you now. You sure showed me. Now you're Alpha of our pack."

"Only until dad gets better," I snap. Her features light right back up with that. Though I want our relationship to improve, she will still be the same Carrie. She will always want power and money. I just hope she wants to be a part of my life and a part of her grandchild's life now as well.

My mate joins us to say hello, and mom actually makes an effort to turn down the charm. It won't work for her anyways. I have this man right where I want him. He is my person, my soul mate, and the father of my unborn child. Life has never been so perfect.

Darien

From the moment our eyes met, I knew Ari was meant for something big. I would have been blessed just having her by my side, loving me, and being mine. My mate is too amazing to not be something more. There have been moments in our short time together, where her power has caught me off guard. She is a strong wolf, but there has always been something else that I haven't been able to put my finger on.

When she told me that she had somehow taken the reins as Alpha over the Canadian pack, it all clicked into place. The only thing holding her back before was her own insecurities about being good enough. In the short time with me and my pack, she found exactly who she was meant to be.

There's still something *more* to her, and maybe someday we will find out exactly what that is, but for now I'm just happy that she's safe. Watching her take on Simon was not easy for me to do, especially knowing she is carrying my baby. I'll be getting an earful from her father once he's strong enough to lay into me. Trace is going to pull through as well, all thanks to Ari. She saved us all.

Seeing the way that she took control of the hand she has been dealt, is nothing short of amazing. She spoke to our new pack members with the confidence I have watched her gain over the last few weeks. However, it was obvious that she was a little more tense speaking to her old pack mates. If only they could have seen who she truly was, they would have tried a little harder to be her friend, and she would have abandoned her idea that she needed to run away.

The moment I found out that Ari Wilder was going to be my mate, I knew things were going to change. Not in a million years would I have guessed that my life would be like this. After watching the relation between my parents, I thought I was destined for a similar fate.

As I watch her take on her new role as Alpha, and even try to make amends with her mother I know just how blessed I am. This wild woman is more than anything I could have imagined. She's my mate. My other half. My wife, and the soon-to-be mother to our pup. She's mine, and the thought makes my pants a little too tight.

I've given her time to mingle, but I'm done sharing her for tonight.

Before she can make anymore rounds, I stalk in her direction. She squeals in surprise when I lift her up and throw her over my shoulder. Without a word, I carry her towards our tent. The witnesses behind us, erupt into laughter and cheers. Ari is going to give me hell later, and I'm going to enjoy every minute of it.

My faith in her is not misplaced, but I could have lost her today. We could have lost the baby. If her command hadn't stopped the gunmen, I would have been shot too, and may not have survived. Though, everything turned out fine, I know very well that it might not have.

My wolf and I need her. We need to feel her strong pulse and smell her unique scent that is combined with my own. Her hormones are driving me crazy, and I need to be inside her.

There's a large, fold-up mat on the ground with blankets. I deposit Ari in the center of it, covering her lips with mine before she can protest. She melts into me, pulling at my clothes, needing this just as much as I do.

In the heated frenzy, I'm not sure how we ended up naked, before I'm pushing my throbbing length inside her. Ari's scream is muffled by my mouth devouring hers.

Her body fits me perfectly, and she's strong, taking every hard thrust I give her. Holding back is impossible as she writhes against me. I pump into her, giving her everything I have before I reach my release. The whole camp probably hears her cry out, and I let out a growl of satisfaction as she pulses around me.

Neither of us moves for a while. We hold each other, lost in our thoughts. Everything feels right in the world again as she snuggles against me.

She sighs contentedly when my lips press against the top of her head.

The future for our pack is unknown, but with Ari by my side, I know everything is going to be one hell of a ride.

Ari

Months have passed since that fateful day in the forest. Any day now, I am due to pop. My stomach is huge. Werewolves don't go to hospitals because humans would discover things they shouldn't. Our pack healers and doctors have most of the things we need, but we don't typically bother with ultrasounds or anything of that nature. Not unless something is wrong. And something is definitely wrong.

Darien thought I was being paranoid, but seeing how swollen I am now, has him worried as well.

He drives me to Mindy, and she sets me up for an ultrasound. I give her a death glare when she comments on my size. She listens with a stethoscope first, and I watch her lips pinch together just the slightest bit, and I about come out of my skin. My pack probably thinks I'm in trouble with all the stress consuming me.

I lift my shirt for her so that she can put the gel on and she gets her wand or whatever it's called and presses it to my belly. An image comes on the monitor, but I have no idea what it is. Darien holds my hand as he watches the monitor with me, waiting for the news.

"Just as I thought," Mindy smiles as she continues to move the wand around my belly. She takes a couple pictures. It takes everything I have not to reach out and strangle the answers out of her. She looks up at us, and smiles.

"WELL?" Darien's impatience beats me to it.

"It's twins!" I stare open-mouthed at her, trying to process what she just said.

"No seriously, what is it?"

"It's no joke. Look," she hands the sonograms to me, "there is the two heads, and more than one set of hands and feet, but the picture can't catch it all. I can't even tell what gender they are because they are so crammed in there."

"Werewolves don't have twins," I state, and it's the truth. I have never heard of wolves having twins. Or maybe I heard that only one twin could survive the birth. I'm not sure at this point.

"Now they *can* apparently, and we need to get these two out. We should have induced you weeks ago." Mindy says calmly, and I look up at Darien who is mirroring my look of terror. The two of us are anything but calm.

Mindy leaves and comes back with some sort of gel and a hospital gown for me to change into.

"Wait, are we really taking them out *now*?" Suddenly the fear of actually taking care of a child hits me, and there's going to be two of them.

"If we don't do it now, we would be putting the three of you in danger. And then we would all be in danger from Darien. So yes, your babies are coming now."

Darien starts undressing me. I turn to slap him, but the crazy in his eyes stops me. He is just as freaked as I am. So, I let him continue to help with the process. Mindy comes back and gets to work, preparing me for birth.

Hours later, I can feel the whole town of our pack members are in the waiting area of Mindy's office.

We didn't want to leave, so we stayed in Priest River, but we made a home in Canada as well, and plan to visit often. Until recently, I have been training them to fight.

As promised, I tried to give Alaska back to my father, but he refused. Apparently, he was enjoying his time off, and for now, wants to do other things with his life. He told me to gift it to his grandchild one day. Little does he know that he has two grandbabies on the way.

Pain rips through me as another contraction comes. I'm pretty sure I broke Darien's hand, which is why he refused to hold mine now. Instead, he gives me a football he stole from a kid; a kid I now owe a new football. I flattened it in seconds, but now I have it balled up into one giant stress ball.

Mindy checks my dilation, and I pray it's time to push. I would rather be shot a dozen times than endure this pain any longer.

"Alright, it's time to push," she says.

"Praise the Lord!" I yell, and don't hesitate to do just as she says.

A few pushes, and I am stretched to my limit as Mindy pulls. Suddenly there's nothing left to pull, and the cry of a baby, *my baby*, fills the room around us. Tears sting my eyes, and I try to find the source of the sound through blurred eyes.

"It's a girl!" Mindy shouts before handing her off to Darien's open arms. He takes her and holds our baby as if she is the most precious thing on this earth. He looks at me with so much love in his eyes as he shows our beautiful girl to me.

I don't get to hold her yet though. It's time to push again. Darien cheers me on, while also cooing to his little girl.

This one is stubborn and doesn't want to come out. It takes dozens upon dozens of pushes before another cry fills my ears, and it's the most beautiful sound I have ever heard. Both of my babies are healthy.

"It's a boy!" Mindy announces, and my heart fills with absolute joy. I never said it out loud because I really would have been happy either way, but I was really hoping for a little Darien. And now I have one of each.

She sets him in my arms, and he is the most handsome little baby boy I have ever seen. I already love him with every ounce of my being.

Darien props him up against my legs and sets my beautiful girl up next to him, and I love her just the same. How can I love something so small, so much, when we have only just met? When I think life can't get any better, something else outdoes the other.

"Look what we made, baby," Darien coos, and it's something I never thought I would see. "They are so amazing. You did good, love," he kisses the top of my head, and it's the last thing I remember before exhaustion claims me.

EPILOGUE

"Be careful, pups," I call out to my spunky children running along the beach. Darien chases after them, and they wrestle in the sand. I take the opportunity to snap a picture.

Alexia has been teaching me how to use my new camera that I got for my 25th birthday. Her and Jerek normally come stay with us at our beach house that I got on my last birthday, but they decided to go somewhere on their own for their anniversary. I'm almost positive that Jerek is going to finally propose.

Darien kept his word that he would take me to the Pacific Ocean. The first time was shortly before the kids turned one. I fell in love with it, so of course Darien bought us our own beach house in Arcata, California. We let other pack members use it when we aren't here, but we go more and more now that the kids are three, and they love it just as much as us.

Life has been hectic with all of the wolves, but with Darien by my side, and the support of all of our friends, life has been just about perfect.

When we had first taken Canada and Alaska, other territories started joining forces, but we didn't move against them, and so far, no one has moved against us. Hopefully that never changes, but it would be a mistake to go against us. I have trained every willing fighter in our pack, male and female, and we are hands down stronger than any pack in the world.

Since Darien and I are both Alpha's, we are able to keep control over so many wolves without much issue, but when the little pups are older, we plan to share it with them rather than send them away to some foreign pack. They have to earn it though, of course. Just because they are of royal blood doesn't mean they automatically get to be Alphas.

The dominance in them is already apparent though, and it's pretty equal between the two. Dylan and Athena are going to be a force of nature when they are older.

Darien has his own team of guards consisting of Trace, Asher, Ben, and a man named Jake from the Alaskan territory. There are probably stronger, more dominant wolves on the Canada side, but they seem to feel more attached to me so they haven't tried to earn a position with him. Well, except for Macen, but he fell short there.

No one has been able to take second from Jerek, and I pray no one ever does. He is my best friend, and I can't imagine anyone else filling that role. I also have Charles, Niko, Macen, and another woman from Canada whose name is Maya. She has become quite the fighter.

"Mama come play with us," Dylan calls to me.

"Yeah, come play," Athena copies her brother, and its music to my ears. I close the distance to them and wrap them in my arms. They shift into wolf pups. Athena's wolf is light brown like mine but she has her father's eyes. Dylan is the opposite, with Darien's dark brown fur, and my hazel eyes. They are a perfect mix of each of us.

"You two change back this instant!" I scold them, though it's hard to be mad when they are so adorable. "You know better."

I lift them by the scruff of their necks, and carry them towards the water, threatening to throw them in. Our beach is private, but there is still the chance of being seen. They follow my orders, and I drop them into the water anyways.

Darien grabs one while I grab the other. They sputter as we lift them to the surface. We all laugh and splash each other as we swim around the ocean just like a normal family. Everything really is better at the beach, but with my family, I am always happy.

"You ready for a third?" Darien asks with the same look of love in his eyes that he saves only for me. My hand rests on the bump of my belly.

"I wasn't ready for two, but look how well that turned out. Maybe we will have a set of twins again," I tease, but it doesn't do anything but bring a bigger smile to his face. He pulls me in for a kiss, ignoring the gagging sounds from our children.

"I love you, Ari," he says adoringly, and with a passion as strong as the day we met, we share another long kiss under the setting sun.

BOOKS BY MELANIE

Light in the Dark

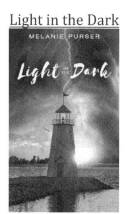

After a rough childhood and a continuous streak of bad relationships, fate brings Sophia Morgan face to face with the sexy and charming Adam Pierce. He's a man who knows what he wants, but she's not sure she has anything left to give.

Adam is a former Marine and now works as a detective in Oklahoma City. With his focus on his job, he keeps his heart locked up tight. When he meets an alluring beauty with a refreshing sense of humor, he can't stop thinking about her.

Afraid of getting hurt, they try to keep their distance, but Sophia is confronted with painful memories of her past when she is attacked by a masked man. When Adam rescues her, neither of them can deny their feelings any   longer.
Their relationship is put to the test when the case of murders Adam has been working on shows signs of Sophia being one of the killer's targets.

Can Sophia embrace her past before it's too late and seek justice for the victims, or will she and Adam be forever separated from the love they never thought they would find?

About the Author

Melanie Purser lives in Spokane, WA with her husband, daughter, and two German Shepherds. She loves to write when she's not teaching teenagers how to drive. She is obsessed with animals, mainly wolves and foxes. She loves the ocean, and anything that is teal or turquoise. Though she hoped to do something sport related with her Bachelor's degree in Kinesiology, and a background of College level softball, her dream was to publish a book one day. At least she was able to do one of those things. This is her first self-published, work. More to come soon.

Follow Melanie @
https://www.facebook.com/authorMelaniePurser/
amazon.com/author/melaniepurser
https://twitter.com/purser_melanie
https://www.instagram.com/authormelaniepurser/

Acknowledgements

Many thanks to my friends and family for your support, especially Mark Purser and Macie Gardner, for being my beta readers. Thank you, Angie Snyder, for the awesome book cover. You all made this possible.

Made in the USA
Middletown, DE
09 February 2021

33358854R00198